The Not So Perfect Duke

The Rakes of Regent's Park #5
By
Karyn Gerrard

Summary

DUE TO HIS FATHER'S untimely demise, Damon Cranston finds himself thrust into the role of the Duke of Chellenham. His loathsome and debauched father was too busy indulging in his vices and left the dukedom in shambles. Damon turns to Althea Galway, co-owner of the Galway Investigative Agency, to assist in unraveling the tangled mess. Since meeting Althea months ago, he hasn't been able to get her out of his mind, for he is captivated by her intellect, compassion, and confidence.

Althea Galway has never been impressed by money or title. Or by looks—although Damon, the devilishly handsome, golden-haired duke, caught her attention at first glance. Arrogant and egotistical, he is called Dorian Gray by society because of his reprobate reputation. But Althea senses deep loneliness, perhaps even inner scars, and is compelled to find the honorable man she believes is hidden behind the cool exterior.

Damon and Althea become swept up into a maelstrom of revelations: a conspiracy involving the late duke and others from the privileged class. Add a personal crisis into the mix, and finding a way to a shared future together seems hopeless. But they cannot deny the scorching attraction between them. Finding a way to make it all work will be a challenge. But the duke and the lady detective are determined to overcome it.

Rakes of Regent's Park Series

IN A PRIVATE MEETING place, in an old bank office behind Colosseum Terrace on Albany Street, a group of gentlemen attended a gathering. It had nothing to do whatsoever with financing, investments, or stocks—unless you counted moral bankruptcy. The central rules of this club: no serious attachments to anyone, and the pursuit of one's pleasures, especially of the carnal variety, were of the utmost importance.

But weariness and boredom were setting in. Along with something more worrying: loneliness. A disquiet of the soul. These bad-boy peers of Victorian London were damaged, hiding their inner torture beneath a thin veneer of devil-may-care dissoluteness.

It takes an exceptional group of women to capture the hearts of such men. To see past the outer shell. The ladies are determined to live and love in their way, with no relinquishment of their independence and no compromises. How satisfying to find that these progressive men are in total agreement.

Author's Note

BOOK #5 IS ALL NEW material! There should be hyphens between the phrase 'not so perfect' since it's a compound adjective, but I decided to leave them off the title for aesthetic reasons.

The Rakes of St. Regent's Park consist of the following books (so far). Will there be more after book 6? I never say never.

Book 1: Protecting the Duke

Book 2: The Baron and the Mistress (Revised Edition)

Book 3: Knight of Christmas

Book 4: The Duke of Pain

Book 5: The Not So Perfect Duke

Book 6: The Viscount of Shadows (coming soon!)

Each historical romance author does their own world-building, much like authors in fantasy, paranormal or other genres. Each author has their own set of characters and peers. That is why my characters from different historical books pop up in my writing. They are all part of my particular historical romance world. See the detailed author's note #2 at the end of this story for specific historical details.

Prologue

IT HAD BEEN SEVERAL years since Damon Cranston, Marquess of Brookton, had any contact with his mother, the Duchess of Chellenham, much less encountered her in person. But here he stood, awaiting her appearance on the veranda of her hacienda. When Damon arrived at his mother's home unannounced, the servants had been dubious about allowing him access to the property. Showing his card and throwing his imperious manner around gained him entry eventually, with a muscular footman keeping watch.

Holding his temper will be a definite challenge. Damn it all, his insides twisted in knots. Feeling like an 8-year-old lonely little boy had him annoyed to the extreme. When was the last time they had met face-to-face? Scads of years. Decades. The chasm between them was insurmountable, at least in Damon's eyes.

His mother breezed onto the patio and stopped cold in her steps. "My God, it *is* you. I would recognize you anywhere," she whispered while removing the scarf from her head. She then turned toward the footman. "Mateo, you may leave us. Bring refreshments, if you please."

"*Si, de inmediato Duquesa,*" the brawny footman replied, giving her a bow. He departed directly, leaving them alone.

How astounding to find his mother had retained most of her youthful beauty after twenty-plus years.

Damon stood with his hands clasped behind his back. "I haven't heard from you in ages, so I thought I would check to see if you are alive." He kept his voice devoid of emotion, as usual.

"As you see. I am well. Come, and sit at the table," the duchess replied as emotionlessly as he had done. Once seated, she asked, "And what brings you here?"

No need for pleasantries or kind words; right to the point. Then so shall Damon.

"I want to know of father's affairs and how many children there are from all his various debaucheries and dalliances."

His mother blinked rapidly but kept her expression neutral. "Before I answer, do you wish to know why I have not contacted you since that lone letter of ten years ago? Of which, you did not reply."

"I don't care to know," Damon sniffed indifferently.

She gave him a plaintive look. The first display of emotion from her. "Yes, Damon. You do. There was no contact before or since that impulsive letter because it was the arrangement I had agreed to."

His brows knitted. "What are you on about?"

His mother sighed. "The only way your father would agree to the separation was for me to depart the country without further communication with you. I had to get away, no matter the cost. The duke gave me this cozy villa and a monthly stipend in the settlement. That cost was—you."

The churning of his guts increased, along with his annoyance. "And when I grew older and came of age, what then? You could have contacted me besides that one time, and I would have assisted with your upkeep. But you did not." The last words ended with a hiss through clenched teeth. "Two sentences in that letter. To say you are well and that you hoped I continued in good health."

"And *you* never responded. Who pays you a monthly allowance?" the duchess shot back. "The duke would have cut you off. Besides, I *made* inquiries through the years and learned that you followed in your father's footsteps by joining a debauchery club and haunting East End brothels and music halls. What is the name, The Rakes of St. Regent's Park?"

She tapped her finger on the table. "I could not subject myself to such again. Not ever. Not if I were to keep my sanity. I barely escaped with a semblance of lucidity, as I had what is called in polite society—a breakdown. Your father threatened me with incarceration in an asylum, and I *had* to leave."

At that shocking moment, the footman entered and laid a tray before the duchess. Damon needed a lull in the conversation to process what his mother had divulged. Of course, this was *not* the picture his detestable father painted. The duke had claimed that the duchess no longer wished to be his mother and abandoned him to travel and seek out adventures—with other men.

Whom to believe?

One was as bad as the other. Or so Damon had supposed. His mother's abrupt departure had affected him so profoundly that he accepted his father's blatant fabrications. At the time, Damon was eight years old, an imprudent boy, hurt and afraid. His father was all he had. Of course, he believed the duke. But be damned if Damon would reveal how much his mother's absence had damaged him.

"Iced tea?" She held the pitcher aloft in question.

"Yes."

His mother poured a glass and passed it to him. "Thank you, Mateo."

The footman departed, and Damon took a long swig of the cold beverage. It should cool the heated uproar spiraling inside of him.

"There are almond biscuits, called panellets, and citrus sponge cake. Please, help yourself," the duchess offered politely. "Where are you staying?"

Still the gracious duchess.

As if he could partake of any food. Regardless, he reached for a biscuit. "I am staying at the Casa Cádiz."

"You are stunningly handsome. You have grown into the beautiful man I always knew you would be. On the outside. I have no clue what beauty exists within you."

"Do not bother delving deep. I allow no one in," Damon replied as he nibbled on the biscuit.

The duchess eyed him askance but gave no reply to his dismissive statement. "Now that we have the pleasantries out of the way. Regarding your father. Inasmuch as I detest the man, it is time I discussed him. It was not a love match at first," she stated matter-of-factly. "But God help me, I grew to love him most desperately. Or it was more of a wild infatuation. Why? Perhaps it *was* his breathtaking golden looks. I was that young and shallow once. Oh, how he took advantage of that vulnerability. He was cruel, the devil incarnate. I assume he still is."

"What, handsome and a devil? Yes, and he has only worsened with age. And yet, you left me in his care. Abandoned me to that overt cruelty," Damon accused. "And his cold indifference." So much for keeping his emotions hidden.

The duchess frowned. "I tried to depart and take you with me. Reach back in your memories."

He sneered. "I banished all memories as far as you were concerned." Perhaps a harsh taunt and not all that accurate, but Damon said it anyway. It appeared he acted as a sullen child, after all. He often lashed out and said things he did not mean—a decided character flaw.

His mother visibly winced. "Yes, you were always adept at pushing away and hiding horrible reminiscences. I envied you for that. Even at a young age, I watched how deftly you tucked away your emotions. Hiding them, denying them, just like your father."

"Stop comparing me to that wretched bastard," Damon snapped.

"Not hiding the emotions now. Think, you were seven years of age. We traveled as far as Euston Station before your father and his men dragged us back, and he thrashed us both for good measure."

The buried and hauntingly disturbing memory pushed through the protective haze and returned in full force. Yes, he recalled it, just as his mother described. His father beat him, the only time he had done so, then made him watch as he battered his mother and—worse.

"Damn you for making me recall that," he whispered dangerously.

"Forgive me. I will not speak of our shared past under your father's harsh and corrupt rule. Do you see why I departed in such haste? And why I couldn't take you, even if I wanted to? I sent numerous letters, but the duke returned them unopened. So, I waited until you reached the age of majority. I honestly believed that you were lost to me, that you are your father's son." The duchess reached across the table and took his hand. "Are you—his son?"

Was he? It was a chilling thought.

Partly, perhaps, but not deep down. At least, Damon hoped that was the case. What was the decades-old proverb or idiom? The apple doesn't fall far from the tree.

"I don't want to be," he whispered. Damon gave his mother an affectionate squeeze of her hand, and tears welled in her eyes. This was the first time he had admitted this to anyone.

"I am glad to hear it. Avoid emulating the duke in any way." Releasing his hand, the duchess dashed away the tear trickling down her cheek. "Let us change the subject. Why do you wish to trace your half-siblings?"

"Guilt. To know some children have been tossed aside—picks at my conscious. Yes, Mother. I have one, impaired though it may be."

She sipped her iced tea thoughtfully. "And have you taken care of your own dealings?"

"I would never act as recklessly as the duke. That is all you need to know."

"What have you discovered so far?"

Damon stared at the serene scenery, squinting at the bright sun. "Father has bragged over the years of a few of his offspring. It was challenging to know what was true and what was not. I know of two half-sisters, or so the claim goes. One refused to meet, and considering the source, I believe the statement was untrue. I have encountered the other. Her name is Olivia Durham. There is no denying it, as Olivia has the same blue eyes and golden hair I imagine all his spawn possesses. We are going to attempt friendship. Perhaps, in time, think of each other as brother and sister. Perhaps we are starting to do so already."

His mother smiled warmly. "I am glad to hear it. Is that the baby adopted by the country vicar and his wife?"

Damon could feel the blood drain from his face. "You knew of her?"

The duchess nodded. "And more besides. I found out about these children *after* my wedding. Your father took great pleasure in bragging about his perfect progeny. You had best pour us a drink, my son. You will need it. And so shall I. There is Brandy de Jerez over on the side table."

Damon rose but gripped the table to steady himself as his legs shook. He wondered if coming here was a terrible blunder: such revelations, such unfamiliar sentiments. Something was to be said for staying removed from family drama and well above the fray. He would be picking at threads best not pulled.

Well, he had come this far.

After pouring the drinks, he handed one to his mother.

She took a sip, then sighed. "You have an older half-brother by three years; last I heard, he is with the Metropolitan Police. You have a younger half-brother working as a footman at Chellenham Park."

The mouthful of brandy Damon had taken sprayed across the flagstones.

A copper—and a footman? A footman at the country seat?

Damon searched his mind for recollections of a blond-haired footman, but he never stayed at Chellenham Park, and he barely even looked at the staff the few times he did.

God above.

He picked up the serviette and wiped his mouth, then took another mouthful of the brandy to steel himself for the disclosures ahead. "How do you know about these children, and what became of them?" Damon asked.

"Your father kept me apprised of their progress through the years, whether I wanted to hear of it or not. With each quarterly allowance statement, he sent a noxious letter bragging of his conquests and the fact he had illegitimate children in every corner of London and beyond."

Damon glowered, despising his father afresh. "I am sorry my father subjected you to that."

"After a few years, I no longer cared. But I read the letters to spite the duke. And to prove that they had no effect."

"How many more offspring are there?"

"I know of seven, no wait, eight," his mother murmured. "But, as I said, I know there are more, considering the infidelities. At first, your father noted locations and names and even continued their maintenance, at least the boys. But later, he ensured they were taken to an orphanage and never thought of them again. Those are the ones you will never locate. There are no doubt a dozen or more of the poor children. At least, that is what he told me. I doubt the veracity, considering the information came from him."

His mother sipped her brandy. "Your father preferred poor, young, attractive women, mostly Irish, so not all the children you may try to locate will have blond hair and blue eyes."

"Good God," Damon muttered. "Rumor states the Earl of Oakby died of syphilis, along with some baronet the earl was friends with. Why is Chellenham so hale and hearty considering his flagrant behavior?"

His mother reached for a panellet. "I have often asked the same. It is why I kept him from my bed after you were born. You know what he is capable of, and I did not trust him to keep me safe and healthy."

"Do you still have any lingering feelings for him?" Damon inquired. "Forget I asked; it is an indelicate question."

"No, I will answer. Not for a long time. That particular destructive fever dissipated a few months after you were born. I have turned my affections elsewhere."

A man in a crisp white linen suit strode across the flagstones toward Damon's mother as if on cue. The handsome man looked in his mid-forties, and his eyes softened as he gazed affectionately at the duchess. The man leaned down to kiss her cheek.

"We have company," his mother beamed. "This is my son, Damon Cranston, Marquess of Brookton. Damon, this is Antonio De León."

The man held out his hand. "Tony, please. A distinct pleasure."

Damon took his hand and shook it.

"I will leave you, *mi corazón*, to visit with your son. You will stay for dinner, my lord?"

"Yes, thank you."

How astonishing that he would agree so swiftly, but the day was full of surprises, and Damon had the notion there were more shockwaves to come.

De León was about to depart when the duchess took his hand. "My love, could you ask Mateo to bring a pen, ink, and several sheets of paper?"

He brought her hand to his lips and kissed it. "I shall."

After De León left, Damon asked, "How long have you been together?"

"Over nineteen years. Tony is six years younger." She bit her lower lip, pausing as if considering revealing a secret. "You have a younger brother. Promise you will never tell your father."

"I swear it."

My God. A secret, indeed.

"Sebastián is away visiting his grandparents far north of here, but we will arrange a meeting soon if you wish. I am so pleased you are staying for supper. Will I see you again? Will you write? Am I in your life again, my darling boy?"

That is what his mother used to call him.

My darling boy.

It took all his inner courage not to fall to pieces, for a rush of memories threatened to overcome him. Yes, in the past, his mother tried to protect him. The affection she had always shown him, the extra hugs and attention. As if making up for the lack of warmth from his father.

But falling to pieces, showing emotion?

It was not the done thing. It was not Damon's done thing.

Regardless, Damon stood and leaned in to kiss her cheek. "Yes, Mother. We will keep in touch. I will stay a few days. And I want to meet my half-brother. How old is he?"

His mother smiled. "Soon to be 17 years old. And yes, please stay, Damon. As long as you wish. I have a guest room overlooking the water. We have so much to catch up on."

"Thank you, I will take you up on the kind offer."

Mateo entered with a tray and sat it before the duchess. She quickly wiped away another tear, then waved the servant away. Damon took his seat.

"Take your coat off, roll up your sleeves, relax in the sun, and sip your brandy. This will take some time. I will write down the children's names and the name of the orphanage. All I know is that the institution is located in the East End." She glanced up from the papers. "Does your father still employ that muscle-bound thug, Silas Browning?"

Damon nodded and removed his coat as his mother suggested. The oppressive heat was starting to make him feel dizzy.

"Question him, for I believe he was involved in this scheme. Also, question any servants, especially those working for your father since our marriage. Although, I imagine there are hardly any remaining."

"Perhaps I will. I do not want the duke to know what I am doing. At least, not right away."

"The people on this list will not thank you for locating them," his mother murmured as she dipped the pen into the ink bottle.

Damon rolled up the sleeves of his shirt and stretched out his legs. "I want to know they are well and will be cautious in my dealings. I merely wish to know if any need assistance, monetary or otherwise."

"You are stirring up a hornet's nest. Perhaps you should hire an investigative agency," his mother suggested.

A slow smile crept across his face as he thought of the lovely Miss Althea Galway.

"I have just the investigative agency in mind."

Chapter 1

Late July 1898

It was an unexpected death but not a shock, considering the circumstances. So, when Damon Cranston, the Marquess of Brookton, was called to his father's town house at two in the morning to identify the body, it churned up a temporary maelstrom of emotions. As his mother noted, Damon was adept at tucking away such bothersome feelings since he was old enough to form cognitive thoughts and understand their meaning.

Some servants huddled together at the bottom of the stairs, whispering furiously. MacClery, his father's butler, took his hat and cloak. The Scotsman had served his father for as long as Damon could remember, and as far as Damon was concerned, the middle-aged man was one of his father's inner circle of collaborators.

"The police await you upstairs, Your Grace."

Damon whipped his head around as if to look for his father. Then it hit him. *He* was the Duke of Chellenham now.

Damn, and blast it all to hell.

After taking the stairs two at a time, he strode nonchalantly toward his father's chambers. A woman's wailing filled his hearing. Of course, his father wasn't alone when he died. What did the working classes call it? He had heard the saying often enough during his many East End haunts.

"He's popped his clogs."

Yes, that was it.

A sudden urge to giggle overcame Damon. Entirely inappropriate considering the situation. But the impulse to laugh evaporated as soon as he entered his father's bedroom. Two uniformed policemen were filling out reports. A man in a suit was setting up a camera while another man in an overcoat stood nearby. In the corner of the room, a young woman wrapped in a sheet sat on the floor, shaking and crying. Then Damon turned toward the bed.

His father was naked and kneeling with a belt around his neck. The other end of the strap was attached to the bedpost and kept him in that indelicate position. The duke's lifeless eyes stared into nothingness. Damon's gaze slid lower.

Good God. *That* he didn't need to see.

The man wearing the long coat stepped forward. "My lord? I am Detective Mitchell Evercreech, Metropolitan Police, B Division."

Damon had to bite his lip to stem the inappropriate laughter from escaping. He had to gain control of himself. What kind of name was that for a copper? Evercreech? And—

It had been only five days since he had returned from Spain. The duchess had given him a list of names of illegitimate children sired by his father. At least the ones that she knew of. Damon had yet to begin to investigate, let alone set up an appointment with The Galway Agency.

Evercreech was one of the names.

No, it cannot be.

The fates wouldn't be that ironic, would they?

The detective was tall, close to six feet or maybe an inch shorter, with sandy hair, more golden than brown, light blue eyes, and sharp cheekbones. His gaze darted from the detective to his dead father and back again. There was a decided resemblance in the jawline and the shape of the eyes. Or it could be Damon's overactive imagination.

Notwithstanding, this was not the time to bring up such a sensitive subject. "I thought the City of London Police would be attending this," Damon stated distantly.

Evercreech shook his head. "This residence is just over the boundary, my lord. You will be dealing with the Metropolitan Police."

"What transpired here, or do I want to know?" Damon asked.

"The young woman claims they were about to indulge in one of the duke's favorite games, oxygen depletion, or as it's known in certain circles, erotic asphyxiation. They had sex multiple times, and according to this woman, she no sooner placed the belt around his neck and attached it to the bedpost when he groaned and went very still. A heart attack, it's assumed. We will know more once the police surgeon has a look at him." The detective pointed to the woman cowering in the corner. "Do you know her, my lord?"

"No. My father had many sexual partners. I have never seen her before." It was surreal standing here having a conversation with his dead father, only a few feet away. "Why do you conclude it was a heart attack?"

"There are no ligature marks around the throat or other signs of strangulation. So, it may have occurred, as the woman states. Sorry to question you here in the room, my lord, but I needed you to observe the scene so I could ask relevant questions."

"And is *that* normal? An aroused state even in death?" Damon waved his arm toward the bed. Typical of his dissolute father, if nothing else.

"It can be, my lord. A doctor explained it to me once," Evercreech replied, completely unruffled at the sight of the late duke. "Blood settles in the lower extremities when a person dies, swelling the dead tissue. Plus, he was no doubt in this state when he expired. It can happen to men when hanged. I've seen it, and it's often referred to as angel lust."

"Leave it to my father to die in such a way," Damon muttered. Better to go in your sleep, in your eighties or even nineties. Suppose a person was fortunate to live that long.

Not—this.

How humiliating.

If Damon ever needed a reason to stem his nocturnal debaucheries—this was it. Not that he had been seeking such pleasures lately, and that stark and disturbing image of his dead father would haunt him for years. What a way to end one's life.

"We will take a few photographs, then take the body to the morgue," Evercreech said, pulling Damon from his morbid thoughts. "If you wish, my lord, you may have your father's physician attend the examination."

"Yes, I will contact him."

It struck Damon that he could involve Althea's investigative agency immediately. Didn't she and her sister have a competent police surgeon for such inquiries? Damon recalled that the man was an actual physician. "I may also have another doctor look into this. How do I contact you to make arrangements?"

Evercreech passed him a card. "I would be swift about it, my lord. We will transport the corpse to St. Thomas's Hospital. Or I suppose I should be addressing you as Your Grace?"

"It doesn't matter. I suppose it is Your Grace, seeing he's dead. I will make arrangements immediately. No one is to touch the body until my doctors attend. And the manner of his discovery is to be kept secret."

The detective shrugged. "We try, but these things can slip out, Your Grace. Best be prepared for the scandal."

"Scandal and I are old friends, Evercreech."

Evercreech turned to attend the photograph session and confer with the other police officers. Damon stared at his father, waiting to feel anything.

Regret. Hate. A hint of sorrow.

There was nothing.

Damon backed up several steps until he rested against the wall. The bedroom door was ajar, voices drifted in from the hallway, and Damon leaned in to listen. The butler, MacClery, was talking to one of the uniformed coppers.

"His nibs will no doubt move in here. The Chellenham town house is larger and entailed." MacClery stated. "And things will go on as before, for the son is near as bad as the father for depravity. You'll be back here in no time at all, mark my words."

The constable tsked in response.

"They are all alike, these nobs. One as bad as the other," MacClery added. His Scottish burr was evident while conversing with the constable.

"True, that," the man murmured in reply.

"I couldn't stand the duke. He was a cruel, unfeeling bugger. And you can quote me on that. But I tolerated his verbal lashings, for he paid well for my silence. Well, he's dead now; who bloody cares? The worms will get him soon enough," MacClery spat.

Damon threw open the door and met MacClery's shocked gaze. He could fire the man on the spot, as he had planned to dismiss his father's entire staff when the time came. But how curious to discover MacClery was not entirely his father's faithful retainer.

Were any of them loyal?

Keeping most of the staff in place, for now, is prudent.

"MacClery, await me downstairs in the library," Damon demanded coldly.

The policeman discreetly moved away.

"If I'm for the chop, tell me now. Your Grace."

"Library, MacClery."

The butler straightened; and, with all the dignity he could muster, made his way to the library. Damon turned his attention to Evercreech.

"Do you need me for anything else?" he asked the detective.

Evercreech shook his head. "No, Your Grace. We will be moving the body directly, and I will await word from you regarding the examination and autopsy." The detective touched his forelock, then returned his attention to the young woman, sniffling quietly.

Damon entered the upper hallway, took a shaky breath, then exhaled.

What to do first?

He would have to contact his mother. She was free of the duke at last. He had no doubt she would marry De León as soon as possible. Who could blame her? Not Damon.

He entered the library, and MacClery stood by the desk, back straight as if preparing for what would come.

"Sit, MacClery." Damon waved his hand toward the chair. "I am not firing you for speaking the truth. Do you wish to stay on here? It will not be as a butler. I have my own whom I trust implicitly. But under butler will suit for now. But only if you continue to be truthful in all matters. Your salary will stay somewhat the same."

"Most generous, Your Grace. Aye, I mean, yes, I wish to stay on."

"There must be several here I can cut, staff-wise. I may not keep the marquess town house. My residence has no entailment, and I might sell it forthwith. I want the senior and loyal members of Clarendon Place integrated here or at Chellenham Park."

"I understand, Your Grace. There is not as many staff here as you may believe, and there has been a high turnover. Current vacant positions remain unfilled."

"Good to know. I want to meet with my father's steward right away. I want an up-to-date accounting of the finances, holdings, and savings. Arrange it."

MacClery nodded. "As soon as possible, Your Grace."

"I will be hiring an investigative agency. If you wish to keep your position, you must promise to cooperate with them in any inquiries they may have, whether personal or sordid. Do you agree?"

"I do, Your Grace."

Damon stared long and hard at the Scotsman. Time will tell if he was sincere. "Any conversations we have, either here, now, or in the future, will stay between us. No—sharing below stairs, especially. You are to be *my* man. Assist me in all things, understand? There must be trust between us, which we must earn—on both sides."

"I understand completely and agree, Your Grace." MacClery hesitated, shifting uncomfortably in his seat. "Begging your pardon, Your Grace, but will you continue with the debaucheries under this roof specifically?"

Damon raised an eyebrow. "What do you mean?"

"Well, the former duke had an orgy here two months past, for example."

"Indeed?" Damon rubbed his temple. A sharp pain tore through his head, as it often did when agitated and overwhelmed. He was inheriting quite a corrupt dukedom. "If I pursue any debaucheries, as you call them, I give you my word it will *not* be under this roof."

Damon never brought women to his home or held depraved parties. All his sexual pursuits were done elsewhere, the East End, specifically.

The man's rugged features visibly relaxed. Damon would have to obtain an accounting of all who attended this orgy. But he would leave that for Althea and her investigative agency.

"See that you pay the woman upstairs to ensure her silence and see her off the premises. She is never to come here again; make that clear. Come and notify me when the body and the police have departed. Do you have a footman you trust?"

"There is one, Your Grace, possibly two."

"Send one of them to me right away."

MacClery stood. "Would you care for a drink, Your Grace? You've had a shock."

The last thing Damon needed was alcohol to cloud his brain. "No, bring a tray with tea, sandwiches, and the like."

"At once, Your Grace."

MacClery departed, leaving him alone. People stomped about in the front hall, no doubt the wagon to take away the body. Damon could hear movement upstairs.

His father was dead.

Again, Damon waited to see if he felt anything. Regarding his father directly—still nothing. Nothing but annoyance at being left with this mess of a dukedom. The finances were probably a muddle as well.

However, strange emotions gripped him at the prospect of seeing the lovely Althea Galway again. He had not seen her in a few months, not since late spring when she assisted Gideon Broyles, the Duke of Watford, with a personal matter.

Anticipation. Excitement.

And a hard—literally hard—jolt of desire.

No other woman had affected him in such an unadulterated way before. Would he still feel the same? Still yearning to hold her in his arms? Whisper in her ear, nuzzle the soft skin of her neck, hold her close in a protective embrace?

Or was his heart completely dead and blackened?

It seems he would soon find out.

Chapter 2

ALTHEA GALWAY SAT IN the office study at 149 Cleveland Street, writing a report on a case that had just concluded. Early morning sunshine poured into the room, giving it a definite summer warmth.

The inquiry concerned divorce. The marriage laws had changed, allowing women to sue for divorce (with particular stipulations), and most of their investigations focused on this matter. Althea had worked on this case exclusively with Archie.

Archie Fitzgerald, their young apprentice, had sprung up four inches in height over the past several months, making him ideal for more undercover work. The lad would be away attending Charterhouse school in the autumn.

Eleanora, Althea's older sister and co-founder of the Galway Investigative Agency, breezed into the room carrying a tea tray.

"My, you're up early," Eleanora stated. "Time to take a break. And the mail has arrived along with a special-delivered note addressed to you. Can you believe we have more clients than we could possibly take on? What a powerful position to be in. Shall we winnow out cases, say three times a week? We can take turns."

Eleanora was unbearably cheery, but this had been her permanent state since marrying Christian Bamford, the Duke of Allenby. Christian was her partner in all things, including the investigative agency.

Althea didn't mind as she adored Christian. She could not ask for a better brother-in-law. Christian had assisted Althea with the Duke of Watford's case. Who ever thought a duke would revel in investigative work?

"And you're here early as well," Althea observed. "I thought you and Christian were late sleepers?" She gave her sister a teasing smile, knowing that the couple was not using their morning time alone to sleep.

Eleanora chuckled. "Amusing. We had other appointments today, so no leisurely 'sleeping' this morning."

"With regards to winnowing cases, Sybil has expressed an interest in staying firmly behind the scenes," Althea said as she sorted through the mail. "She will run our little office and select clients. We trust her judgment. Besides, her courtship with our doctor friend is slowly but surely intensifying."

Their cousin, Sybil Nolan, assisted with their investigative venture when not spending time with her parents in Yorkshire. However, she has been in London more often lately. Part of that reason was Doctor Corbett Buchanan, a Canadian whom Eleanora and Althea called on when medical matters needed addressing in any particular case.

Corbett had been a drinker and suffered from various mental issues from his turbulent time serving in The North-West Mounted Police as a surgeon on the Canadian Prairies. He had been sober for almost a year and had taken on a position as a police surgeon at their Uncle Reece's police precinct in Bethnal Green. Accordingly, Sybil was not rushing into anything with the good doctor.

"Then, by all means, Sybil can handle it. I was wondering if we should enlarge the office area, and you can turn my old bedroom into a sitting room," Eleanora suggested.

"Yes, we will discuss it with Sybil."

Althea had other plans concerning the agency, but that was a conversation for another time.

Eleanora sat and passed the sealed envelope to her. "Open it, Sister. My curiosity is piqued."

Taking the letter opener, Althea carefully slid it under the wax seal, then unfolded the note. She read aloud:

My Dear Miss Althea Galway,

I require your services for two matters of personal import concerning life and death, and I will pay any fee you care to name. I prefer to speak to you alone, if at all possible. Please send word when you are available today, and I will come to Cleveland Street at your earliest convenience.

"The note is signed, Damon Cranston, Duke of Chellenham. My God, his father must have passed, but when?" Althea pondered.

"Must be recent. I've seen nothing in the papers," Eleanora replied as she poured their tea. "And you read the society pages more than I do."

"It must be *very* recent," Althea frowned, staring at the note.

"Well. The Marquess of Brookton is a duke now. You, or more specifically, we—have a soft spot for dukes," her sister teased. "And pretty men."

"What are you on about?"

"Well, I married a duke. And you flirted with Gideon Broyles, the Duke of Watford, not a few months past."

Althea snorted. "For all of five minutes. Then I discovered he was most decidedly taken. I will admit he *did* appeal. The threads of gray at the temple, those sharp cheekbones, and an even sharper aristocratic nose. The cool demeanor."

"Yes, the haughty, imperturbable duke—who secretly smolders deep inside," Eleanora laughed.

"You're describing *your* duke," Althea responded. "Besides, I was not put out about Gideon's unavilability, not at all. I have made friends with Olivia, his bride. I stood for her at their wedding. That was a first, a case concluding with matrimony."

"Indeed. All the best to Gideon and Olivia." Eleanora raised her teacup, then took a sip. "Months ago, you told me that Brookton appealed and aroused your interest in more ways than one. Is that still the case?"

"And what if it is? Is that not my business?" Althea replied with an even tone.

"I must confess I had Brookton; I mean, Chellenham investigated some months ago. By Uncle Reece."

"Why? When, exactly?" Althea couldn't believe this. Eleanora went to their police detective inspector uncle?

"Shortly after Christian's case concluded. I saw how you looked at Chellenham. I wanted to know more about the man to see if he was truly as horrible as he presented and as his reputation states. Uncle Reece discovered nothing beyond the gossip. I am sorry I didn't tell you before this. I hope you are not angry."

Althea folded the letter and placed it on the table. "No, I am not angry. I understand your reasoning. Yes, the new duke still interests me. However, if you recall, I also told you that the then Marquess of Brookton disgusted me. And that we could not involve ourselves in the lives of these troubled men. I still hold by that observation."

Eleanora chuckled. "Too late for me. Well, for both of us, actually. We've become involved by taking cases and becoming friends with some." Then she sobered. "Will you take Chellenham's case?"

Althea shrugged. "Common sense states that I stay clear of the man altogether. But when has common sense ever stopped me? I will take the meeting as I am curious enough to hear what he has to say."

"Do you wish me to sit in on the consultation, even though he requested a private audience?" Eleanora asked as she sipped her tea.

Althea considered it. Her sister would act as a buffer and perhaps keep those bothersome sparks from coming to life in Damon's presence. Yes, she thought of him as Damon, another warning bell indicating that she should refuse to see him.

But Althea was drawn to the man.

Seeing it was Shakespearean in origin, she could use the moth-to-flame allusion, but it wasn't adequate for the almighty pull she felt whenever near him. Perhaps she could use Greek mythology, the Icarus flying too close to the sun-wings melting thing.

No, still not satisfactory enough.

Damon was unbearably handsome, too perfect for words. But it was more than that. She sensed his loneliness, and yes, he was troubled. Multiple complicated layers that Althea yearned to peel back. Utterly *ached*. Her insides quivered at the thought. Damon was not so perfect underneath, which made him captivating. Her fascination was complete folly.

"No, I will see him alone. But I would like you to be nearby if needs must," Althea stated.

There, I made the decision.

Althea confided to her sister since she was old enough to form sentences, but Althea had *not* mentioned the few times her path had crossed Damon's the past several months. When Archie returned in half an hour, Althea would ask him to deliver her message to the new duke.

"I think you can handle Brookton, or Chellenham, well enough. But I will stay on the premises," Eleanora grinned.

Althea's eyes narrowed. "You are like the cat that swallowed the proverbial canary. Spit it out, Ellie."

"I know you exchanged barbs with Chellenham a few months past at Gideon's. Gideon asked Christian if there was anything between you because the electricity in the room was *not* from his newly-installed overhead lighting."

Althea shook her head in disbelief. "And, of course, Gideon relayed the exchange details to Christian, and he told you."

"Of course," Eleanora declared. "Christian tells me everything. I thought *you* did as well. Why not tell me about this? I am quite put out."

Althea chortled. "No, you're not. You're amused more than anything. And curious."

Eleanora took on a serious but concerned look. "Reject the case. I could not bear it if this scoundrel hurt you in any way. I remember you distinctly said: 'He's everything I loathe in a man: his wealthy class, his arrogance, his blasé lifestyle, he's immoral to his core.' Then you claimed: 'I can never be alone with Brookton, for there lays the danger. To my sanity and most especially my heart.'"

"Do you remember everything I say verbatim?" Althea huffed, annoyed at being reminded of her early impressions of Damon.

"Regarding this, yes. My dear sister, the alarm bells are clanging at full peal. Can't you hear them? You obviously harbor mixed emotions concerning this man. I want you to be certain you can remain detached and professional regarding Chellenham."

Althea raised an eyebrow. "Like you did with Christian?" She waved her hand dismissively. "I don't want to argue. It's my decision to make. I warned you about becoming involved with Christian, but you drew your own conclusions, and I respected them. All I ask is that you esteem *my* choice. Whatever it may be."

Eleanora sighed and reached for a ginger biscuit. "I also knew you spoke common sense, but my heart told me something else. Just be cautious."

Precisely. Althea's heart ruled her options here; she might as well admit it. She would hear Chellenham out and go from there. As far as hiding her emotions, that may be more formidable to accomplish.

DAMON ARRIVED AT CLEVELAND Street promptly at eleven. Althea's housekeeper-cook, Mrs. Bartle, showed him into the office.

"His Grace, The Duke of Chellenham," Mrs. Bartle announced imperiously. Then she gave Althea a playful wink and closed the door behind her.

The new duke did not breeze into the room with his usual arrogant, confident air. Damon was more subdued, solemn, and closed off. But what did she know of him, as they only conversed a few times? But those exchanges were heated, and not only the conversation. As Eleanora said—electricity. Already, Althea's emotions were pinging in all directions.

"Please, take a seat, Your Grace." Mrs. Bartle had brought a tea tray before Damon arrived. "Would you care for tea?" she asked politely.

"Yes. Although, that is all I have been drinking for hours now."

As Althea poured, she said, "May I offer my condolences on your loss?"

"Right. Condolences. Thank you. As far as being duke, it is not official until I am issued a Writ of Summons from the Queen, where I have to go through some trivial ceremony to take my seat in the House of Lords." He took the proffered cup and saucer.

"You didn't already sit in the house, Your Grace?"

"First, let us dispense with the Your Gracing. If you take my case, it will become tedious for us both. Damon or Chellenham. I prefer Damon when we are alone for various reasons, one being that hearing the Chellenham title reminds me of my father. And I would rather *not* be reminded." He exhaled. "Brookton was a courtesy title, and I could not sit in the house unless given special dispensation."

Althea was baffled by all the intricacies of aristos and titles. "Then why didn't Whinstone take his seat in the House of Lords?"

Sanford Ellingford, the Duke of Whinstone, was Gideon Broyles, the Duke of Watford's stepfather and the key villain in the case she had taken this past spring.

"The dukedom was bankrupt, and so was his soul, for that matter," Damon responded. "Bankrupt peers cannot be seated, and neither can lunatics. Supposedly. It will be a few months before The House of Lords strips his title from him. I heard Whinstone is in a reform prison, given good meals and a warm bed. Yet, a poor man is sentenced to prison in a drafty old castle, like HM Prison Oxford, where he spends his days walking a treadmill or turning a crank, given gruel to eat and a pallet for a bed. Though I hear that hard labor practice is finally ending."

Althea smiled, delighted that the new duke knew of such particulars and how it affected the lower classes. "Perhaps that is a deserving subject you can get behind in the House of Lords, further reform for prisons."

Damon adjusted his cuffs and sniffed. "I would prefer to discuss what I came here for. To hire you and your agency."

And there was the haughty, imperturbable duke.

Why she kept trying to see any good in him was beyond her typical sound reasoning. Disappointed, Althea fussed with her notebook and pencil.

"Then, by all means, let's keep this professional. What can I help you with?" Althea replied using her business-like voice.

"I want you specifically to handle the case. Wenlock and Watford sing your praises. And Allenby, obviously." Damon reached into his coat pocket and removed a small cloth bag. "The first payment. Twenty gold sovereigns."

"Money, though welcome, is not an inducement for me to take *any* case. I will need more information first."

"The money is a bonus for the stipulations that will be part of this investigation. I want to be involved every step of the way, as Allenby was with his situation. This is non-negotiable."

Althea scowled as she detested anyone establishing conditions on her inquiries. "Won't that interfere with your thoroughly debauched lifestyle? How will you cope?" she replied sarcastically. Honestly, this man brought out the worst in her, and Althea did not like it.

"Still interested in my private life? Do you wish to ask me probing questions as you did in Allenby's case?" Damon replied with mockery in his tone.

Althea shook her head, embarrassed at her statement. His personal life was none of her business.

She was ready to apologize when he said, "I will make a pact here and now. Throughout this case, I will live as a proverbial monk, be at your beck and call, day or night. For the investigation, of course."

"I will not ask for such a sacrifice from you, but I will involve you should I take your case. What can you tell me?" She held her pencil, ready to take notes.

"First. In the matter of death. My father passed away late last night. I was called to his home at two this morning and have not been to bed since. Please send your police surgeon to St. Thomas's to assist with the autopsy. My father's doctor will be in attendance as well."

"Was the death suspicious?"

Damon explained the details of his father's death as Althea furiously took notes. Good Lord, these peers were a depraved lot.

"It could be a heart attack, as the detective alleged. How old was your father?" she ventured.

"Fifty-seven. As far as I am aware, no heart problems. But how am I to know? We were not close. We rarely spoke, let alone exchanged private information regarding health or other sensitive topics."

She looked up and met his gaze. Damon was watching her rather intensely. "To be clear, you wish Doctor Buchanan to assist in the autopsy. Is the mortuary doctor at St. Thomas's aware of this?"

"Yes. And yes."

"Is your carriage outside?"

"Yes."

Damon looked weary; no wonder with no sleep. Besides all the other conflicting emotions he brought forth, he also awakened the protective instinct within her. Blast it all for feeling concerned about his welfare and state of mind.

"Doctor Buchanan is at my uncle's precinct this morning. I will write a note, and your driver can take it to him. What time do you wish him to be there?"

"Two o'clock. I am sorry for the short notice. My father's physician, Doctor William Breaks, will also be there. I want a complete report. And I want Buchanan to thoroughly question Breaks as to the state of my father's health."

Althea continued to write her note. Without looking up, she said, "It has been my experience that many doctors do not reveal their patient's health details unless compelled to do so."

"Then write in your note if he doesn't give details to Buchanan that he will deal with my team of solicitors," Damon snapped. "That should compel him."

Althea met his gaze, an eyebrow arching at his irritable tone.

Damon rubbed his forehead. "I apologize."

"Damon," she said softly. His penetrating gaze grew heated at her saying his name. "No apology is necessary. You said in your message that your being here concerns life and death. Is there something else beyond your father's death you wish to hire the agency for?"

"Yes. It is rather complicated and does concern my late father."

"Then we will deal with your father's death first. You're exhausted. Go home and sleep for a few hours. As soon as I have any information, I will come to you. Will you be at 10 Clarendon Place?"

He rubbed his temple. "Yes, perhaps that is wise. And I will be at the Brookton town house."

"After your driver drops you home, he can deliver the note to Doctor Buchanan, and I will take it from there. If you haven't guessed, I will take your case."

"Thank you. I will try to catch some sleep and await your arrival." Damon stood and turned to leave but halted. "I thank you for your compassion."

He was gone, and Althea sat back in her chair. Never had she seen him so vulnerable. It touched her deeply. She made a vow then and there. To be more sympathetic in her dealings with him. To not allow him to infuriate her or, worse—arouse more than her exasperation.

For she was correct, Damon Cranston, the new Duke of Chellenham, *was* a danger to her heart.

Chapter 3

AS FAR AS DREAMS WERE concerned, Damon experienced them so rarely. Or if he had, once awake, he could not recall them. When he remembered the dreams, however, they were vivid.

Like this one. It was in living color, etched in Damon's mind for all eternity.

Of course, it involved his wretched father. Why wouldn't it after the doings of the past twenty-four hours?

In the dream, he was a small boy, going from room to room at Chellenham Park to locate his father. While growing up, his father only beat him once. So physical abuse was not at the core of their contentious relationship. It was the neglect. The lack of affection. And if he deemed to give Damon any attention, the duke showed disdain.

His mother tried to make up for it, but she was gone when he turned eight years of age.

Regardless, back to the dream.

HE SEARCHED EVERY ROOM. Then he came to the duke's bed chambers. His small hand wrapped around the lion's head doorknob. With a twist, the door popped open, revealing complete darkness. Damon looked toward the window. A slight cool breeze ruffled the draperies. The room itself was cold, for he could see his breath.

Tentatively stepping inside, Damon headed toward the window, tugging the draperies apart. Moonlight washed the area in a subdued but eerie illumination.

Damon's eyes adjusted to the lighting enough to make out a shadow on the bed. The clouds parted, revealing more of the full moon as light crawled across the wood floor until the shadow was revealed.

It was his father in the exact position he had been found in.

Naked. On his knees. A belt around his neck.

His lifeless eyes stared into nothing, although they now had a milky film over them. His father's skin had a light gray tinge. With a snapping crick, the head turned, and those horrid eyes locked on Damon. The mouth twitched, and the hinged jaw dropped in a ghoulish silent scream. Out of the duke's mouth poured loose earth—it pooled on the bed before him—mounds of moldy-smelling earth. A fat worm slithered through the dirt. Then he heard MacClery's voice, "The worms will get him soon enough."

DAMON BOLTED UPWARD, his hand over his mouth as if to silence his bloodcurdling scream. Perspiration poured from his temples as chills curved about his spine.

Christ, what a nightmare.

Why even have it? His father was not even in the ground yet. When was the last time he had a nightmare? It had been many years, but if he recalled correctly, it was somewhat similar. He was going from room to room looking for someone. For what purpose?

One of those new innovative physiological doctors would have material to dissect here.

Trembling, Damon took a fistful of the sheet and wiped his brow. A sudden knock on the door made him jump. What time was it anyway? His gaze swung to the timepiece on the fireplace mantel. It was close to five o'clock. In the afternoon, obviously.

"It is Kingsley, Your Grace."

His butler had a standing order never to barge into a room without knocking as butlers were wont to do.

"Yes, what is it?"

"There is a Miss Althea Galway and a Doctor Buchanan to see you, Your Grace. I informed them you were resting, but they claimed you asked them to stop by."

Damon had been so weary when he returned from Cleveland Street that he neglected to inform Kingsley that they would be by later in the afternoon. Well, he wasn't going to bellow at a closed door.

Damon stood, grabbing the bedpost as his legs shook. "Where is Baldwin?"

"I am here, Your Grace," came the muffled voice through the door.

His valet. Now able to stand on his own two feet, Damon reached for the dressing gown at the foot of the bed and draped it over his nakedness.

"You may both come in," he announced, pulling the tie across his waist. "Where are they? Miss Galway and the doctor?"

"I put them in the drawing room, Your Grace," Kingsley replied. "You have not eaten. Shall I bring a tray? Mrs. Stewart has breakfast foods ready as per your instructions."

"Is there enough to offer the guests?"

"Yes, there is, Your Grace."

"Then see it laid out in the dining room. Fetch me when the meal is ready, then escort my guests to the dining room. Then we are to be left alone."

"I will see to it at once, Your Grace." With a slight bow, Kingsley departed.

"Well, Your Grace. You do look a little ragged, I must say," Baldwin said wittily.

Why he kept Baldwin around, *he* could not say, for the man spoke his mind. Although Baldwin occasionally tsked about Damon's lifestyle, he never outwardly admonished him or showed disrespect. At least, not too much of it.

"No more than usual, you mean?" Damon replied sardonically.

Baldwin moved to the wardrobe and flung open the doors. "Under the circumstances, it is understandable—my condolences and my sympathy, Your Grace. For the dukedom, and all that responsibility is now yours. Perhaps sooner than you thought or hoped."

"Yes," Damon murmured. "Far too soon for my liking."

"Well, here is your chance to replace me. The late duke's valet requires a position." Baldwin turned to face him, grinning impishly. The middle-aged man was as thin as a needle; his dark black hair slicked back against his skull. He had heard whispers that Baldwin dyed his hair, but who cares?

"Why would I replace you? To train someone all over again to know my likes, dislikes, and preferences for freshly laundered shirts and pressed silk cravats? I cannot be bothered."

"But of course, Your Grace. Shall I shave you?"

"No. And I don't give a toss that it is improper to greet guests in such a state. This is a business call, and besides, I am utterly famished. The sooner I dress, the better. An afternoon coat and waistcoat will do."

Baldwin held up a black suit. "Tradition states that you should wear black, Your Grace."

Damon grunted. "For six months to a year? I think not. I will wear black to the funeral, but that is all. And no armband."

Baldwin snapped to it, selecting a gold taupe vest and a brown coat. In assisting in dressing Damon, his finishing touch was a light beige cravat.

"Those fair whiskers are hardly noticeable and even give you a dash of danger. You look good enough to eat, Your Grace. Not to me, obviously."

"I am relieved to hear it." Damon strode toward the door, then halted. "I will be meeting with my late father's steward soon. I want you there. You handle my personal finances, and I want a second opinion on what the steward has to say. And I want your estimation of the man. If I should keep him on or not."

"I am at your disposal, Your Grace."

"Also, I am going out as soon as I am finished with my guests. See that the carriage is ready."

He must see his half-sister, Olivia Durham, now the Duchess of Watford, and his friend Gideon's new bride, before their father's death was announced in tomorrow morning's papers. Not that Olivia ever met the old duke or had wanted to. But it would be a courtesy to inform her personally.

"And the funeral ought to be organized," Damon continued, his mind eddying in all directions. "We will need to contact my father's solicitor. Get the name from Kingsley. Set up an appointment right away. I want you and my solicitor to have an initial meeting to get the lay of the land, as it were. We must also collect the body from St. Thomas's when they have concluded their inquiries. See it done."

"At once, Your Grace," Baldwin bowed.

Kingsley arrived and escorted Damon to the dining room. Thank Christ he had employees handling these tedious details.

Althea and the doctor entered the room. Damon piled his plate high with bacon and fried eggs. As he turned, Damon's breath caught in his throat as it often did in Althea's presence. It wasn't so much her looks, though she was attractive with her dark brown locks threaded with gold.

But it was her carriage, the confidence, the frank and open way she gazed at him. And the fact that she didn't bother to hide that she found him attractive. Her innate empathy and, when warranted, her compassion. And her intelligence, the fact that she co-owned and operated an investigative agency. Damon was mightily impressed by that, regardless of what he might have said in the past. Or may say in the future, considering his many defects.

"Miss Galway, and Doctor Buchanan, I presume. There is an assortment to choose from. If you are feeling peckish, do help yourself. I am afraid I slept most of the day away."

Althea placed her large case and reticle on a nearby chair and strode to the sideboard. "Thank you, I will. Corbett? Come, fill your plate."

The doctor moved next to Althea. "Breakfast at a quarter past five in the afternoon. The first time for everything. And not unwelcome," He smiled as he grabbed a couple of scones, ham, and a small ceramic pot containing shirred eggs.

After gathering the foodstuffs and drinks, they sat at the table.

The doctor looked down at his plate. "This is hardly fit conversation at a meal."

"No," Damon stated. "But there it is. How did he die?"

"I was present for the autopsy and assisted with it, Your Grace. Afterward, I spoke to your father's doctor as you instructed. Doctor Breaks was most forthcoming. Your father suffered from a recently diagnosed heart ailment. Doctor Breaks instructed him to curtail his sexual extracurricular activity, drinking, and smoking. Your father gave up none of it. The autopsy showed major damage."

"What kind of damage?" Damon asked as he cut into his fried egg.

"The heart is encased in a sac-like membrane called the pericardium. Inflammation can cause this sac to tighten and become rigid, and this rigidity impairs the proper blood flow needed to keep the heart beating. It is a rare condition and, ultimately, fatal."

"I see," Damon murmured.

"Your father manifested some of the symptoms of heart failure," Buchanan continued. "Difficulty breathing, swelling in the legs. That is what Doctor Breaks thought it was, the beginnings of heart failure. But constrictive pericarditis is difficult to diagnose, and it is only after an autopsy that a final diagnosis is rendered complete. As it was here."

Damon digested the information. "Not to sound like the selfish being I am, but is this something I will have to look forward to as I grow older? Heart conditions are passed on in families, are they not?"

The doctor cut his ham into small pieces. "They can be, but it is not the case here. Doctor Breaks informed me that your father had scarlet fever as a child. The damage to his heart was done then, and it steadily worsened the older he grew until the heart ceased functioning. Nothing to be done, Your Grace. As I relayed, it is ultimately a fatal condition."

Damon had no idea about the scarlet fever. But as he observed earlier, he and his father never had any conversation of consequence, primarily related to anything personal or medical.

"I appreciate that you could attend at such short notice and collect this information for me. You seem a learned fellow. Can I ask you something completely off the topic?"

The doctor sipped his coffee. "Of course."

"A doctor told me at St. Bartholomew's Hospital that work is underway to classify blood types in Vienna. Theoretically, at some point in the distant future, you will be able to classify people according to these types, and these categories could show commonality through the paternal link. Is this accurate?"

Althea looked at him as if he had grown another head.

The doctor nodded. "Yes, Your Grace, I have heard of the theory. But that will be years away, decades, even. Blood study is long, tedious work and won't happen overnight."

Damon took a sip of tea. "So, here in 1898, there is no medical or scientific way to prove if someone is related."

Buchanan raised an eyebrow. "Have you a paternity suit being pressed?"

"Ah, no. God forbid. I am merely curious," Damon nonchalantly responded as he placed the cup on the saucer.

"There is no definitive way to prove it, though there are quacks aplenty who will testify as to nose and finger lengths being communal features as well as hair and eye color. It proves nothing, and neither does hair and eye color. Even the roof of the mouth is measured. I have seen black-haired parents give birth to a red-haired baby, and the mother was not unfaithful." Buchanan popped a ham in his mouth, chewed, and then swallowed. "A simple investigation found redheads in past bloodlines."

"There is much we do not know, Your Grace," the doctor continued. "In 1889, a Swiss chemist, Johann Friedrich Miescher, discovered and isolated a material from white blood cells called nucleic acid. Again, this will take years to research, though they have given it a scientific name: deoxyribonucleic acid. This substance may also hold the key to common features passed on to families or even recessive traits, but who knows?"

"You seem to understand a good deal about it," Damon said. "For a police surgeon."

"I am a physician, educated and trained. I like to keep up with the latest discoveries or theories. Any doctor worth his salt would do so," Buchanan said matter-of-factly. He did not take what Damon said as an insult.

And how astounding to discover Damon had not meant it as one.

Damon glanced at Althea, who was busily constructing a sandwich. "What *are* you doing, Miss Galway?"

"Making my favorite sandwich. Bacon and cheese on toast. It is my comfort food, as it were." She neatly sliced the sandwich into two wedges, then passed him the plate. "Here. This is for you, and perhaps it will also comfort you."

And there was that compassion.

That Althea cared enough to offer him a sandwich made from her hands caused a lump in his throat. Not like him at all. He could be callous and refuse her sweet gift. But for the life of him, he could not do it.

Damon took the plate. "Thank you," he whispered.

He bit into it, and it was delicious.

Comfort, indeed.

ALTHEA LOOKED AWAY and started to make another sandwich for herself. What possessed her to do that? The room was quiet for several minutes as everyone ate. She cast the occasional clandestine look Damon's way. He was unshaven, and even though he had slept for hours, he still looked exhausted. Althea had the impulse to hold him close and protect him from the world. How ludicrous.

Corbett laid his napkin across his empty plate. "I must return to Bethnal Green. Another autopsy awaits. Althea, are you coming with me?"

"Could you wait one moment, Miss Galway?" Damon asked. "I would like a word."

"I will hail a hansom," Corbett interjected.

Damon stepped forward and held out his hand, and Corbett took it. "Thank you, Doctor Buchanan. I am glad your services are available to The Galway Agency, for I may need them again. If it is acceptable, I have another appointment and can drop Miss Galway at Cleveland Street or wherever she wishes." Damon turned to look at her. "Is that satisfactory with you, Miss Galway?"

"Yes, it is. You return to your work, Corbett. I'm fine," Althea replied.

Once alone, Damon kissed her gloveless hand, causing heated waves to roll through her. "And thank *you* for taking my case. There is no time to go over what the next part will entail, but if you can glean any idea, it's from my questions to the good doctor. I recently visited my mother in Spain. She gave me a list of the illegitimate children that she knew of. Ones that my father sired. I suspect there are more than what is on her list, and I want to trace them."

Now *that* topic she did not expect.

Althea had many questions and gazed into his light blue eyes for answers. His emotions were hidden, although she could read warmth in them as if that heat was for her and her alone.

Before she could reply, the butler came to fetch them, so she gathered up her bags and was quickly whisked into the carriage, and they were off. They would be on Cleveland Street within minutes.

"I have a favor to ask," Damon said, his voice low. "Will you attend my father's funeral with me? I need you by my side. I cannot explain it. But I cannot get through the dismal affair unless you are there."

Damon looked at her almost beseechingly, and it caused her heart to stutter. How could she say no? "Send the information to me when the plans finalize, and I will attend."

"Thank you. After the funeral, we will go into the case details, and I will make certain bacon and cheese on toast sandwiches are available."

Althea laughed gently. Then she sobered. "I *am* sorry about your father. Whether close to him or not, he was your father. Death is so final. There are always things that were not said or done. Such a maelstrom of feelings. Even for you, Damon. Oh. I did not mean that the way it sounds."

"Nevertheless, how astute of you. Ah, here we are at Cleveland Street." He held out his hand and helped her stand. Then, he kissed her on the forehead as the door opened. "Until later, Althea."

As the driver assisted her from the carriage, she absently touched her forehead where he had kissed her. Althea's skin tingled under her touch. Sighing wistfully, she turned to watch the carriage disappear down the street.

Oh, this won't be easy, keeping things professional. And finding illegitimate children? Why would he care? The man was such a delicious puzzle. Already her heart was engaged. There was no denying it. How much of it was involved was another question entirely.

Caution would have to be the watchword.

But it may already be too late.

Chapter 4

OLIVIA GREETED HIM warmly. It was the first time Damon had seen his newly discovered half-sister since returning from Spain.

He recalled what he had said to her when he had discovered their blood connection: "Shall we become acquainted? Could we be friends? Will we, at some point, think of each other as brother and sister? Can it be achieved?"

When Damon said those words aloud, they sounded foreign to his own ears. Not only the uncharacteristic vulnerability, but when had he articulated with such compassion or even formed such anomalous thoughts?

Friends? Brother and sister?

It beggared belief and was far removed from his previous apathetic behavior. Had some horrible shift taken place within him? Or was kindness and vulnerability always within, waiting for an opportunity to escape? Isn't this why he wished to locate half-siblings? Was he that desperate for some blood connection, no matter how dubious? Did he desire to cobble together some kind of family?

He never had a family, not in the truest sense. All this turmoil of emotion made him feel pathetic and exposed, and Damon nearly stood to depart. But Olivia's warm and sincere greeting kept him rooted to the spot.

He took her outstretched hand and squeezed it gently before releasing it. "I shall not stay long, but I want you to know before it makes tomorrow's papers. The Duke of Chellenham is dead. Our common father, although he was not a father at all, was he? If ever a more loathsome, reckless, and self-centered man ever lived, I do not know him. Wait. That is not completely true. There is a couple worse in some respects and more than a few on equal footing."

"How true," Gideon murmured. "I am sorry for your loss, at any rate, for that pushes you into the dukedom limelight. Welcome to the club. Come, let us take a seat."

They sat in the parlor, Damon in one of the chairs, Gideon and Olivia on the sofa opposite.

Olivia frowned. "I do not feel anything."

"Exactly my reaction," Damon replied. "And perfectly normal under the circumstances. You didn't know him. Be glad of it. Blast it. I did not know him, either. We were strangers. I will spare you the details of his lurid discovery, all I will say is that it was late at night, and he wasn't alone." He mentioned in general terms of the autopsy and its discoveries. "His heart ailment is not passed on to family members, so there's a mercy."

"That is good to know," Olivia murmured.

Damon exhaled. "There will be a funeral. I will not ask you to attend. I do not expect you to appear."

"The only reason I would is to be there for you," Olivia replied.

"Ah. I truly am touched by that, more than you know. I don't expect either of you to attend. Continue with your summer plans. I will have someone by my side to offer support. With Parliament not sitting, you are heading to Foxmont for the remainder of the summer, correct?"

"That we are; until the middle of September," Gideon replied, taking Olivia's hand. "We depart tomorrow. I can postpone it, stay behind, attend the funeral, and join Olivia later."

"I thank you, but no. Do not alter your plans."

"Damon, why not join us after the funeral?" Olivia asked. "Just stay for a week, rest, and get your bearings before facing the dukedom and all its responsibilities?"

The heartfelt suggestion caused his heart to hitch. Perhaps this is why he wanted to find any siblings. To have someone give a damn.

"You are thoughtful, Olivia. I will take you up on it later; never fear. But I am afraid all those responsibilities are weighing on me already. There is much to address. Including the current financial situation and other matters. My father told me nothing, prepared me—for nothing."

"You know you can ask Christian and me anything," Gideon offered. "We will assist you in any way we can."

Christian Bamford, the Duke of Allenby, was married to Althea's older sister, Eleanora, and a former member of The Rakes of St. Regent's Park. Damon considered both Christian and Gideon friends. Well, especially Christian; they had known each other since they were boys.

"Believe me; I will take you both up on that. I also have one more matter to discuss. I've hired The Galway Agency to look for any half-siblings."

He told them about visiting his mother and the list of names.

"I have a favor to ask," Damon continued. "I will understand if you would rather keep our connection secret. But the duke is dead. There is no need to keep our association cloistered away. I wish to tell Althea Galway for investigation purposes, and eventually, I want to recognize you as my sister. But only when you are keen, if at all. What are your feelings on any of this?"

"I don't mind Althea knowing. She is my friend and will keep my confidence. You can tell her sister and her husband since they are part of the agency. As for making it public, I need time, Damon. Is that all right?"

"More than all right."

"The invitation is open at Foxmont. Come for a week or more if you wish. Will you keep me apprised of your investigation? If you find any more siblings?" Olivia asked.

"Well, I may have found one."

He mentioned Evercreech, the police detective that attended his father's death.

Olivia's eyes grew round. "What are the odds?"

"I have a feeling that there are many more out there. I will certainly keep you informed." Damon stared at them, sitting close on the sofa, holding hands. "The two of you look unbearably happy. It's most annoying."

Olivia and Gideon laughed as they showed him to the door.

Then Olivia grasped Damon's arm, stood on the tips of her toes, and kissed his cheek. "Dear brother," she whispered.

He patted her hand and turned to depart before he fell to pieces. Regardless of his outward chilly demeanor, his inner emotions balanced on a knife's edge.

OLIVIA WATCHED AS DAMON disappeared into the main hall. Gideon stood beside her and slipped his arm about her waist.

"A heartfelt goodbye. Your relationship with your newly discovered half-brother is advancing faster than I imagined," Gideon observed.

"It is, isn't it? I think the emotion involved has surprised us both," Olivia replied softly.

"I will wager that the person he asked to support him at the funeral is Althea Galway," Gideon mused, a smile curving about his mouth.

She turned slightly and looked up at her husband. "No, truly? Oh, that would be wonderful, as I adore Althea. She would be perfect for Damon. Just the type of lady to keep him grounded. She is honest and caring, just what Damon needs. Someone to love him unconditionally." Olivia paused. "I am not sure why I feel that, as I hardly know him."

They headed toward the drawing room. "You know, after Damon and I met with Huxley and were heading home, he said something quite extraordinary—for him," Gideon said reflectively. "I am not certain he knew that he had said it aloud. 'I always wanted a sister. I always wanted someone to love.' Damon is a little lost. Lonely. Perhaps—damaged. Like most of the members in The Rakes of St. Regent's Park, at one time or another."

Olivia covered her face with her hands, the emotion overwhelming her. She wanted to run after Damon and hold her brother close. Protect him.

"Oh, my love," Gideon crooned as he gathered her in his arms. "You feel things so deeply. It is one of the many, many things I love about you. Never fear. I believe Damon will find his way. How can he not do so with you in his life? And his friends. In fact, I will stop in and see Christian before we leave for Foxmont and ask him to keep a close eye on Damon."

Olivia dabbed her eyes as she looked up at him. "Oh, will you? That would make me feel much better."

"Then, I shall."

"Perhaps I should attend the funeral and offer my support," Olivia said, her brows knotting in uncertainty. She wanted nothing to do with the man who had sired her. Why attend his funeral? Since she never wanted to meet him, looking down at the dead duke lying in a casket did not appeal.

"No, you heard Damon. He does not expect you to. You can offer support in other ways. Write him frequently, and if you wish, we will return to London when you say."

"Oh, I do love you," Olivia affirmed as she leaned against his chest. "I think we will return in a few weeks after we take care of business at Foxmont."

"And who knows, a summer romance may flourish between Damon and Althea. Nothing like falling in love to set a person on the correct path," Gideon teased.

If only such would occur. Olivia wanted Damon to find love, peace, and happiness.

THE MESSAGE ARRIVED two days later, stating the date and time of the Duke of Chellenham's funeral. Since Christian and Eleanora were attending, Althea would travel with them. She wore the same black gown she had worn to her father's funeral nearly four years ago, and Althea did not care a whit of its out-of-style look.

As they entered the Southwark St. Saviour church, Althea marveled at the gothic arches and spires, for its medieval roots were visible.

A man stepped forward. "Your Graces, Miss Galway, if you would follow me."

The usher escorted them to the front of the church, where Damon stood in the first pew. He stepped forward and held his hand to Althea, and Christian and Eleanora followed. Once seated, Althea was astonished that he still clasped her gloved hand.

"Thank you for coming," he whispered in her ear.

It was challenging to be heard over the organ as the sound reverberated off the stone walls.

"As you see, I am the only one to represent the Cranston family," Damon continued in a low voice. "My aunt, my father's older sister, married an American decades ago and hasn't returned to these shores since. I do not know her or her children. My grandparents on my father's side long passed, and no one from my mother's side is attending, obviously."

"I don't mind," she whispered in reply.

As Althea started to move away, he briefly nuzzled her neck, sending fissions of awareness all through her. His enticing scent enveloped her senses, a mixture of his soap, cologne, and his own earthy essence. How tempting it would be to crawl into Damon's lap and bury her face into the curve of his neck. It was inappropriate to experience such a wanton sensation while at a funeral. Reluctantly, Althea shook such feelings away and turned her attention to the front of the church.

Appropriately somber pallbearers carried in the fancy oak coffin. How strange Damon was not one of them. Wasn't the son expected to act as such? What did Althea know of peerage funerals?

The rest of the service passed in a blur. The church was barely half full, and no one spoke except the Anglican priest, although Althea wasn't sure what went on in church services since, while growing up, her family hardly ever attended except at Easter and Christmas and not every year.

As they stood for the final prayer, Damon finally released her hand. Everyone stood silent as the pallbearers carried out the coffin, and the pews started to empty, beginning with theirs. Damon took her arm and slipped it through his.

Walking behind the coffin with the new duke, wouldn't that stir speculation? She could hardly decline, for it would draw even more unwanted attention, so Althea allowed Damon to lead her down the long aisle.

"The graveyard on these grounds has been closed since '53, but they are making an exception for my father. He will be buried next to his parents in the Cranston crypt," Damon murmured close to her ear. "Because of it, there is no need for an elaborate procession with hired mourners, horses, and a fancy hearse. Saved a few pounds there."

Althea glanced at Damon, but his expression showed no emotion at all.

After the priest gave the final blessing at the crypt, a man stepped forward and said, "There will be a brief reception in the church library. Tea and biscuits are available."

"Good Lord," Damon muttered, "I want this over. Will you stay for the reception?"

"Yes, of course."

Some mourners departed, but the rest headed toward the upstairs library. It was a serene spot, with walls covered with books and sunlight pouring through the stained-glass windows.

Damon gave her hand a gentle squeeze. "I must greet the mourners; you will stay with Christian and Eleanora?"

"Yes, of course."

Asher Colborne, Baron Wenlock, and his wife, Lady Chastity, approached Damon just as she walked away.

Damon seemed oddly detached as if he was not here. Althea knew enough that he wore multifarious masks to hide how he truly felt, and the newly minted duke wore one now.

Their first consultation occurred this past autumn at The Rakes of St. Regent's Park's meeting place on Albany Street, where she and Eleanora took on Christian's case. Damon had been the Marquess of Brookton, then. Damon's handsomeness had struck Althea, but when he opened his mouth to speak, it ruined the illusion, and her dislike germinated. He had acted boorish, dismissing the usefulness of women running an investigative agency.

That should have ended any interest right there.

The next time Damon and Althea met was shortly after that at Cleveland Street. Before Damon had arrived for the meeting, she said to Eleanora: "Outwardly, the man is too perfectly gorgeous.

Inside? I will lay coin there is an empty pit, with an unquestionable rot of what is probably left of his soul."

Once he had entered the room, Althea interviewed him rather pointedly about his personal life because it had a bearing on the case. And, truth be told, she was curious. He acted detached and dismissive until she began probing him deeper. Damon became agitated. One could even say emotional.

"Regarding my preferences, there were sexual activities in my past where men were participants. If that makes me this bi-sexual that you described, so be it. If you must know, I prefer women, but I also do not deny myself any pleasure."

He had spat those words at her, clearly hoping to shock her. Knowing he indulged in such dissolute activities should have slammed the door shut permanently on any inkling of attraction. But it had only made him all the more mesmerizing.

"Why stuffy virgins would read such claptrap is beyond me. I believe on-hand experience is always best."

He then gave Althea a wicked grin. He had been referring to a physiological book she quoted about the recent classification of sexual preferences. So, she retorted about him having a portrait in the attic, calling him out on his nickname in society.

His smile had evaporated.

"I am beyond weary of the Dorian Gray references. It's not amusing. And it is insulting. I may be debauched, but I would never sink to the depths of that gothic fictional character."

He had been angry then, his eyes like blue chips of ice. The interview continued, and the sparks flew about. Mixed in with the annoyance on both sides was a decided attraction.

Then as he rose to leave, she had as well, and the hem of her skirt caught on the toe of her boot, causing her to stumble. Strong arms held her upright and enfolded her in a masculine embrace—Damon's strong arms.

Time had stood still.

"Are you well?" Damon murmured to her, genuine concern in his tone.

"Do not think this is some parlor trick to have you rescue me from a faux fall. I don't play games," she whispered into the folds of his silky cravat.

Damon then nuzzled her neck. "I would not care if it was a game."

He had smelled wonderful. Exactly like today. Freshly laundered linen and a hint of expensive cologne with a woodsy and bergamot aroma. Very appealing. Damon holding her close had been a revelation as if her desire sprang free from its moorings. Leaning against all that solid masculinity had her insides tumbling.

They haven't stopped tumbling since. Unconsciously, Althea laid a hand across her midsection.

"Sister, are you not feeling well?" Eleanora asked worriedly.

Althea was torn from her reminisces and brought into the present. She cleared her throat. "I'm fine. Let us fetch a cup of tea; then, we can be on our way."

A large table sat at the front of the room with tall men wearing livery standing nearby. On that table were platters of sugar biscuits decorated with icing crosses and thin slices of dark fruit cake with a marzipan topping. Althea did not feel like eating for her innards were scrambled like Mrs. Bartle's Sunday morning eggs.

All thanks to that man.

The new Duke of Chellenham.

Chapter 5

ASHER HELD OUT HIS hand. "My condolences. Not only on your father's death but the dukedom being thrust upon you."

Damon took his friend's hand. They had known each other since they were boys. And because of it, Asher partially understood the dynamics of Damon's so-called relationship with the old duke.

"And thrust upon me it truly has. Thank you for coming. You did not return to London specifically for this? God forbid."

"Afraid so. We haven't seen you in months, and we wanted to be here for you," Asher replied.

Damon's gaze slid to Asher's pretty wife. He took her hand and kissed it. "Lady Chastity. Thank you."

Damon spoke sincerely, softening the lady's expression further.

"Anything you need, Your Grace, do let us know." Chastity moved away, but Asher lingered.

"Allow me to arrange a dinner party. You, me, Christian, and Gideon," Asher murmured.

"Gideon has returned to Foxmont for a few weeks, but yes, a dinner or luncheon with the three of us."

Asher nodded and joined his wife by the refreshments.

"Your Grace."

Damon turned toward the deep voice. It was Oliver Wollstonecraft, a recent prospect member of The Rakes of St. Regent's Park.

"May I offer my condolences," Wollstonecraft said gravely. "My grandfather, the Earl of Carnstone, and my father, Viscount Tensbridge, also offer their condolences." The honest words were more than he had exchanged with Wollstonecraft since the man joined the group.

Damon took the outstretched hand and shook it. "I appreciate it. My sincere thanks to you and your family."

"I don't habitually attend funerals but wanted to offer my commiserations."

"Not much of a funeral. My father wished for a low-key event," Damon lied with ease. "And I followed his wishes."

Oliver Wollstonecraft nodded and moved away, and Damon found himself moved by the sympathy offered. He should show Wollstonecraft a little more respect at the next meeting. Stranger after stranger cooed their sympathy. And as if he were an automaton, he shook hands when offered and responded appropriately.

His gaze kept sliding toward Althea, following her about the room and tracking her movements. She stood with Christian and Asher and their wives, speaking familiarly. When the mourners gathered their tea and edibles, Damon strode purposely toward the group.

Grasping Althea gently by the arm, he steered her away from the others. "Just need to speak for a moment," he called back. "A matter of business."

She pulled her arm out of his grip. "What are you doing? You are attracting notice," Althea huffed with exasperation.

"What do I care about it? And more importantly, since when do *you* care?" he responded incredulously.

"Since you are now a *duke*. Society will scrutinize your every move along with whom you see in society. I should never have agreed to stand with you today."

Althea's curt tone caused his heart to sink like a stone. But being adept at tucking such disappointment away, he instead showed infuriation. "I do not need your pity or your counterfeit empathy. As I said, this is business. Say so here if you do not wish to take on my case. I will find another agency, perhaps one more competent. One run by a man."

He inwardly winced at the jaundiced statement. Althea and Eleanora had proven that they were more than capable. He was hurt and lashed out, something a petulant child would do.

Something *he* would do.

"Hell, ignore that. I do not mean it," Damon murmured. And he spoke the truth. Why Damon responded in such a way puzzled him exceedingly. Instead of dismissing his crass behavior as in the past, perhaps it was time for further self-reflection. And soon.

"I wonder," Althea whispered, her lovely eyes alive with flames of fury. "Sometimes, when emotional, people say things they genuinely believe, but in normal circumstances would never voice aloud. Or it could be that you are just an arrogant, ignorant bastard deep to your core."

Ouch.

No one put Damon in his place quite like Althea Galway. And he deserved her wrath—every bit of it.

"Perhaps I am both. Nevertheless, I do apologize. It was uncalled for, and I had no business uttering such misogynistic drivel. For I do not believe it, I assure you. I never have, regardless of what I may have said now or in the past."

Her mouth twisted. "Hmm. Well, considering the circumstances of your father passing away, I accept your apology. This time. But if you ever speak such misogynistic drivel as you call it, ever again, our association is at an end."

"I have been duly warned. Now, come with me to Clarendon Place to discuss the case."

"No."

"Now, who is acting petulant?"

"You haven't heard a word I've said. After being by your side at the funeral service, I cannot go into your house alone. If this is business, then come to Cleveland Street instead."

Damon exhaled, frustrated. He had ordered a luncheon prepared with her favorite sandwiches. There was no use arguing. Looking about the room, it appeared Althea was indeed correct. They *were* attracting attention.

"As you wish. When?"

"In two hours, at three o'clock. And we will not be alone. Eleanora and Christian will be there," Althea said, her voice firm.

"What?" he said a little too loudly, attracting even more scrutiny. "Whatever for?"

"They are part of the agency, and I may need them on this case. Until then." She inclined her head and moved away.

Disheartened and aroused, he growled low in his throat. He marched to the food table, grabbed a funeral biscuit, and nibbled on it.

Christian came to stand next to him. "Damon, you certainly know how to provoke speculation. Althea put you in your place once again?" he mused sardonically.

"Once again. And I loved it," Damon replied, causing Christian to chuckle.

Then Christian sobered. "Althea told us you wish to hire the agency. You do not mind that Eleanora and I will attend the meeting?"

"Whether I mind or not is of no consequence. Althea set the terms. I will see you at three."

Christian shrugged and returned to his wife. Damon tossed the half-eaten biscuit on the table, and one of his footmen swooped in to gather it for disposal.

Damn his degenerate father for leaving him in this position. The next several days contained various meetings and conferences with solicitors and stewards, let alone preparations for the autumn session of Parliament. He had received the Writ from the Queen to take his place in the House of Lords on the first day of that session, Monday, October the third. That carefree, devil-may-care life he led since reaching the age of majority was at an end.

Nothing to be done about it.

Not that he had been with a woman lately. While in Spain, he remained celibate. Hardly proper to be haunting Cádiz's nightlife while visiting his mother. But he had not gone out to seek female company since returning, either.

Eleanora, Christian, and Althea headed toward the exit. Damon's intense gaze followed them.

Turn around. Look at me.

But the headstrong Althea continued out the door. Perhaps he was deluded in thinking she was interested in him, even a little.

And it made her all the more incredibly appealing.

Chapter 6

WHEN ALTHEA RETURNED home, she changed from the black gown into a more serviceable navy wool skirt and white blouse with a matching short jacket. Eleanora had changed as well. They waited in the study office with Christian.

Already the duke was late. How typical.

"What is going on between you and Chellenham?" Eleanora demanded.

"El," Christian laughed.

"Well? He held her hand throughout the service. Althea walked down the aisle with him, and they conversed confidentially at the reception. You know this will make the society columns," Eleanora replied pointedly.

Althea groaned, covering her face with her hands. Her sister was correct; this *could* make the papers. And she should have thought of that before agreeing to attend the funeral. But she felt sorry for Damon and wished to support him. What a quandary.

"I have known Damon since we were boys at school," Christian interjected. "Our friendship has ebbed and flowed over the years—not on my end, but on his. If he feels too much, he pushes people away, literally or by saying something insulting to make the other person retreat. Why put up with such a capricious person? Most don't. It is why Damon has never had a serious relationship with anyone, including women. It is why he seeks his pleasures with strangers. No attachments of any kind."

"Then why be friends with him at all?" Eleanora asked, clearly bewildered. "He is not worthy of your friendship and compassion and is thoroughly unlikeable."

"It is a legitimate question. I can only speak for myself, but since I've known Damon for so long, I know there is goodness in him, although well hidden. He does not show that part to just anybody. Why be friends? Because I value our relationship and accept him, flaws and all. And because of those sporadic moments when Damon does show emotion," Christian replied. "That brief glimpse is so radiating you want to bask in it. Because you know there is much more beneath the surface."

What her brother-in-law disclosed about Damon was how she felt when with him. Althea *knew* that more was secreted away, and she wanted to be the one to—what, precisely? Tear off those masks? Peel back those onion-type layers? Or whatever metaphor fits. The new duke possessed a fair number of protective coverings.

"Damon is complex, to be certain, but he has changed in the past year," Christian continued. "Don't get me wrong, he can still make cutting remarks to anger the most serene of personalities, but he has made more of an effort within our circle of friends. A small beginning but a good one. That variation began when he met *you*, Althea."

Her eyes widened. But before she could contemplate that remark, let alone form a response, Mrs. Bartle entered the room.

"The Duke of Chellenham," she announced.

Damon strode into the room with two footmen following behind, carrying a large hamper. "Set it up there, on that table," he ordered.

Christian rose and waved his arm at the footmen busily laying out the food. "What is this?"

"I thought we might be a bit peckish after those dreadful proceedings, so I brought along some of our favorites." He handed his coat to Mrs. Bartle. "My good lady, if you could bring tea, it would be greatly appreciated."

The housekeeper blushed. "Right away, Your Grace." She hurried out the door.

When the footmen concluded setting out the repast, Damon said, "Return to Clarendon Place and have the driver come here in an hour."

Once the servants departed, Althea made her way to the table. There were platters of sandwiches and sweets. Along with the food were matching plates and cups, and saucers. There was also grapes, sliced apple, and assorted cheeses. In truth, she was rather famished and—

Sitting on one of the platters were toasted bacon and cheese, her favorite. Her heart beat a little faster at the discovery. As Christian related, Damon said or did something thoughtful—now and then.

Damon stood beside her. "Allow me to apologize once again," he murmured so only she could hear. "You are the most competent, intelligent woman I have ever met, and I believe that you—and your sister and cousin—are more capable than any ten men together. That is why I want you on this case." He moved away before she could respond.

And there it was.

That moment of intense radiation. Althea closed her eyes and reveled in his sincerely spoken words.

"Beefsteak sandwiches for Christian, ham and egg for me, and I apologize, Eleanora. I am not aware of yours," Damon said.

"And cheese and bacon for Althea?" Eleanora responded. "I like all three, so I am lucky there. Thank you for this, Chellenham."

Althea cast a glance toward her sister. Being polite to Damon and thanking him? Would wonders ever cease?

With tea food collected, they took their seats at the long table. Eleanora would be taking notes.

"What is all this about?" Christian asked.

"I am not sure how to explain it," Damon began. "During my East End sojourns, I was astounded to find that many working at music halls and brothels were orphans, raised in orphanages, workhouses, or even the streets. And more than a few were the illegitimate children of peers or other wealthy men. It did not seem right to me. These children were tossed aside like so much rubbish, left to fate, only able to find work in the gutters or one or two steps above it."

Damon's sipped his tea. "Men of means have acted recklessly in this fashion for centuries. How many of these unwanted children belonged to my father? It began to haunt me. It appears I have some semblance of a soul after all. I traveled to Spain a few weeks past to visit my estranged mother. She gave me a list of eight names she knew of, along with the name of an orphanage. My mother claims there are more children out there, now adults. I do not intend to know these people personally; I want to assist them. If they want or need it. Set up a trust account, I suppose. I haven't worked it all out yet."

Eleanora and Christian glanced at each other. Althea could understand their surprise, for his narrative also riveted her. Then Eleanora returned her attention to her notes.

"Damon, while it is admirable that you wish to assist these illegitimate children or adults, if word gets around, you will have people lined up with their hands out," Christian said gently. "There is no way to prove your father sired them."

"I am aware. Doctor Buchanan made that very plain, scientifically speaking," Damon replied. "It is why we must do this discreetly. Starting with the names on the list and investigating the orphanage."

"If the orphanage even exists," Althea interjected.

Damon swung his gaze toward her. "What makes you say that?"

"Your father could have given your mother the name of a fictitious orphanage to assuage her concerns about where these illegitimate babies were winding up. Did she ever inquire?"

"My God, you have a dark turn of mind," Damon marveled, his eyes sparkling. "My parents had an acrimonious split, with my father threatening incarceration in an asylum. My mother was effectively exiled to Spain and banned from contacting me. I just found this out during my recent visit. So no, I doubt she had the time nor inclination to check the validity of my father's statements."

"He was a miserable bastard, your father," Christian fumed.

"The very reason I gave him a bare-boned send-off," Damon replied acerbically. "He did not deserve all the pomp and circumstance a duke usually receives. Good riddance."

"I believe the place to begin is for me to take the lead on this case. And when needed, involve Christian and Eleanora," Althea stated. "They are on a case now involving fraud at a railway company, but it is a drawn-out one, so they will have time to assist here and there. We have recently hired a competent young woman I can use to gather the needed information. I will start with the orphanage. Do you have the list?"

Damon pulled a sheet of paper out of his side coat pocket. "There is one name you will all recognize, and until she wants it made public— if at all—you are all sworn to secrecy. It is Olivia Durham, Gideon's wife."

To say that Althea, Eleanora, and Christian were stunned was an understatement. Damon explained the circumstances of her birth and that a country vicar and his wife adopted her. Eleanora was furiously taking notes while Althea tried to wrap her head around this shocking development.

Her new friend was Damon's half-sister?

But, now that she knew, Althea could see the resemblance. The hair and eye color obviously, but also the shape of the mouth, the full lips, the sharp cheekbones.

My. God.

"Do you wish me to contact this nunnery and the sister that Olivia spoke to a few years ago?" Althea asked.

"Yes, and I want to go with you when you do. The nun told Olivia she was well aware of my father's name. I want to know how," Damon replied. "As I said, I want to be involved in this investigation as much as possible. Regrettably, I have many meetings in the next two days. Solicitors and the like."

"Why don't I start with this orphanage? I should have some information for you once your conferences have concluded," Althea suggested.

"Yes, that is a sound plan," Damon responded. "There is another name on the list. You will not believe this."

Damon explained how the Metropolitan Police detective from B Division, Westminster, that attended to his father's death was the same name on the list, Mitchell Evercreech.

"My mother said one of the names was a copper. And the name just below it? August Donaldson? A footman at Chellenham Park."

"Are you certain you wish to pull on these threads, Damon?" Christian asked.

"I know there will be some who will be angry. Perhaps this is a selfish endeavor, as egocentricity has ruled my life. Olivia has accepted me with open arms. But I understand she is the exception, not the rule. Do not approach anyone as yet. As Althea said, the orphanage and the nunnery to start."

Christian stood. "Then we will let you get to it. Eleanora and I are available if and when required. Please, say seated." He said to Damon and Althea as he held his hand to Eleanora to assist her standing. "Condolences once again, Damon. Ash mentioned the dinner. We will arrange it next week. Do you wish us to stay, Althea, until Damon departs?"

Bless her dear brother-in-law for the offering. Althea glanced at the mantel clock. "Chellenham's carriage will be here in less than ten minutes. I will be fine." She smiled as she glanced at Damon. "Mrs. Bartle is within shouting distance if needs must. Our housekeeper uses her broom as if it was a broadsword."

Christian and Eleanora laughed as they departed.

They were alone.

Althea wished she had asked them to stay, for the air between her and Damon was awkward yet electric. They gazed at each other, sitting in opposite wing chairs.

"Damon, I am sorry I was snappish with you at the reception. At your father's funeral, of all things. It was not well done of me." She meant it. The fact that her emotions were all over the map when in his presence proved she would have to be more cautious from now on.

"I deserved your wrath. Always speak your mind with me. Never change that."

"It is admirable that you wish to find any siblings."

"Is it? I wonder. Guilt is fueling my actions. There was another time in my life I did not act when I should have. I will not turn away this time."

"Can you tell me about it?"

Damon exhaled. "The drowning episode of so long ago."

During Christian's case, the investigation led to a former friend of The Rakes of St. Regent's Park. The summer the boys were sixteen, Ford Whitney held one of their friends underwater until he drowned.

"While I lay there, drunk, thinking I was dreaming, Ford fought with Hayes Addington. I was oblivious to the tragic incident playing out under my very nose. Then, I shrugged and moved on. What does that say about me? Not much. I will not do that again nor abdicate my responsibility."

"I admire that, and thank you for sharing it," Althea replied softly. This confession made him all the more alluring. Layers to peel back, indeed.

Damon stood, took her hand, and pulled her slowly toward him. "Indulge me. For on such a day, I wish to feel alive. Just a brief kiss of farewell. Will you allow it?"

"To what purpose?" Althea whispered, thrilled to her toes by the suggestion.

"Because, my Thea, you have attracted me as no other."

My Thea.

Oh, she liked that—very much.

"I will indulge you because of the day." As if she could say no.

This attraction had been building since that investigation interview in this room almost one year ago. That meeting where Althea, in not so many words, called him a deviant Dorian Gray, and Damon called her a stuffy, judgmental virgin. When she had stumbled, and he caught her from tumbling to the floor, Althea had wanted him to kiss her then with those sinfully full lips.

Damon cupped her face, the pad of his thumbs caressing her cheeks. Her face burned hot, and the anticipation grew as he moved toward her. Heat pooled low in her belly and lower still. Her breasts felt heavy, and she ached to press them against him. Althea did not close her eyes as she wanted to see everything and commit it to memory.

Damon's lips touched hers, a feathery contact, then he softly nibbled on her lower lip before taking the kiss a little deeper. A perpetual flame burst to life inside her. The tenderness of it had her near to swooning as it was as tinder to flint and steel.

The kiss was deft and gentle, revealing a hint of the devil within him. He then kissed deeper, and the evident hunger spurred her desire. One of his hands trailed over the curve of her hip, leaving heat in its wake. Then he cupped her rear, bringing her in tight against him. Against that extremely hard masculine part of him.

Althea eagerly kissed him in return, her entire body throbbing with need. Briefly, their tongues tangled, and a husky groan came from deep within him. Soft whimpers of need escaped her lips as she plunged her fingers through his silky golden hair.

More. Althea wanted more.

She yearned to push him against the wall and touch him all over. Kiss every bit of exposed skin. Reach under his shirt and waistcoat and run the tips of her fingers across his flat stomach and lower until she boldly wrapped her hand around his erect shaft.

But it was over before she could blink, and a regretful moan escaped the corner of her mouth as Damon backed up a step.

No!

Althea nearly reached out to grab the lapels of his coat to pull him back.

"I will await your report." His voice shook a little, showing he was affected by their kiss as much as she had been. Damon glanced out the window. "My ride is here. I will send the footmen later to collect the dishes and hamper. Keep the food. Good afternoon."

Althea closed the study door behind him and let out a shuddering breath.

Never had she felt so alive.

Chapter 7

DAMON SAT IN HIS FATHER'S study at an elongated, rectangular table, half listening to the droning voice of his father's solicitor, Mr. Nigel Hendricks. He had heard words like 'bequeath to my only son and heir,' Damon nearly snorted at that.

Only *legitimate* son, more like. Legitimate in the eyes of the law and society.

The reason he was only half listening?

Althea.

He recalled that spectacular kiss over and over. How he ached for more. Damon wanted them rolling about the floor, limbs tangled, with him thrusting and Althea moaning with delight. By God, she was eager. Althea was passion incarnate in his arms. But he ended it; more fool him. Why? He had no idea.

"Your Grace? The will?" Mr. Hendricks questioned.

Unfortunately, that question pulled Damon into the present. "Continue. I am all attention."

The will was straightforward, as the late duke left everything to Damon. No mention of the duchess, his long-suffering wife, the duke's older sister and her family, or any faithful retainers. Not that any of the servants were long-term or all that faithful. Who could blame them?

"My mother was left with nothing?" Damon asked.

"Except what is standard in the primogeniture. Everything goes to the eldest son and heir. However, the widowed duchess is entitled to a small income from the dukedom, usually from the rents and such," Mr. Hendricks replied.

His mother would probably receive a pittance, which meant her upkeep would fall to him as the new duke. Blasted inheritance rules needed to be changed.

"And what of her dowry? Surely my father made provisions for that?" Damon asked.

Mr. Hendricks held up an officious-looking paper. "There was no dowry, Your Grace. It is all here, signed by your grandfathers and the late duke."

His mother was the granddaughter of a viscount, and Damon's grandfather was not even close to being either the heir apparent or the presumptive. There were three brothers before him, and they all had multiple sons. The viscountcy was and is insignificant and underprivileged according to peerage standards. One of his uncles was the viscount now, but he rarely ventured to London. Not even to attend Parliament. Damon had no contact with that side of the family for years, not since his mother's exile in Spain.

He could not recall the names of some of his cousins. How strange that he never came across any of them in London, but then, it was a populous city, and Damon rarely socialized with the upper crust. However, he wouldn't know his now adult cousins if he fell over them.

"Give me a summary. What is the financial state of the dukedom?" Damon glanced from Mr. Hendricks to the steward, Mr. Lionel Luckett.

There was an awkward silence.

"Good? Moderate? Fair to middling? Poor? Dire straits? Come now, speak," Damon barked, losing patience with this entire process.

"As you are aware, Your Grace," his valet Baldwin stated, "Mr. Crowle and I had a meeting with Mr. Hendricks and Mr. Luckett. The financial state is middling, leaning toward poor. The good news is that there are no significant outstanding debts. Your father recently tried to borrow against this town house but was refused because of the entailment. Although, I surmise that the duke was rebuffed more for his lack of funds and collateral."

Benjamin Crowle was Damon's solicitor. "And Mr. Crowle, are there any savings?" Damon asked. "This Queen Anne's Gate town house is paid for, surely."

"No savings of any consequence, Your Grace. There are thirty-five pounds in the account. And yes, the mortgage was paid by your grandfather decades ago."

That couldn't be right about the savings. Damon never knew his grandfather; he had passed away before Damon was born. Damon's father had boasted more than once that he had inherited tens of thousands of pounds.

"And the debts?"

"Mostly to the wine merchants, grocers, and other incidentals, Your Grace," Mr. Hendricks interjected.

"And most of these are past due and amount to 130 pounds," Mr. Crowle added, glaring at Mr. Hendricks. "If this is a true accounting."

Mr. Hendricks sputtered. "Of course, it is. How dare you—"

Damon raised his hand. "Enough. What else about my father's finances or lack thereof?"

Mr. Hendricks cleared his throat. "There have been a few ill-advised investments through the years, Your Grace, particularly a railroad scheme some fifteen years past. Regardless of these circumstances, the duke met his obligations, like your monthly allowance and other expenses."

Railway schemes. How many clueless peers have lost money in the past decades over such speculation? Damon thought his father was many things but never imprudent.

His father's solicitor reached into a folder and slid a piece of paper across the table toward Damon. "This is a list of the holdings, Your Grace. Your father sold many properties during the past decade for ready cash. It is how the late duke funded his lifestyle and the dukedom."

Damon took the paper and glanced at it. "And Chellenham Park? Are there still any tenants? Farmers? Is it making money at all?"

"Like most peerages, there has been a steady decline in income. Such is the case of your late father, Your Grace," Mr. Luckett replied gravely. "Eight tenants are left, and they pay the rent on time, and three farmers turned a tidy profit last year."

"And these rents are not enough to maintain the upkeep on Chellenham Park, correct?"

This situation was worse than Damon thought. He *had* been left with a muddle of a dukedom. It also meant he was accurate that his mother would get next to nothing.

"No, Your Grace," Mr. Luckett replied. "Chellenham Park is in dire need of maintenance. All that remains is the barest minimum of staff. The horses have all been sold but three. Your father hadn't been there in quite some time."

Damon growled low in his throat. Chellenham Park had some of the finest horses in East Sussex. Located outside the small village of Westmeston, the manor was somewhat isolated, which was why neither he nor his late father used the place. How can one live a debauched life in the middle of rolling hills, dense forests, galloping deer, and foraging foxes?

"What about the villa in Spain that my mother lives in? I was under the impression that my father bought it for her as part of the separation agreement. And what about the monthly stipend she is receiving?"

"That property was sold long ago, Your Grace. The stipulation was that your father would pay rent on it for as long as he lived. That pact will end once we contact the owner," Hendricks stated. "As for the allowance, that stopped more than fifteen years past. When the duke discovered she was living with a man."

What an odd condition of the sale.

As if reading his mind, Hendricks added, "The owner possesses many buildings in that area and will be glad to have the agreement at an end as it was to your father's advantage. He can rent the place at a higher price now. Or sell it."

So, not only would his mother have little to no income, but now she would be homeless. De León must have some coinage. How else had his mother been living these past years?

"You are not to contact the owner until I inform my mother of the circumstances and make other arrangements. I will continue to pay the rent until then." Damon paused. "With all the properties sold through the years, just what have you been the steward of, Mr. Luckett? What is this property on the list? Chellenhome? Never heard of it." Damon pointed to the paper. "And Chellenhome Farm and Flour Mill? Where in hell is it located? Why didn't my father sell this property and business?"

Hendricks and Luckett shifted uncomfortably in their chairs.

"Now we come to the meat of it, Your Grace," Baldwin said. "As these two gentlemen would not give us a straight answer. Perhaps they will, to you."

"The home is in Barking, Your Grace," Mr. Luckett replied.

"That tells me nothing," Damon retorted.

"It is a small town outside the East End of London, heading toward Essex," Baldwin replied. "We've had no time to inspect it, Your Grace, and these two have been closed-mouthed about it all."

"Only because we've had no dealings with it, Your Grace," Mr. Hendricks interrupted. "Your father handled all currency concerning that particular place, and I was only aware he possessed them. I have seen no records or financial statements; I only have the deeds to prove he owns them. They are now yours."

Weary from all this talk, Damon dismissed his father's solicitor and steward. "I want all final statements and papers sent to Mr. Crowle and the transfer of deeds done immediately."

"Will you be keeping us on, Your Grace?" Mr. Luckett tentatively asked.

"I will let you know in due course."

The men gathered their papers, and Kingsley escorted them from the room.

"Good Christ," Damon muttered.

"Indeed, Your Grace," Baldwin agreed. "Let us say your finances are in fine fettle, at least compared to the late duke. Your investment in the Daimler Motor Company has already paid dividends and will only rise in the foreseeable future. It is more than enough to keep the dukedom afloat."

"For now," Damon replied. "I suppose I will have to move into this horrible place. Have you worked out the staffing? Who will be kept on?" It was tradition to keep on the staff at the duke's residence, but Damon was determined to run things his way.

"We are still working on that with Kingsley and MacClery. We have discovered that Queen Anne's Gate and Chellenham Park do not have the full staffing one would expect for a duke's residence. So there will not be as many to dismiss as originally thought," Mr. Crowle stated.

Damon had noted the decline in housekeeping here and noticed a few expensive artworks were gone. No doubt sold by his late father for ready cash. "I wish to see the staff list before you act on it."

"Of course. You are selling Clarendon Place then, Your Grace?" Mr. Crowle asked.

"What choice do I have? I want every stick of furniture and wall coverings stripped from this place and sold. There still might be something here of value. Arrange to have the Clarendon Place furnishings moved here. I will not sleep in the same room as my father, so other rooms must be altered to suit me. This town house is to be fumigated, painted, and scrubbed clean before I move in."

He paused. "There is a footman at Chellenham Park I wish to keep on for now. August Donaldson. See it done. Also, my father's hired bully, Silas Browning. Keep him on for a few weeks as yet."

"Yes, Your Grace," Crowle answered as he took notes. "Will you be keeping on Luckett and Hendricks?"

"Do you want to be the steward, Baldwin?" Damon asked.

"Alas, no, Your Grace. Being a personal valet to a duke is as high as my ambitions climb. Presiding over a dukedom's holdings is more than I care to handle," Baldwin responded.

"I will venture to find you a competent steward, Your Grace; never fear," Mr. Crowle replied. "And selling Clarendon Place is a wise decision. The mortgage is nearly paid, so you should have a tidy sum left over."

"A tidy sum I will have to invest into the dukedom, as in alterations to this place. And Chellenham Park. Eventually," Damon frowned, annoyed afresh.

13 Queen Anne's Gate.

He hated this place as it held horrible childhood memories. Well, he would only move in once all alterations were complete. Too bloody bad he couldn't sell it. Perhaps he could rent it, but the income would be minuscule compared to selling Clarendon Place outright.

God, his head ached. Damon rubbed his temple. He wanted this meeting done. The men must have taken the hint because they started to gather their papers.

"We will investigate this Chellenhome immediately, Your Grace. Perhaps we can sell it as well," Mr. Crowle stated.

Investigate.

Althea Galway entered his mind. In truth, she never left. That soul-stirring kiss had kept him awake most of the night. Awake and aroused. As he pondered earlier, the kiss ignited those simmering flames into roaring, eternal bonfires.

"I will ask The Galway Agency to investigate Chellenhome. You two concentrate on the other matters at hand, like finalizing my father's so-called estate and starting renovations here. I also want to see all expenditures. As far as staffing, a little better than the bare minimum, but not as in years past. Those days are gone."

Keeping MacClery on was extravagant enough, for who had under butlers anymore?

"We shall move on your requests immediately, Your Grace," Crowle stated. He bowed and left the room.

Baldwin lingered. "You still wish for me to oversee your personal finances, Your Grace?"

Valets did more than dressing. They handled social engagements, appointments, and personal financing.

"Absolutely. You will be working hand-in-glove with Crowle and the new steward. I will give you a raise and a bonus when all this falderal is complete."

"Oh, thank you, Your Grace." Baldwin gave him an exaggerated bow.

Damon's mouth twitched with amusement. "Let us return home, as there is much to do."

For he also had a meeting with the bank tomorrow. And as soon as he completed these damned appointments, he would contact Althea.

For he yearned to see her again. Most desperately.

Chapter 8

ALTHEA SPENT ALL OF yesterday looking up records for St. Nicholas Orphanage in the East End and around the peripheries of London, and no accounts turned up in her search.

Then Althea got the idea to look up churches called St. Nicholas. She found four main ones. Churches that ran orphanages sometimes named them the same as the church itself. The churches in question were Roman Catholic and Anglican. Althea decided to investigate two, and have their newest employee, Edwina Callen, explore the others.

She stood before St. Nicholas Church in Chiswick. Chiswick was a bustling town outside the west of London in the county of Middlesex, with a thriving shipbuilding industry and fast becoming a desirable district. The church property had a long and varied past. Ancient gravestones, leaning every which way, surrounded the light gray stone church. Centuries-old gnarled trees encircled the property, giving it a decided gothic look.

"May I assist you, miss?"

Althea started and turned to face the person who spoke. A pleasant-looking young man, perhaps in his middle thirties, gave her a polite smile. He wore a black cassock.

"I was admiring the church and the grounds," Althea responded.

"A church has stood on this land since 1181. The current church was rebuilt, with construction concluding in '84. If you look toward the west tower," Mr. Willis pointed, "It was built in the 15th century. Inside are architectural features from the same era, like the parapets."

"How fascinating."

"I am the curate here. Mr. Willis."

Althea smiled. "Good day. I am Althea Galway of the Galway Investigative Agency. I'm exploring the name of an orphanage for a client. St. Nicholas Orphanage. Have you ever heard of it, Mr. Willis?"

"No. Not ever. There are a few orphanages in the immediate area, but none with that name."

Althea sighed. "I have turned up nothing. I believe my client was given a fictitious name after all."

"It would be a good name for an orphanage," Mr. Willis mused. "St. Nicholas is the patron saint of sailors, merchants, thieves, and prostitutes. But he is also such to children. Father Christmas has St. Nicholas in its origins. Children used to be left small gifts on St. Nicholas feast day in centuries past. But you did not come for a tour or a history lesson."

"No. But I found the information interesting, nonetheless," Althea smiled.

Mr. Willis chuckled softly in response. "I know this is not something a curate should know, but a parishioner mentioned a brothel in the East End unofficially known as St. Nicholas's or Nicky's."

Althea hurriedly retrieved her notebook and pencil. "Do you know the location, Mr. Willis?"

"Why, yes. Wellclose Square in Whitechapel. Mind you; this was more than a few years past; I am not sure if the establishment is still in operation. I know that it is a poverty-stricken area, Miss Galway, so caution is in order."

She extended her hand, and the curate shook it. "Thank you, Mr. Willis. You have been most helpful. And informative."

"If you have time, I can give you a tour of the interior. We have many unique memorials and statues within."

"How kind. But I must dash. The investigation awaits."

After hailing a hansom cab, Althea traveled to Whitechapel. As Mr. Willis had stated, grinding poverty was evident everywhere. Prostitutes were plying their wares on the street corners near The Mahogany Bar Mission. What a strange name. Someone at the mission could assist.

She stepped inside the building and encountered a long queue of people. The sign on the wall said, "East End Mission of the Methodist Church." This was a soup line, and judging by the ragged clothes on the men, women, and children, this could be their only hot meal. It angered Althea to see that in a prosperous city such as London, so many went without. So, so many.

A rather stern older woman stepped forward. "Back of the line, please, unless you are here for another reason."

Althea offered her card. "I would like to speak to someone with historical knowledge of this street and the nearby buildings."

The woman took the card and studied it. "Investigative agency? Well, that would be me. I've been here since the mission opened thirteen years ago." She turned toward a man standing nearby. "Mr. Clapham? Please see to the door while I speak with this young lady?"

"Miss Althea Galway, I co-own the agency," Althea interjected.

The woman glared at Althea over the top of her spectacles. "Do you, indeed? Well, I am Miss Malvina Purcell. Come this way. Hurry along now. I've not all day to dawdle."

Althea had to pick up the pace to keep up with the formidable Miss Purcell. She headed to the rear of the building. "Then I will get straight to the point. I'm investigating the name of an orphanage my client was given, and it has brought me here to Wellclose Square."

The office was so tiny that there was hardly room for a desk and two chairs. Miss Purcell motioned toward the chair in front of the desk and closed the door.

"There has never been an orphanage here. This spot was Wilton's Music Hall until it burned down in '77. A rebuild of the surviving structure started, but they ran out of money eight years later. The church bought it as there is a crushing need in this area. Before it was Wilton's, it was known as The Mahogany Bar. We use the name for this mission seeing that alcohol was and is the main cause for the East End's social ills."

Well, that answered her question as to the name.

"We are actively involved in improving the lives of those in the area," Miss Purcell continued. "During the '89 London dock strike, we provided a thousand meals daily to starving workers and their families. But you have not come here for a litany of our good works."

"No, but I applaud your labor here. Someone suggested I come to this street, claiming there is a brothel named Saint Nicholas's or Nicky's. If so, could you direct me to the building?"

To Miss Purcell's credit, she did not flinch or act shocked at the mention of a brothel, but why would she if she has been here thirteen years? For the woman had no doubt seen and heard plenty. Miss Purcell sat and clasped her hands, resting them on the desk.

"Ah. Nicky's. A famous spot when Wilton's was open. It closed eight years ago. It was located across the street, on the vacant lot. The council tore it down six years past; the building was in a shockingly rundown condition."

Miss Purcell took off her spectacles and cleaned them with a cloth. "Many a fancy nob came to Wilton's and Nicky's for cheap thrills," she continued. "Especially those of the peerage eager to wallow in the gutter." Miss Purcell glowered. "If any area could use an orphanage, it is here, considering the number of unwanted children on the streets. It's been like that for decades. Probably centuries."

From what Althea could glean about Damon's father, this could be his idea of a cruel joke. Edward Cranston would have been at the height of his vigor twenty years ago. He was undoubtedly a brothel regular and gave the name to his duchess. The shocking revelation of it all if she investigated. How ironic to call the brothel St. Nicholas, seeing as the curate said he was the patron saint of sailors, merchants, thieves, and—prostitutes.

Where did Edward Cranston leave his illegitimate children? On the street as Miss Purcell had suggested? Oh, that would be too awful to contemplate.

Althea opened her reticule and peeled off two pounds from her small roll of notes. "Please take this, Miss Purcell, for your mission."

"Thank you. I am sorry I couldn't be more assistance."

Althea stood. "On the contrary, you were most helpful."

Damon will be disappointed. She wondered how he had made out with all his conferences and meetings. Althea departed and started walking until she could hail a hansom.

Then that heated kiss wandered into her mind again, as it did on and off since it occurred. Does she encourage more kisses? Perhaps initiating a few herself? What about more? Entering into a physical relationship with a man who had been with numerous women? An unrepentant notorious rake? One that attended orgies and who knows what other deviant enterprises? Should it matter what his past is as long as they enjoyed being with each other in the present?

For there could be no future for them. They were too wildly different in countless ways.

Of course, many said that about Eleanora and Christian, but Christian happily embraced Eleanora's life and became part of it without demanding that she become part of his. Althea could not see Damon Cranston, the newly minted Duke of Chellenham, doing the same. She could not see him even meeting her halfway.

And that made her sad and full of regret. If only Damon were different and not so self-centered. And not a duke.

Althea told her sister once that she had a weakness for pretty men.

And Damon certainly was that.

So why not enjoy his attention for as long as it lasts? Why not see where this attraction goes? Why deny herself? That reason certainly overshadowed all her other trepidations.

As she hailed a hansom coming into view, Althea was satisfied that she had made the right decision.

See where this goes, indeed.

Chapter 9

ALTHEA SAT AT THE DINING table eating breakfast when her cousin, Sybil, rushed into the room. She held a newspaper aloft.

"You thought you escaped scrutiny regarding your appearance at the late duke's funeral. Well, sorry to say, you haven't."

Sybil sat across from Althea, laid the folded paper on the table, poured a cup of tea, and reached for a piece of toast from the rack.

Althea frowned. "I am reluctant to ask, but read it aloud, Cousin."

Sybil held it up again. "The *Daily Mail*. It came into existence two years ago with one of the highest circulations in London."

"Wonderful," Althea muttered.

"It is only a paragraph. 'The presence for the Duke of Chellenham's funeral was rather sparse, with few peers in attendance. Not surprising, considering the duke was not popular among his own because of his scandalous reputation and abysmal voting record in the House of Lords. Long estranged from his duchess, who was not in attendance, the only family member present was the bored heir with an equally shameful status, Damon Cranston, the new Duke of Chellenham. By his side was a woman, who, we have since learned, is the younger sister of the Duchess of Allenby. Miss Althea Galway, co-owner of The Galway Investigative Agency.'"

Althea groaned loudly.

"There is a little more. 'The couple were together and seen to be speaking intimately both at the funeral and the short reception following. Will Chellenham follow in his friend, the Duke of Allenby's footsteps, and take up with a lady detective? Or was Miss Galway there in a business capacity? Only time will tell.' There, not so bad," Sybil concluded.

"And to think I used to relish reading the gossip. Never again," Althea grumbled. "And not only because they have focused on me, but the snide remarks about Eleanora and her supposed lowly status. A curse on London society."

"Eleanora doesn't care, and neither does Christian. And neither should *you*," Sybil stated firmly. "It is no one's business, although," Sybil gave her a knowing smile. "Were you speaking intimately? What is happening? Come, Althea. Do tell. I haven't had a chance to speak to Eleanora."

Althea chewed on the corner of her mouth. "I suppose we were speaking in such a way. We argued at the reception, as usual. Then we came here to speak about the case with Eleanora and Christian. They departed, and as Chellenham waited for his carriage, we—kissed."

"And a kiss is how it starts. You were attracted to the new duke from the first," Sybil nodded.

"I don't deny it. Although, there is something about Chellenham beyond his looks," Althea pondered.

Sybil chuckled. "That is what Eleanora said about Christian. This situation all sounds so familiar. Well, I must prepare. I'm seeing potential clients this morning. I believe we should install that telephone contraption we have been discussing. And Eleanora mentioned expanding, turning the parlor and study into permanent offices. Our finances are robust, and we can afford some alterations. We can even cut down on the size of the dining room."

"Yes, we could. Or we can see about setting up an office nearby, and we will discuss it soon. How is Edwina Callen working out?"

"She is extremely efficient. I like her. Today, she is assisting Eleanora with the fraud case but will be available after tomorrow for anything you wish."

"And Archie?"

They had taken on a street lad that used to sell them information. Archie was turning into a capable investigator. Now fifteen, he worked part-time for the agency.

"He is collecting information on a divorce case for me," Sybil replied.

The doorbell rang.

"Goodness, my appointments already?" Sybil stated, standing.

But Mrs. Bartle entered the room and said, "The Duke of Chellenham wishes an audience, Miss Althea."

Sybil snickered at their housekeeper-cook's faux superior tone. Mrs. Bartle replied with a cunning smile.

"By all means, show him in," Sybil replied. "And I will take my leave. Have fun, Cousin."

Sybil was exiting as Damon strode into the room. He stopped to give her a slight bow, then looked at Althea as he removed his gloves and hat. Mrs. Bartle took them and his long coat, then left them alone.

He stood, staring, and Althea's nerve endings pinged with awareness. As usual, Damon left her breathless. He was not wearing mourning black but a day suit the shade of dark caramel, with a brown vest and fawn cravat. In a word, he looked glorious and enticing, like a slice of butterscotch cake.

In attempting to stand, she stumbled. But this time, Damon was not near enough to catch her. Embarrassingly, Althea wound up sprawled on the carpet.

He was kneeling at her side in an instant. "God, Althea. Are you hurt?"

All that was injured was her pride. "It's nothing," she said as she tried to get up.

But Damon halted her. Grasping her leg, his hands moved under her skirt. Deftly, he unbuttoned her short boot and removed it. He gently shifted her stocking-clad foot from one side to the next. His touch scorched, sending heat upward to settle between her legs.

"No discomfort?" he asked, his voice quiet yet husky. "I am checking for a possible sprain."

"No. No pain at all."

His fingertips moved halfway up her lower leg. "I feel a bump, and does it hurt when I touch it?"

Althea flushed with embarrassment. Nothing like having your flaws pointed out. "It has been there for a while, and no, it doesn't hurt."

"You should have that seen to by Buchanan."

Althea raised an eyebrow. "Are you a physician now, Your Grace?"

Damon slipped one arm under her legs, then the other at her back, and stood, cradling her in his arms. If Althea was flustered before, now her skin ignited, sending heat through her. He strolled over to the sofa and gently placed her on it.

"I am too heavy. You shouldn't be doing that," Althea admonished. "You could do serious injury."

"Not at all. Light as a feather. It would be best if you stayed off that leg. Allow me to send for Buchanan."

"No."

"No?"

Althea jumped to her feet and paced back and forth before him. "See? No discomfort, no problem. I can be clumsy, is all."

Damon placed his hands on his hips. "This is not the first time I've seen you topple over."

"And it probably will not be the last. Why *are* you here? We do not have an appointment." Anything to change the subject as Althea felt foolish enough about her ungainliness.

"I was passing by and took a chance you would be in. I wish to go to that convent. During the journey, we can fill each other in on what has happened the past few days. Are you available? It is not far. Fifteen miles from central London, in Elstree."

Damon reached into his side pocket and retrieved a piece of paper. "I have the directions here from Olivia. It is a Roman Catholic order at the Borehamwood Priory, and we will seek out Sister Rose."

"Don't you have various dukedom duties to see to?" Althea questioned.

"That is why I have employees. I am not needed today for anything of import."

Sitting with him in a carriage—alone?

She was tempting the fates, to be sure. But Althea was eager to delve further into the investigation. "Very well. We will travel to Elstree."

Damon called for Mrs. Bartle, and once he retrieved his coat, hat, and gloves, and Althea selected a lightweight cape and bonnet, they headed north. The air had a coolish bite for early August, a sign that autumn drew near.

"Look there," Damon said, pointing out the window. "There are more and more automobiles on the road. Thank providence Christian urged us all to invest in the Daimler Company. I bought more shares than anyone except for Christian."

"Like the telephone, I believe the motorcar is here to stay. How very prudent of you."

"It may keep the dukedom afloat." The carriage no sooner pulled away when Damon started a lengthy narrative concerning his meetings with the solicitors, steward, and others—explaining that there was little to no property or money and how the primogeniture effectively shut his mother out.

"What will happen to your mother?" Althea asked. "Will she return to London?"

"I highly doubt it, and I imagine the duchess will marry her love at the first opportunity. I wrote to her two days ago, sending a copy of my father's death certificate. Now I must inform her that the villa sold long ago and that she must vacate. I will send my new steward and manager, Willis Arrowsmith, to meet with her. He will deliver a letter from me, offering any assistance. My mother and I never communicated those years she spent in Spain, a true estrangement, but I will not abandon her, for none of it was her fault."

And her opinion of Damon shot another few notches upward. "I am glad to hear that. Wait, marry her—love?"

Damon told her of the man his mother had been with for years and that he had a half-brother.

"I will say this; your life is not dull by any stretch. And well done for financially and otherwise supporting your mother." Althea gave him a warm smile for good measure. "And I am glad the duchess found happiness."

"So am I. My devil father wreaked the estrangement between us. May he rot."

"I still cannot believe that Olivia is your half-sister. Were you shocked to hear it?" Althea asked.

Damon nodded. "Shocked hardly describes it. Especially since I made a rather coarse suggestion to her when I came across her and Gideon in the park, and this was before I discovered our connection. Obviously."

Althea shook her head in disbelief. "I am surprised Gideon didn't pound you senseless."

"He was fetching ice cream and didn't hear all of it. I acted as a complete arse, but what's new? This behavior has been my standard means of operation since I was out of short trousers."

How self-aware, and it was another good sign. "Did you apologize to Olivia?"

"Yes. To my utter astonishment, Olivia accepts me as I am, flaws and all. I do not deserve it." Damon grimaced. "To say this will haunt me the rest of my days is an understatement. I inadvertently and possibly could have had physical relations with my half-sister if she agreed to my crass suggestion. As I said, this was before I discovered our blood relations. It has certainly curtailed my nocturnal adventures and made me examine my damaged soul. That, and seeing how my father died, is not how I wish to end up."

Althea's look softened. "And it made you all the more determined to seek the illegitimate progeny of your father because their unknown fates haunt you as well."

Damon met her gaze. "You seem to know the inner workings of my twisted mind. And to my amazement, you are not judging me. At least, not in this. Yes, it haunts me."

"Then we shall do all we can to ease your strife," she replied firmly. "I am glad you told me this. I will keep your confidence, also concerning your financial situation. I have only known Olivia for a short period, but she is a good judge of character."

"Thank you. Now, what have you been up to these past couple of days?" Damon sat forward, giving her his full attention.

He wished to change the subject. To admit to all of this showed that he trusted her. How interesting to discover that the duke's death and the manner of his discovery put the final nail in Damon's erotic escapades, along with his encounter with Olivia. Althea was glad to hear it.

People always scoff that a leopard cannot change their spots, but there was a profound shift within Damon over the past several months. Discovering Olivia and other possible half-siblings, meeting with his estranged mother, and his father's untimely death all contributed to this long overdue self-examination. If a more empathetic man emerged, all the better; the prospect made him all the more fascinating.

Another thing she had noticed. The ease at which they conversed, as if they had been friends for ages. It continued to astound Althea. All class, status, and gender barriers disappeared whenever they were alone. Althea spoke of investigating Saint Nicholas properties, the information the curate gave her, and her visit to the mission in Whitechapel.

Damon sat back. "As I said, may he rot. The duke gave the name of a brothel. My father never sent those children to an orphanage. Damn him."

"Miss Purcell said many illegitimate children end up on the streets, and there would be no way to trace all of them. I am sorry, Damon."

He pulled aside the curtain and looked out the carriage window at the passing countryside. "It is a lovely day. Perhaps we can share a meal at an inn later."

"We have to speak about the kiss."

He whipped his head around to stare at her. "Is this the part where you say it must never happen again? Because I will not have that kind of dismissive talk."

With the speed of a jungle cat, he sat next to her. Cupping her face with his hands, he gazed into her eyes. The heat and unfamiliar emotions swirling about in the light blue depths had her breath catching in her throat. Wait, those feelings were not wholly unknown. Althea observed passion, yearning, and an almighty heat, and it caused her heart to speed up in response, for she was experiencing the same.

"It will happen again, I assure you. Whenever we are alone, I will be kissing you," Damon said, his voice low and gruff.

And to prove his point, Damon did just that. He captured her lips and gave her such a thorough and deep kiss; Althea couldn't stop moaning. She tunneled her fingers through his thick, golden locks again, grabbing fistfuls of it as he took the kiss deeper. Oh, those overwhelming waves of desire rippled through her again. Their tongues tangled, and the carriage stopped just as Althea moved to sit in his lap.

"Damn it all," Damon muttered as he returned to his side of the carriage.

The door opened, and the carriage driver assisted Althea. Damon stepped out, buttoning his long coat. His hair stood up in places where she had thoroughly mussed it. Reaching up, she smoothed his hair, giving him a teasing smile.

"Let us wait a moment," he murmured. "I cannot walk into a nunnery in this condition."

"What condition—oh." Althea blushed. "Just from a kiss?"

Damon took her arm and slipped it through his. "Just from *your* kiss."

And how that statement thrilled her to her toes. For she had been affected as well. Althea curled her fingers and stroked the sleeve of his coat.

"You keep touching me that way, and I will never recover," he said in a husky voice.

Her reply was to move closer. Damon chuckled low in his throat.

They strolled at a leisurely pace, taking in the grounds. A wrought iron fence and gate surrounded the property. One of the three brick buildings was the chapel with a tall wooden steeple. Plenty of stately and ancient oaks dotted the property, with manicured gardens in full bloom containing harebells, cornflowers, and lilies of the valley. It was quite a serene spot, perfect for quiet contemplation.

Damon stopped, picked a cornflower, and handed it to her.

"For me?"

He nodded. The look he gave Althea was penetrating, causing her insides to tumble.

She rubbed the blossom against her cheek. "This flower is as beautiful as your eyes, though a deeper blue shade."

Damon gave her an amused grin. "Flatterer."

After carefully tucking the flower in her reticle, Althea slipped her arm through his as they continued along the walkway. He had given her a flower, and the sweet gesture caused her heart to skip a beat or two.

As they strolled along the stone footpath, a nun in a black habit came forward to greet them. "May I help you?" she asked politely.

"We wish to see Sister Rose," Damon replied.

"Come with me, please," the nun stated.

Once inside, the nun escorted them to an office and told them to wait. Five minutes later, an older woman entered. As Damon rose from his chair, she waved at him.

"Please, stay seated. How may I assist you?"

Althea passed her card to the nun. "I am Althea Galway from the Galway Investigative Agency, and this is the Duke of Chellenham."

"Good heavens. It is not often we have a duke on the premises." Sister Rose took the card and sat at the desk, facing them.

"You spoke to a young woman a couple of years past, Olivia Durham, concerning the circumstances of her birth here at the priory," Damon said.

"Yes. I remember. Good heavens, Chellenham. I remember the name."

"It is the name Olivia's mother gave you. Can you give us any more information?" Damon asked.

"Well, the birth incident took place well over thirty years ago. We do not often see a birth here, but the young woman was clearly distressed, and we could not turn her away. I don't know her name, as she never answered our questions. Was she from this area, and that is how she knew about us? I cannot say, Your Grace."

Sister Rose sighed. "It was a difficult birth, and it soon became obvious that she would not survive it. We sent for the village doctor, but he arrived too late, though he said there was nothing he could have done. All the young woman said was to contact the Duke of Chellenham, that he was the father and would look after the baby."

"And you contacted my father."

"Yes, Your Grace. His man of business arrived the next day with the name of a vicar and his wife looking to adopt a baby. He wanted to take the baby then and there, but we insisted the vicar come to the convent."

"Can you remember what this man of business looked like?" Althea asked.

"Yes, I do, for he looked rough, despite his new suit. A little taller than average height, built like a dock worker, his speech was strange, as if he were trying to mimic a posh accent. I wouldn't hand the newborn over to him, for something about him disturbed me. The man said he represented a charity home for foundlings sponsored by the duke."

Althea and Damon exchanged astonished looks.

"Chellenhome," Althea whispered.

Chapter 10

DAMON'S BLOOD RAN COLD. Could that be what Chellenhome is, a charity home for foundlings? It made perfect sense. He told Althea the details in the carriage and mentioned the nearby farm and mill. Was it supplying food to the occupants? Is that where his father tucked away his illegitimate children? And why he kept the place and its doings from his solicitor and steward?

The rough-looking man was none other than Silas Browning. Silas worked for his father for decades; he must now be in his middle fifties. Silas was and still is a bully. As a young boy, Damon stayed clear of him. Browning was the man for the job if there was any dirty work.

"Sister Rose, you told Olivia that you knew of my father. Can you tell me how?" Damon asked.

"I heard his name mentioned twice before the birth, Your Grace. I believe he was a marquess then. It is a story as old as time: a young man in a position of power with title and money taking advantage. Some young women from this area who had gone to London to work in manor houses were seduced, dismissed, and sent home in shame. It is reprehensible."

Damon's cheeks grew hot as that stinging rebuke could also apply to him. Although he never dallied with the help or anyone within his sphere—and he always took precautions. Regardless of making excuses, Damon experienced shame for his past disgraceful behavior and all the prominent men who had done the same and will no doubt do so in the future. It turned his bile.

"You are acquainted with Miss Durham?" the nun asked. "And accept her as your half-sister?"

Damon nodded, still unable to speak.

"I wish you peace on your journey. Love bears all things, believes all things, hopes all things, endures all things. Corinthians 13:7." The sister looked at Althea, and she gave her a sad smile. "Be courageous, be strong."

The interview was over. Damon stood and offered his hand to Althea, and they thanked Sister Rose and departed, swiftly heading toward the carriage.

"My God. Chellenhome," Damon murmured. "We must go there at once."

"Where is it again?"

"The East End. Handy for his doings," Damon grumbled. "Outside of the town of Barking, specifically. The location is off the main path. I will give the directions to my coachman. Luckily, I have the handwritten instructions on me. Better if we arrive unannounced. A meal at an inn will have to wait."

Once inside the carriage, they were off, and Damon's mind spun in all directions. To know his father's reputation began at a young age and reached the far-flung countryside—and to nuns in a secluded priory—gave Damon pause.

When had he ever considered his actions?

Granted, he took precautions to avoid unwanted children and diseases, but there was no guarantee. Damon always told himself he was seeking his pleasures with strangers. What was the harm?

"You are deep in thought," Althea observed.

He met her inquiring gaze. "Perhaps too deep, as self-examination is not something I typically indulge in."

"The names your mother gave you. Will you be contacting any of them?"

Damon snorted. "I'm now having doubts. Perhaps it is a scab best not picked at. Please excuse the vivid description. All my sanctimonious talk of setting up a trust. First, there is no money for such a scheme, and God knows how many names there are beyond the ones my mother knew of. It boggles the mind."

"Perhaps you should approach Detective Evercreech."

Damon cocked his head. "Why?"

"Considering the circumstances, you should inform him about your father. He was attending to the death scene and whatnot. From what you told me of him, he seems a decent sort. Why not get to know him?"

"I cannot think about that now. I am dreading what we will find in Barking."

Althea shrugged. "Or it could be an empty property in need of repair. Or rented to someone. Although, strangely, the solicitor and steward have never been there or any dealings with it."

"Strange indeed. Which means it has been kept secret for who knows how many years. Come here. I do not want to discuss this any longer. I want you in my arms. Here. Straddling me." He patted his lap, already becoming aroused at the prospect. "Sit facing me, and kiss me, my Thea. I am being too bold, but if my father's death proved anything, time is short, and I do not wish to waste it."

Her look softened. "I do like you are calling me that," she whispered. "And I want to be in your arms. And kiss you. Where will it go from here? Don't answer. If we are to have an affair or dalliance, I must have a promise from you that you will remain faithful as long as we are involved in whatever way. I cannot give my undivided attention to a man who is indiscriminate in his sexual dealings."

Good Christ.

"Even if all we share is kisses?" he asked.

"Even if. I have never become involved with a client in *any* way. This is a line that I swore I would *never* cross. I must have assurances from you, or we keep this strictly business, and I conduct this investigation on my own."

God, he admired her. She was so honest, so he would do the same.

"I have not been with a woman for over a month, and before you scoff, that is a long drought for me, not that I am bragging," he began. "The trip to Spain, my father's death, all reasons to be certain. But having just turned 31 years of age, I gave a brief thought to the notion that this was becoming tedious. Our group, The Rakes of St. Regent's Park, is all but defunct. Even Gideon, an original founding member, has married. It gives one pause."

"Does it?" Althea said, her voice gentle.

"But what has given me pause more than anything is you, my Thea. From the moment we met. From the moment you most decidedly put me in my place during that interview last year. From the moment I first briefly held you in my arms. You haven't left my thoughts, day or night. Especially the night."

"And yet, you've been with other women."

Her tone was not an admonishment but a statement of fact.

"Not as many as in the past. Saying it all meant nothing is crass, but I fear it is true. Sometimes I traveled to the East End to attend a musical and partake of a meal. Then I would come home."

"I know."

Damon's brows raised. "You know?"

"During Christian's case, we had all The Rakes followed briefly. Your report over a two-week period had you visiting a brothel only once. You did the dinner and a show and home routine the other two times."

Damon sputtered. He could not believe this. "You had me followed as if I were a suspect?"

Althea shrugged. "As I said, we shadowed all of you, as it is standard procedure in most investigations. And your fellow rakes were not as active as *you* might think."

"Are you having me followed now?" Damon asked sarcastically.

"There is no need to be annoyed. And no, you are not under surveillance. So, can you? Stay exclusive?"

"How can I not?" Damon cried. "I will be suspicious of every freckled-faced lad lurking about the alleyways, thinking he is working for you!" Then he exhaled. "But beyond my paranoia, I respect you too much to act the cad." The truth was that he wanted no other woman *but* Althea. But he wasn't ready to admit such a susceptibility at this point.

She gave him a pretty smile, then vaulted off the bench and landed in his arms. Grabbing the hem of her skirt, she pulled it upward until she could snuggly fit against his raging erection.

Damon was ready to blow apart. An almighty heat flamed within him. A few rubs against his arousal, and he would come in his trousers, and no mistake.

"Yes, right there," Damon murmured, nuzzling her neck. He then nibbled on her delicate earlobe, causing a soft whimper to escape her lips.

"What do I do now? As you correctly observed last year, I *am* a virgin," she said breathlessly.

"But by no means stuffy," he murmured. "Rock against me. Back and forth. All that is between us is bits of cloth. I can feel you. This activity is stimulation to produce arousal."

"I'm aroused now," she moaned.

"As am I."

Althea started to move, tentatively at first, then faster, causing his head to spin. Damon thrust upward to meet her frenzied motions. God, he was so hard.

"Come for me. Let yourself go. Embrace the feeling overcoming you," Damon demanded. "You are wet for me. I feel it. Just soaking wet."

"Oh, yes," she moaned. Althea held nothing back as her face radiated sheer bliss as her peak built.

"It is like when you touch yourself. And you have done so, I know it. Many times. You have touched yourself thinking of me."

"Yes," Althea moaned again, only louder. No doubt Dawson, his carriage driver, could hear her, but Damon hardly cared.

Damon growled low in his throat. "And I have done the same, thinking of you while I pull on my cock and—"

Her climax hit hard, and with a ragged cry, her arms encircled his neck as if to hold on for dear life. He understood her intense response because mere seconds later, he followed, and they breathlessly shuddered while embracing each other.

"Oh, dear God." Althea moved to scramble off him, but Damon was not having it. He wrapped his arms around her and held on as if she were the only thing keeping him from drowning.

"Hold me," he whispered raggedly. "Just a moment longer, I beg you." Never had he begged anyone for anything ever before. So much for keeping his vulnerabilities to himself.

Althea stayed in his embrace, smoothed a lock of hair from his temple, then tenderly kissed his forehead. After several moments, she pulled away, shaking out her skirt. "That was—quite incredible," she sighed. "But it left you in a bit of a mess."

"I'll keep my coat buttoned, which I often have to do when in your presence."

She chuckled while taking the seat opposite. Then Althea opened the curtains. "We must be nearby, for the skyline of the East End is far in the distance."

Damon took the opportunity of Althea gazing out the window to tidy himself. What an intense climax, just from rubbing against each other. What would actual sex bring? He may not survive it. But he wanted nothing more than to be joined with her in all positions. To explore them, to show Althea how one could have sex. Or make love, not that he had ever referred to it as such. But with Althea? Yes, it could very well be that.

The carriage turned onto a narrow path completely encased by immense trees. The branches scraped against the sides of the conveyance, the leaves slapping against the windows. Finally, they came into an open area. A two-story wooden structure stood in the clearing. A fair size; although Damon was no expert, he could see that the construction was somewhat shoddy. As he assisted Althea from a carriage, a woman bustled toward them.

"Is it the duke at last? I've written so many letters." She pointed to the crest on the carriage door. "Where is Chellenham?"

Damon turned to face her. The woman in her late forties was modestly dressed in a wool skirt and a frayed blouse, both covered with a well-worn, crisp white apron.

"I am the Duke of Chellenham as of a few days ago."

The woman deflated. "Oh, no. What will become of us?"

Althea stepped forward. "This is Damon Cranston, the new duke. He only learned about this place at the reading of the will when his solicitor showed him a statement of property holdings. I am Althea Galway of The Galway Investigative Agency, and we are here to inspect and make inquiries regarding Chellenhome. And you are?"

"Mrs. Reba Seddon, manager of this home. You had best come in."

As soon as they crossed the threshold, Damon could smell mold and stale air.

Mrs. Seddon must have noticed him wrinkling his nose, for she said, "Many of the windows do not open, so when the weather is nice, we keep the doors ajar to allow fresh air to enter." She pointed to the walls that were in desperate need of painting. At least they seemed reasonably clean. "As you can observe, Your Grace, we require repairs and standard upkeep. I have written your father numerous letters over the past several months to no avail. Come here into the sitting room." It was a rather cramped area, but they sat on the sofa on the far wall while Mrs. Seddon sat opposite on a rickety wooden chair.

"How long has this place existed, and what is this place, specifically? Please be as forthcoming as possible," Althea instructed.

Mrs. Seddon exhaled. "This is a charity home for foundlings, and as far as I'm aware, it has existed since '63."

His father would have been 22 years old. That horrible feeling that had been plaguing him amplified further. Damon sat back, content for Althea to take the initial lead in the questioning.

"I've been here close to nine years," Mrs. Seddon continued. "It was a thriving enterprise up until a few years ago. The money dried up, and we were not receiving as many children as in the past. We charge a fee for fostering and adoptions, you see. Some well-heeled patrons made donations, but they dried up as well."

"This property also includes the farm and mill, which I assume is not far from this place," Althea stated.

"It's but half a mile away. But there has been no money to pay the tenant farmer, so he left months ago. The fields have foundered. We have done what we can, but having young children working in the fields is not ideal. We managed to grow a few carrots, but that is all. We need food, Your Grace; the children are hungry. I've appealed in Barking, and a kindhearted merchant, Mr. Penn, gave us food donations, days-old bread, and the like, but I cannot keep asking them for contributions."

"We will address the situation immediately," he replied. "Perhaps before speaking further, you should take us on a tour of this place. How many children are here at the moment?"

"Altogether? There are seventeen, Your Grace. Three girls between the ages of 6 and 7, two boys aged 6, seven boys between the ages of 10 and 13, four girls between the ages of 10 and 13, and one 15-year-old girl. Come with me, then," Mrs. Seddon replied in a low tone. "If they are not adopted by age eight, we start with training toward certain occupations."

The first room they entered must be a schoolroom. Damon counted ten children working studiously at their tables.

"Please stand and greet His Grace."

They did, and all eyes swiveled toward him. Out of the ten children in the room, three of them were blond with blue eyes. They were thin, and their prominent cheekbones were all the more evident from malnutrition. Their eyes were lifeless, and Damon felt a pain shoot through him as if a hot poker had been slipped under his ribs.

How many of these poor children were related to him?

A potent fury overtook him. A rage filled with disgust at his father's reckless behavior. For his ignorance and the fact that he never bothered to care how others lived—or barely lived. Damon had his comforts; when had he been concerned about others? Shame joined the rage, and it deepened his ire.

He grasped Mrs. Seddon's arm and pulled her none-too-gently toward the sitting room. Once they were all inside, he slammed the door. "This was—and is—a mill for my father's illegitimate children. I will wager that these donors you speak of also send their unwanted progeny here for a fee. The babies were sold for a profit, and the older children were adopted or sent into service or other occupations when trained for further fees. Do I have the gist of it, Mrs. Seddon?" Damon roared.

Mrs. Seddon flinched at his tone, but Damon hardly cared.

"Or were the children sold for more nefarious purposes? I would not put it past my miserable bastard father."

Mrs. Seddon's eyes widened in horror. "Oh, never! I would never allow or condone such a scheme. You must believe me, Your Grace. You see, I was the brothel madam at Nicky's in Whitechapel. I understand the life and would *never* permit it. I followed up on all the children under my care. I ensured their placement in loving homes or good work situations. I swear it. I can't answer about what went on before I arrived."

"I want to see all the records, every transaction. I wager my penny-pinching father kept meticulous accounts to squeeze out every farthing. Collect them, Mrs. Seddon, now!"

The woman jumped to her feet and dashed from the room.

Damon's fists clenched, his insides in turmoil. He needed to smash something. Immediately.

As if sensing that very thing, Althea came to stand beside him and gently laid her hand over his tightly clenched fist. "Stay calm, Damon. We will get to the bottom of this. Together."

Once again, she kept him from that horrible drowning feeling. Taking her hands in his, he turned to face her and touched his forehead to hers. "Good God, what have I found here?" he whispered, his voice revealing the misery he was experiencing.

He felt all at sea, and Althea was his lifeline.

Chapter 11

ALTHEA HAD NO IDEA what to say. For she came to the same immediate conclusion that Damon had, that this isolated place in the woods was a haven for the illegitimate offspring of the late duke and his select list of elite friends and other wealthy acquaintances. A mill churning out homeless and abandoned children, selling them for profit to either adoptive families or businesses. How the scheme worked was still a mystery, but as she said, they would get to the bottom of it.

Since 1863? Thirty-five years?

Just how many children could Edward Cranston produce in that period? With multiple women, it didn't bear thinking about. Even if there were two a year, that could mean—seventy children. No, surely not. But they could be looking at thirty, forty—or more. Or perhaps the children numbered in the hundreds. *That* was the more likely scenario. But who was to know?

Althea gazed up at Damon. He looked livid, crestfallen, and weary all at once—quite the potent mix.

With the backs of her fingers, she gently stroked his flushed cheek. "What you have found is the dark underbelly of the Victorian era, where the wealthy and powerful do as they please without a thought for others or society at large. The abject recklessness. The arrogance. And the fact that there is no price to pay, no consequences for these corrupt men, is a stain upon humanity. I am sorry to say this, my dear Damon, is your legacy."

Damon took her hand and kissed it. "Don't be sorry. You are right. It *is* a stain, one that will never wash off. And it is my legacy. I cheerfully followed the same path, thinking it was expected of me. I knew no other way, and I never bothered to *learn* any other way. As you said, arrogance. I am thoroughly disgusted with my fellow men. With myself."

Releasing her hand, he growled and kicked the chair Mrs. Seddon had been sitting on, and it clattered across the floor and hit the wall.

Mrs. Seddon entered the room and flinched at the noise. She clutched a ledger close to her chest. "This is all I have," she squeaked, "However, your father kept a safe here, and I do not have the combination." She held out the ledger, and Althea took it from her.

Althea flipped through the pages. The entries began in 1863, and the information was vague. It stated whether the child was a boy or girl, where they came from, and some even listed the mother's name. Althea stopped on the year 1869.

"Damon, look."

She pointed to the entry, and he came to stand and look over her shoulder.

Boy age 5
Mother: Dora Mitchell-deceased Evercreech, Somerset
New Name: Mitchell Evercreech EC
Adopted 1870 to Gerald Simpson, London
00456

"Explain this entry," Damon snarled at Mrs. Seddon.

Tentatively, she came to look at the page Althea held toward her.

"It means someone brought the child here because his mother died and then fostered or adopted the next year. These adoptions are not legal as there are no laws. In the early days of Chellenhome, the youngest children were often given new names. This boy's name was an amalgamation of his mother's last name and the village they came from. I do not follow that practice, Your Grace. If a child comes here with a name, they keep it."

Mrs. Seddon took a step closer. "Please, believe me, Your Grace. I was an orphan myself. I love children, but thanks to a botched procedure when I was fifteen, I cannot have any of my own. All the children here are under my care, and I do my best for them. At first, I tried to remain distant, for I didn't want to become attached to any of the wee ones. It was all for naught. I cared for them anyway." She dashed away a tear.

Althea watched her closely. Mrs. Seddon seemed sincere, but she could also be a fraud.

"What is this EC after his name?" Damon demanded, taking the ledger from Althea and waving it toward Mrs. Seddon.

"Oh," Althea said softly. "Edward Cranston. It means this child is his. Is that correct, Mrs. Seddon?"

"Yes, or it could mean he was the one who referred the child. He never explained his reasons for anything. The late duke gave me the information to enter into the ledger. But if I were to guess, yes, the child is his."

"And the other initials next to other children's names?" Althea asked.

"I do not know. The duke never gave me a list of donors, so I couldn't compare. That is what the duke, or the late duke, begging your pardon, called the other initials. Donors. You will see the recent transactions and the lack of funds at the back of the ledger. There are more ledgers like this one, as I saw them when Mr. Browning removed items from the safe."

"Silas Browning?" Damon asked.

"Yes. I never liked the man. The duke himself had not been here in over five years. I want to assist you and will answer any questions I can. Please, Your Grace, sit. And Miss Galway. I will do my best to relay what I observed here."

Grumbling, Damon nonetheless sat on the sofa, handing the ledger to Althea. She flipped to the back and quickly glanced at the numbers. Edward Cranston had abandoned Chellenhome to its own devices in the past four months—miserable man.

"Your father was a steady customer of mine at the brothel. When Wilton's Music Hall closed due to a fire, Nicky's felt the brunt of the loss. We were out of business in no time at all. Not knowing what would happen to me, your father mentioned that he sponsored a charity home for street waifs, and would I be interested in running it? Well, I jumped at the chance. To leave that life behind?" Mrs. Seddon shook her head sadly.

"When I arrived, there were forty-two children and babies. The farm was a going concern and supplied fresh vegetables, meat, and fruit. But I could see a slow but steady decline, which I found surprising, for I knew there were more homeless children than orphanages."

Mrs. Seddon exhaled on a shaky breath. "There is no legal adoption in Great Britain, so these children are not protected under the state. Many are left on the streets, turning to crime and prostitution. There is no continuing education available. Several are forced into horrible labor conditions. Many die. Alone."

"Good Christ," Damon muttered, clearly dismayed by this information.

"The woman who ran the place before me was called Mrs. Loretta Parsons. I have no idea what happened to her. She kept meticulous records, the place was clean, and the children were healthy. I barely saw her recent records before Browning ripped them from my hands. He gave me a new ledger—the one Miss Galway is holding—which contained a list of the children, past and present. I use the term adoption, but in reality, the children were sold. I received a small salary and one percent of any fees. I never kept that remuneration. I put it back into the home for food, clothes, and the like."

Althea laid the ledger on her lap, reached in her bag for her notebook and pencil, and took pertinent notes of the conversation. This case was very distressing.

Damon crossed his arms, clearly still angry. "My father was corrupt, incapable of anything so basic as human emotions."

"Yes," Mrs. Seddon replied in a quiet voice. "He was that, Your Grace. The duke told me more than once that he had a superior lineage, and it was his right and duty to ensure that it continued so that his progeny would exist in every corner of England. He sought attractive, vulnerable women so his children would be good-looking. It was crucial to him. I said, 'But the children will not have your name.' He laughed, 'It is the bloodline that is paramount, not a name.'"

Althea shook her head. Most in the peerage claimed the name and title were everything. What a twisted worldview the late duke possessed. "He was purposely reckless, and that's why the late duke kept exacting records. He wanted to know how many children he produced and where they were. Is that right, Mrs. Seddon?"

"Yes, you have the right of it, Miss Galway. I don't know if he knew about all of them, though."

Damon stood. "Show me where this safe is. If it is not too large, I will have my driver assist me in placing it in the carriage. Miss Galway and I will head into Barking and buy food until I can send further assistance. We will hang on to this ledger for now."

Mrs. Seddon burst into tears, then dabbed at them with the corner of her apron. "I'm sorry to cause such a scene, as it's a relief to have any assistance. Thank you, Your Grace. Miss Galway."

She led them into an adjoining room, but the safe was too large for two men to handle.

"Dawson! We need to head into Barking. Find us a grocer immediately!" Damon called to his driver as he assisted Althea into the carriage. Once seated, he reached into his pockets. "Damn it, all I have is six pounds."

Althea reached into her bag. "And I have one, and that will buy more than enough to hold them over until you send additional aid." Most people would think they were flush with money to have six pounds in their pockets. But to Damon, it was a mere pittance. When they conversed as if they were old friends, it was easy to forget Damon's status in society.

"Hell, what a bloody mess. If possible, I would dig the late duke up and murder him with my bare hands," Damon growled.

"Your father died sooner than he might have. Maybe that is one sort of punishment. But it means you are indeed left with a muddle. We need to find someone who can crack a safe. If Browning will not reveal the combination."

"I will beat it out of him if I have to," Damon spat.

"You must control your temper. You are allowing your feelings to run amuck. For a man supposedly adept at hiding his emotions, you are allowing them to cloud your judgment. On the other hand, if it were me, I would be furious, too."

He sighed. "What do you suggest I do next? Beyond sending assistance?"

"Hopefully, there is a list of donor names in the safe—men who have sent their children to the home. Shame them into contributing money. See that kind people take the children in. You cannot take on this responsibility yourself."

"They are my half-siblings," Damon replied. "At least, some of them are."

"I know it," she replied delicately. "But there are too many of them. Let us say half those children now at Chellenhome are your father's. What are you going to do? Will you take eight children into your home? What about all the others that came before?"

Damon plowed his fingers through his hair in exasperation. "I don't know, Althea."

"Ultimately, the decision will be yours. I am only offering my opinion. Take the time to think it through."

"Wisely spoken."

The carriage halted, and the window slid open. "Here is a grocer, Your Grace," Dawson said.

"Good." Damon took her hand and assisted her from the carriage.

Damon strode into the grocer and snapped his fingers. The proprietor must have seen the fancy carriage, for he immediately came over to Damon, eager to serve.

"May I help you, my lord?"

"Your Grace," Damon replied icily. "Chellenhome. Do you know of it? Make any deliveries there?"

"Yes, Your Grace. But not for a couple of months. I did give Mrs. Seddon some bread, onions, and potatoes recently. Complimentary like."

"Thank you for your generosity." Damon's tone warmed, but just a little. "Does the home owe you money?"

"No, Your Grace. Mrs. Seddon always settled upon delivery."

"Very well, Mr.—?"

"Mr. Walter Penn, at your service, Your Grace."

"Mr. Penn. I have seven pounds here. Gather an order: flour, sugar, salt, tea, fruit, vegetables, meat, milk, firewood, and anything else Mrs. Seddon had previously ordered. I want it delivered immediately. I am sending a man tomorrow; to set up an account with you to guarantee steady deliveries."

Mr. Penn's eyes lit up, no doubt thrilled to have a duke as a regular customer. "At once, Your Grace. My wife made sugar biscuits today, and I will send them along at no cost. For the children."

Damon slipped on his gloves. "Yes. For the children." He took Althea's arm and stood against the wall, watching Penn and his assistant gather food and other items, packing them in wooden crates. Damon pointed to a display of wool blankets. "How much for those?"

"Six shillings a piece, Your Grace. I can add them to the order, or your man can pay me tomorrow."

"Good man. Add it to the order. See it done."

Damon leaned in and asked Althea, "Can we leave Mr. Penn to see to this order? I want to return to London and have you question Browning."

"I believe we can. Mr. Penn gave the home food donations. The grocer desires your business, so you can trust him," Althea replied. "Again, that is only my opinion."

"I trust your opinion, and I concur about believing the man. Let us depart."

After making arrangements with Mr. Penn, they were off to London. Damon stared out the window, not speaking. Althea left him alone with his thoughts, for he had much to work through.

And Althea had plenty to keep her occupied. Setting aside the case for a moment, what possessed her to suggest terms for an affair? For that is what she had done. Then to eagerly rub against him, coming to a soul-stirring climax? It was the most extraordinary moment of her life. And she wanted to experience and explore more with the handsome duke sitting across from her. His very presence sent her nerve endings on full alert.

She glanced at Damon. So pensive yet guarded.

But not so much in this carriage when he had come to his own intense peak. Lord, when he held her close, begging her to stay in his arms. Althea had melted inside. And she may never recover.

A half-hour later, they arrived at the dukedom town house at Queen Anne's Gate. Good lord, it was far fancier than Damon's present home: all that brick and wrought iron.

Greeted at the door by the butler, Damon marched into the front hallway, with Althea trying to keep up with his long strides. Seeing he was outpacing her, he slowed, then gently took her arm. That thoughtful gesture had her insides melting a little more.

"I want Browning brought to my study immediately," Damon ordered.

The butler frowned. "I am sorry, Your Grace, but he is not here."

Chapter 12

DAMON STOPPED IN HIS tracks. "What?"

"We have not seen him since the day before last, Your Grace," MacClery stated. "And when I went to his room above the stables, his meager belongings were gone."

Stay in control.

Because Althea was correct in stating his feelings were running amuck. It was not like him at all. On the journey back to London, he tried to pack away all those unwanted and wayward emotions, most of which had Althea as the cause, but it was a fruitless endeavor. It was as if he had opened Pandora's Box, and there was no stuffing anything back into it.

"What if he heard about your father's death, and he is heading to Chellenhome?" Althea said worriedly. "What if there is money in the safe? I learned from Gideon's Whinstone case that certain people remain loyal to unethical men regardless of circumstances. What if Browning feels that pull and goes to destroy the ledgers?"

Damon gave her an admiring smile, for he approved of Althea's suspicious turn of mind. It made her an excellent investigator. "You may have the right of it. Can you remain here and question the staff?" he asked her.

"Of course," Althea replied.

"MacClery, bring that footman you confide in. We must leave immediately for Barking. What we spoke of? The trust? This is it."

"There is another I trust almost as much, Your Grace. I will bring him as well. Thomas and Patrick. I'll fetch them." MacClery disappeared down the hall.

"Be careful," Althea whispered to Damon as she briefly slipped her hand into his. He squeezed her hand affectionately and kissed it. The fact that she initiated touching him gave him a decided thrill, straight to the toes of his boots.

"Always. There is one incident that took place here a couple of months ago. You can question MacClery and the footmen about it when we return. My dissolute father hosted an orgy, and I want to know who attended. It may be that some of those corrupt men are involved with Chellenhome." Damon gave her hand another brief kiss before releasing it.

To Althea's credit, she never reacted to the word orgy; she retrieved her notebook and pencil as he had seen her do numerous times.

MacClery returned with two strapping young footmen who looked more than up to the task. "Miss Galway, Mrs. Dunbar, the housekeeper, will set up the study for your interviews. She will also see to it that a footman brings a tea tray. Continue down the hall. It is the third door to your left."

"Thank you."

"We must dash. Will you wait until I return?" Damon asked.

"I will try. But I cannot promise."

Once he gave their destination to Dawson, they were off. The three men crowded on opposite bench seats, and Damon found it mildly amusing.

"Ever hear of Chellenhome, any of you?" he asked, watching their reactions closely.

"I have, Your Grace, in passing," MacClery answered. "I stood at the door to listen once when the duke summoned Browning to the study. That was not very well done of me, but I never liked the man.

I couldn't hear much. Something was said about delivering sensitive merchandise and collecting fees."

In other words, children.

Damon's gaze slid to the brown-haired footman. "Thomas?"

"I am Patrick, Your Grace. Browning never interacted with the staff, and we believe he had accommodations elsewhere, for there were days we never saw him. He rarely stayed in the room above the stables and never took his meals with us, either."

Damon looked to the black-haired footman. "Thomas?"

"It's as Patrick and Mr. MacClery said, Your Grace. He was a bully, helping himself to food from the larder, growling at the kitchen maids, and frightening them. I saw him shove the cook, Mrs. Canning, and I intervened. He had me against the wall, his hand around my neck before I could react. Browning said he would visit me at night and slit my gizzard if I got in his way again."

And the staff couldn't very well go to the former duke, for Silas Browning was his father's man. Browning held a position of inordinate power and used it to act as a tyrant.

"I want you to relay all that to Miss Galway at the first opportunity. Did my father have many visitors, other peers, or wealthy men of means?" Damon asked.

The footmen looked to MacClery. The butler cleared his throat. "Not so much in the past few years, as many of his acquaintances became ill or died."

In other words, they were too old and sick to fornicate and make babies. Damon's insides roiled further. "And yet my father hosted an orgy here a few months past."

"Yes, Your Grace," MacClery replied. "And it was all younger men in attendance. It was as if he were recruiting new blood. The men wore full masks; I couldn't describe them to you. The men were young, judging by their carriage and build."

"There were eleven of them, Your Grace," Thomas interjected, "And as many women. They also wore masks and fancy gowns, so it was hard to tell if the ladies were hired or of the aristocracy."

"Browning told us to stay below stairs for the night. Many of us left to either go to a pub or visit family," Patrick said with loathing. "We weren't even allowed to go to our rooms. Browning came down several hours later and told us to clean up. I nearly quit then and there. But I need the job, Your Grace. I'm supporting my mother and two sisters." Patrick's cheeks flushed. "I am sorry. I didn't mean to reveal that. About my family. Mr. MacClery said to be honest with you."

This proved that one never knew what happened behind the elites' closed doors. Or what a servant's life entailed. Damon imagined servants in many grand houses could tell hair-raising tales of woe to shock the most jaded population.

"Your position is secure—all of you. I appreciate your honesty and will not forget it," Damon said resolutely.

"And the rest of the staff, Your Grace?" Thomas asked, looking Damon in the eye.

"Thomas!" MacClery rebuked.

"No, it's all right," Damon said. "I have my staff at Clarendon Place to see to and those at Queen Anne's Gate. I cannot keep on everyone; that is the reality. I will offer retirement or a transfer to Chellenham Park in Sussex, but some will lose their positions. I will do all possible to see them placed elsewhere with compensation and good references. Regardless of what you may have heard, I am not a completely heartless bastard."

The carriage grew quiet, and the only sounds were the horses' hooves clopping on the cobbles and the harness jingling.

"Your Grace," Patrick said, his voice low. "It will be my privilege to serve you and the Chellenham dukedom."

The statement oddly touched Damon.

"As am I," Thomas added. "Your Grace."

"Aye," MacClery replied in his gravelly voice. "And me and all, Your Grace."

"Good, and my sincere thanks. Because I am in quite a fix, thanks to my late father, I will need all the assistance you can offer."

The carriage came to a standstill, and before they could even step down, Damon heard screaming and crying. He threw open the door and found Mrs. Seddon sitting on the ground, surrounded by squalling children. The oldest girl knelt next to Mrs. Seddon as if attending to her. The men rushed toward the rambunctious scene.

"Mrs. Seddon, are you injured?" Damon asked worriedly.

"That horrid man was here! Mr. Browning," the older girl blubbered. "He hit Mrs. Seddon and knocked her to the ground!"

"Helena," Mrs. Seddon said in a subdued voice. "I will tell the duke what transpired if you could try to calm the children. Take them inside and help unpack the groceries. Feed them bread and honey until we can arrange a meal."

Something latched onto Damon's leg.

What the hell?

He looked down, and a diminutive girl with an abundance of golden curls was hanging on to him for dear life. Damon's first instinct was to shake off the annoying little waif or push her away. When had he ever interacted with children? In his experience, they smelled of sour milk and had perpetual runny noses.

Bothersome little beings.

But when he heard shaky sniffles, his heart melted.

He remembered Oliver Wollstonecraft conveying to the club how decades ago, his grandfather, the now Earl of Carnstone, went undercover in a cotton mill to investigate shoddy labor practices. Aidan Wollstonecraft came out of that experience by taking in a couple of orphans and making them part of his family. At the time of the telling, Damon could hardly keep from rolling his eyes, for he could not stand rank sentiment of any kind.

"Chloe, come away and leave the duke alone," Mrs. Seddon said as MacClery assisted her to stand.

"No," Damon whispered. "She's fine."

He scooped up the small girl into his arms. She weighed nothing at all. Their gazes met, and his heart hitched. Tears trickled down her pale cheeks. The eyes staring back at him were the exact shade of his own. This small child was young enough to be his. Instead, she could be his half-sister. What a sobering thought.

"Chloe, all is well," he crooned tenderly. "The bad man is gone."

A ragged sob escaped the girl, and she wound her thin arms around his neck, hanging on for dear life.

Blast it, and blast adorable moppets for pulling on my heartstrings!

"Come, let us go inside. How long ago was Browning here?" Damon asked, still holding Chloe, gently patting her back.

"Must be close to thirty minutes, Your Grace. He came for the safe," Mrs. Seddon replied as MacClery assisted her to a chair. "But he did not get it. When Mr. Penn and his assistants delivered all the crates of food, I asked him to take the safe to his store and that you would consider it a favor."

"You are indeed clever, Mrs. Seddon. Well done," Damon replied. "Again, I ask, are you injured?"

"No, Your Grace, nothing is broken, but there will be bruising. I'm certain of that."

The table in the dining area could accommodate more than thirty people, so there was more than enough room for everyone.

Mrs. Seddon moved to stand, but MacClery laid a hand on her shoulder. "Mrs. Seddon. Please stay seated. You've had an ordeal. Allow me—and Thomas and Patrick—to unpack the food and bring something to eat for the wee ones."

"Thank you, Mr.—?"

"MacClery, ma'am. Gilroy MacClery at your service." MacClery gave the woman a sweeping bow, and she rewarded the butler with a warm smile.

"Nate, Byron, Adina, and Molly, please assist the gentlemen in the kitchen. The rest of you, watch the younger ones," Mrs. Seddon asked.

Mercifully, the children had fallen silent and even more so when Helena, the oldest of the group, brought out the sugar biscuits and gave two each to the children. A small smile curved about Chloe's lips as she took the biscuits and immediately shoved as much as she could into her mouth.

"Steady on, poppet," Damon murmured. "Eat slowly."

The little girl nodded and took tinier nibbles.

"Helena is 15 years old," Mrs. Seddon said as they watched the older girl return to the kitchen. "She should have been sent into service two years ago, but I needed the help as I no longer had employees to assist me. I also enlisted the 13-year-old children, Merrill and Molly, as assistants. Perhaps selfish on my part, but these past months—horrible."

"I am sorry for the hardships. I had no idea this place existed. Tell me what occurred when Browning came," Damon asked.

"Well, Your Grace, Mr. Penn arrived with a wagon full of food, and you can imagine the excitement. It occurred to me after you departed, what if there was money in the safe or important papers beyond the ledgers? What if Browning caught wind of you hiring an investigative agency?"

Damon smiled. "I believe Miss Galway could use you on her payroll."

"Mr. Penn was only too happy to assist the Duke of Chellenham, his exact words. My, he no sooner left when Browning arrived. They may have passed each other on the road. A good thing Mr. Penn covered the safe with a tarp and surrounded it with crates."

Mrs. Seddon sighed. "Your Grace, never have I been so frightened when I saw that bully jump down from his horse. He immediately grabbed some of the younger boys, shaking them, demanding to know who had been there. But they never said a word. When Browning found the safe gone, he broke furniture, snarling and yelling. Thankfully, he never went into the kitchen and saw the food. Anyway, he then came toward me. He slapped me twice, shook me, threw me to the ground, then kicked me for good measure."

"The miserable bas—I mean, man. I will try and have Browning located. Which direction did he ride off?" Damon asked. It was challenging to keep his anger hidden. How dare his father's hired bully ride in and terrorize everyone?

"The opposite from which he came, Your Grace, away from London. But that means nothing because he could circle about and return to the city."

"Yes, he could." Damon felt a pull on his sleeve, and he glanced down.

Chloe held up half a biscuit. "Share."

Blast it all.

His heart melted a little more. "No, sweetheart, it is all for you. Enjoy. Eat slowly."

"She has taken to you, Your Grace," Mrs. Seddon said softly. "Chloe hardly speaks or interacts with anyone."

"How long has she been here? And how old is she?"

"She could be between 5 and 7 years of age; I am not sure—"

"I'm five!" Chloe stated firmly, her mouth full of biscuit. A few wayward crumbs fell to her pinafore, and Damon absently brushed them away.

"Are you, poppet?" Damon replied, amused.

"I'll be six when it snows, and Christmas comes. That's what Mama said." Chloe nodded to punctuate the point and took another bite of the sugar biscuit.

"Well," Mrs. Seddon gaped, "That is the most she has said since she arrived four months ago."

"I believe Chloe understands more than she let on. Where is your mama, sweetheart?" Damon asked.

"Dead."

Succinct and to the point. If the tiny tot even knew what death meant.

Damon sat Chloe on the chair next to him just as MacClery, Thomas, and Patrick entered the room with plates, utensils, and a food platter. Behind them, the older children carried glasses, a milk container, a teapot, and mugs. The children cheered.

God above, it resembled a maudlin scene out of a Dickens novel, with starving orphans, well-meaning adults, and villains aplenty, with the likes of Browning, his late but *not* lamented father, and the unknown hubristic men involved.

"Me and lads aren't much for cooking," MacClery announced. "But we managed scrambled eggs and sausages."

The footmen moved efficiently around the table, laying the dishes and serving the food. Damon picked up a knife and fork and cut Chloe's sausages without thinking. He looked up to find Mrs. Seddon smiling at him.

"This looks wonderful, Mr. MacClery. Thank you all so much." Mrs. Seddon dabbed at the corner of her eye with the hem of her apron.

"Mrs. Seddon, there will be much to plan and discuss on how to go forward," Damon said solemnly. "This place will have to be assessed to see if it is fit for long-term habitation."

"If it is all the same to you, Your Grace, I would like to be involved in this project. Being an under butler is a dull duty and unnecessary at Queen Anne's Gate," MacClery said, sliding his gaze toward Mrs. Seddon.

She blushed in response.

Well, throw a budding romance into the Dickens blend, Damon thought with amusement. But MacClery had a point regarding the under butler position. Would Chellenhome become a permanent concern? As Mrs. Seddon said, there were more children alone on the streets than orphanages to take them in.

All Damon knew? He wanted nothing more than to discuss all this with one person—Althea. He yearned to see her. Talk to her. Hold her.

Admit it.

Romance was bourgeoning for him, as well. And for once, he embraced the sentiment.

Chapter 13

ALTHEA SAT IN HER STUDY, reviewing the ledger and taking copious notes. It was past eight o'clock, and no sign of Damon. She had stayed at Queen Anne's Gate as long as possible, but there was quite a flurry of activity there. Workers carried out furniture, and she could hear hammers and saws off in the distance. As it grew close to the dinner hour, Althea decided to head home, as it wasn't fair that the staff should see to her meals.

During the afternoon, Althea interviewed everyone. However, nothing she gleaned from the discussions could assist with the Chellenhome aspect of the case. Many staff were recent hires and not privy to most of the goings on. Only a few had been there longer than five years: MacClery, the butler; Mrs. Canning, the cook; and the upstairs maid, Roberta.

The late duke pursued most of his activities off the premises. He only occasionally brought his vices to the Queen Anne's Gate residence, but it was enough to disturb and horrify the staff, such as the recent orgy.

Sybil entered the room carrying two mugs of tea and placed one on the table before Althea. "Still pouring over that ledger?" she asked as she sat at the desk.

"Yes. You remember me speaking of Olivia Durham?"

"On the Duke of Watford case? The lady who married the duke?"

"The very one. We became friends. Olivia is away right now in the country. I found her name in here." Althea turned the ledger around to show Sybil.

Girl infant
Mother: Katy McKinnon—deceased East End
Adopted 1864 to The Reverend William Durham, Hertfordshire
New Name: Olivia Durham EC
00165

"Olivia never knew her mother's name," Althea said.

"What does the number mean?"

"I am not certain. A notation for the transaction? It is probably in another of the ledgers. Most of the listings have numbers. Do we know anyone who can open a locked safe?"

"A safe?"

Althea explained about the safe at the charity home and that Damon and his men had gone to retrieve it.

"Archie might know of someone during his time living on the streets. I will ask him. We have two cases lined up. Will you need Edwina tomorrow? Divorce case for a banker's wife and a baronet's wife."

"No, have her start. I may be a little longer on the Chellenham one."

Sybil sipped her tea, giving Althea a crafty smile. "Do tell."

Thankfully, the bell rang, for Althea did not want to discuss her intense and growing feelings for her infamous rake.

Her rake? Staking a claim already?

"I will see to the bell," Sybil jumped up.

A few moments later, Sybil entered the room with Damon behind her. The summer breeze had tousled his golden locks, making him look glorious.

"Mrs. Bartle is gone for the night, so may I take your coat, Your Grace?" Sybil said with an amused smile on her face.

"No, thank you, Miss Norton. I will not be staying long."

"Then I will leave you to it. I am just upstairs should you need me." Sybil gave her a wink. "Just shout out." She departed and closed the door behind her.

"Does your cousin think I am going to ravish you?" Damon asked as he removed his coat and tossed it onto the sofa.

Althea came to stand before him, laying her hand flat against his chest. "Are you? Society dictates we should not be alone, but I can look after myself. And I am capable of making up my mind. And taking what I want."

"Are you?" Damon said huskily. "Going to take what you want?"

"Eventually, yes. But for now, I will settle for a kiss."

Damon immediately gathered her into his arms and kissed her soundly. Their tongues clashed as he tasted every inch of her mouth. He was very skilled. Easing off to tenderly nibble on her lower lip, then suddenly plunging in again to take complete possession. Althea felt like she was swimming in the ocean, and wild, rogue waves threatened to overwhelm her. It was exhilarating. Utterly exciting, and her insides turned to custard.

Breathless, Damon broke the kiss. "What you do to me."

Althea grabbed his lapels and pulled him closer. "What? Tell me."

"You have me completely confused. I have never felt like this; it is utterly terrifying, yet never have I felt so alive. And I have never discussed my emotions or supposed lack of them to anyone before."

She laid her head against his chest, and the comforting sound of his rapid heartbeat soothed her. "You can tell me anything."

Damon smoothed her hair. "Until I met you, I lived a certain way, free from turmoil and emotion. I often never even bothered to learn a person's name, regardless of any so-called intimacy shared. Because to me, there was no warmth involved. A temporary selfish pleasure, nothing more."

He exhaled. "I am a cad, even with my friends. I've no idea why they still offer friendship, for I have done nothing to deserve it. My mother asked me, 'Are you your father's son?' and I had to think about it because, in many ways, I am." Damon cupped her cheeks, tilting her head upward to catch his gaze. "But I don't want to be. Not since I met you. You have infected my very heart and soul."

"You make me sound like a disease," she teased.

"If you are, then I welcome it. Slowly but surely, you have changed my life. I want to be a better man. One that deserves—you."

Tears welled in her eyes, and Althea blinked them back. "Oh, Damon. What is happening between us?"

"Something—extraordinary. But we will take this at a slow pace. Or whatever pace you wish. You set the terms, and I will follow them. I will follow *you*—to the ends of the earth."

He captured her lips, but this time, the kiss held all the tenderness and reverence Althea had no idea Damon even possessed. Then he ended it, took her hand, and kissed it. Oh, she loved it when he did that. Without thinking, she grazed the back of her fingers across his cheeks. Already golden stubble was evident along his jawline, and the roughness of it made her skin tingle.

Althea could not stop touching him. Damon moaned and leaned into her touch, and they stood that way for several moments as if reveling in the connection. Finally, perhaps even reluctantly, Damon took a step in reverse. A bond was forming between them, and Althea could sense it.

"I want more, but as you said, a kiss—for now. I have much to tell you," Damon said. "Come sit on the sofa with me, for I want to hear about the servants' interviews. You go first."

Once they settled, she turned partway to face him. "There is not much to report. Most of the servants are recent, as there has been a high turnover through the years, according to the cook, Mrs. Canning. She knows of your father's reputation and some of the rumors. The party he gave a few months ago was the first one of that type in years."

"MacClery believes he was trying to recruit new blood, as it were, for his charity home," Damon said. "Many in his circle are too elderly or have died. Chellenhome had no money for the past four months, and my father died with only thirty-five pounds in his account and over one hundred pounds in unresolved debts. The walls were closing in on him. There was no more property to sell except for Chellenhome. And you have seen it. It is not worth selling."

"And what did you find at Chellenhome? Did you bring the safe?" Althea sat enraptured, listening to the unbelievable narrative of all that had transpired.

"We have the safe. We retrieved it at Penn's Grocer. With all the renovation at Queen Anne's Gate, I should bring it here, would you mind? That way, once we open it, you can access the contents easily."

"Of course. We are trying to find someone who can open a locked safe. But poor Mrs. Seddon. Is she well?"

"I offered to have the village doctor drop by, but she claimed the man was incompetent. Do you think Doctor Buchanan would consent to examine her and the children? They have been deprived of proper food for weeks. I will pay him for his time."

Althea nodded. "I will contact him at once."

"I wish to be there. And I would like for you to be with me."

"Yes, of course. The young girl that latched onto you—"

"Chloe," he replied fondly. "The little imp pulled on those tight heartstrings. Apparently, I have them, much to my astonishment."

"Chloe? Wait, I'll fetch the ledger." Flipping through the pages, she found it and passed it to Damon. "She is the last entry."

Girl age 5
Mother: Máiréad O'Connor prison Newgate
Name: Chloe O'Connor EC

"EC. Edward Cranston. So, she *is* my half-sister. My God."

"Chloe's mother was incarcerated. Which means your father kept in contact, probably through Browning."

Damon nodded. "Mrs. Seddon stated Chloe arrived four months ago, brought by Browning. The girl was withdrawn and hardly spoke. Chloe said her mother is dead."

"To a 5-year-old child, dead may mean gone—in the broadest sense. I will go to Newgate and ask to see Máiréad O'Connor and find out the particulars. They keep the women prisoners in a separate ward so I will be safe enough. I will go first thing tomorrow morning. Now, the seventeen children living at Chellenhome." Althea wasn't sure how to broach this.

"Yes?"

"Besides Chloe, there are four more with the EC initials by their names. Have you thought about what you are going to do?"

Damon sighed. "I have thought of nothing else. To assist any of my father's progeny, perhaps I should concentrate on those who need the most support, those at the home. Perhaps the past is best left—in the past. The simple but alarming fact is that I cannot help them all. The dukedom is not all that wealthy. I thought it was only the names my mother gave me, maybe a few more beyond that, but it is literally dozens and dozens. Perhaps hundreds."

"And once they left Chellenhome, who knows where they went from there? It may be impossible to trace, especially the earlier ones." Althea took Damon's hand and squeezed it gently. "It is heartbreaking. What your father did was monstrous."

"You have no idea. Among the duke's papers, I found a book published in 1883 by Francis Galton, a cousin of Charles Darwin. Concerning eugenics."

Althea cocked her head in question. "What is that?"

Damon curled his lip in disgust. "Galton coined the name. I was horrified to read part of it. 'The practice or advocacy of improving the human species by selectively mating people with specific desirable hereditary traits.' Galton approached many in the British elite to 'better mankind through proper propagation.' My father and a few others embraced this, but most dismissed the man and his ideas. I hear it is taking root in parts of America, however."

"Oh, that is horrific," Althea gasped.

"The late duke was obsessed with eugenics. My father underlined certain passages and made notes in the margins. He wasn't concerned with intellect as such. He just wanted attractive offspring. This practice has been around since ancient times. 'Natural selection and selective breeding' are enough to turn one's bile."

"So, your father followed this line of thinking even before the book was published. Good God." Althea thought she couldn't be more shocked by the late duke's immoral behavior, but this? Beyond the pale. The level of arrogance.

"Have you noticed that some of the rakes and those associated with us have father or stepfather difficulties? Asher's wife, Chastity, with her evil stepfather. Gideon's stepfather, Whinstone. Olivia's adoptive vicar father, and the one who supplied the seed, my loathsome father," Damon stated.

"But there were just as many good men in that group," Althea replied gently. "Christian respected his late father, as does Asher. Brandon Knight also loved and respected his father and sought revenge on his behalf. Then my—and Eleanora's—father, who was the best of men," she concluded.

"Well, Christian did not know his father all that long before he passed, but generally speaking, he was considered a decent sort. And all in the past tense. All those good and noble men died far too young," Damon interjected, squeezing her hand in return.

"There is my Uncle Reece, my father's younger brother. I do not remember my mother, who died eighteen months after I was born. Uncle Reece moved in with us and helped his brother to raise his girls. My uncle is also the best of men, but thankfully, he is still here."

"I am glad you have your uncle. Not having a mother in one's formative years is not easy."

"No. It isn't. And you know that. I am sorry your mother was unavailable to you when you needed her. But she can be part of your life now."

Damon nodded but did not reply.

"So, what will you do next?" Best to change the subject for now.

"I *will* meet with Evercreech since we have already spoken. I cannot go through the rest of my life pretending he doesn't exist. And the footman, Donaldson, at Chellenham Park? Do I reside there at some point, knowing my half-brother is pouring my tea? If I were a heartless cad—and for years, I was—I could do it. Other men through the centuries no doubt acted the same."

Althea nuzzled Damon's hand against her cheek. "But you are not heartless, are you?"

"No, not entirely. I will speak with Evercreech and Donaldson soon and see what transpires. If nothing emerges from the meeting, so be it. I will offer to find other employment for Donaldson. He cannot stay at Chellenham Park. But all the ones who came after? Close to three decades worth?" He shook his head sadly.

"It is not your guilt to bear. Assist the few you can. It's more than most would do. I think you have found your cause when Parliament convenes in October. There is no formal or legal adoption law, and homeless children still roam these streets and have done so for centuries. There is a need for more orphanages and better education on controlling birth rates. There is much to be done," Althea urged. "And you are up to the task. I *know* you are."

"Thank you for that. Well, I will have some assistance. MacClery wants to assess Chellenhome to see if the building is viable. He is quite smitten with Mrs. Seddon and wants to be nearby."

Althea smiled. "Oh, I think that is brilliant. Yes, put Mr. MacClery in charge. Why not sponsor a home for foundlings? He could also find a tenant for the farm and mill, maybe one of your tenants at Chellenham Park!" She clapped her hands together enthusiastically. "Think of the good you can do here in the present."

"I know what I would like to do. Right now, in the present," Damon said in a low, husky voice.

"And you *are* still a bit disreputable. I like that, as long as it is only for me. For now."

Did she want to be involved with him beyond the case? Realistically, that is as long as it could last. It had been a relief to discover there was more to Damon than the handsome surface.

But for them to mesh their lives together?

At some point, Eleanora and Christian would have children if they were able. They could keep their investigative partnership for several years, but Christian needed an heir. So does Damon. Althea had no desire to have children. Or at least, she gave it little thought.

Althea had assumed she would be alone on this investigative agency venture because Eleanora was already married. And Sybil may soon be if her courtship with Corbett came to its obvious conclusion. Althea was fine with that and wished her sister and cousin all the happiness in the world.

Althea had plans.

Further expansion, hiring more investigators—preferably women. Opening a large office somewhere in the West End. She only wanted to run this investigative agency until she was too old. It consumed her waking thoughts.

Well, not *all* her waking thoughts.

Exhaling, she met Damon's gaze. He was crawling far too close to her heart. Perhaps suggesting physical intimacy was a grave mistake on her part. Althea had the feeling that if and when they shared a bed, it would merely deepen what was already occurring between them, and it would upend all her plans for the future. How arrogant to think she could enjoy a brief affair and move on with her investigative agency strategies. Toss Damon from her life and selfishly steam ahead, not caring for his feelings. They agreed about the dalliance; perhaps she should leave it at that.

"What are you thinking about? You have that pensive furrow of your brows when you are deep in thought," Damon teased.

"Merely organizing my upcoming tasks. Shall I report to you after I see Chloe's mother?"

"I have a late luncheon tomorrow with Asher and Christian. Can you come to Clarendon Place at seven?"

"Yes. I will also contact Corbett and arrange the visit to Chellenhome the day after tomorrow. I will tell you the exact time when we see each other at seven."

Althea stood, and Damon did as well.

"Time for me to go?" he questioned, picking up his coat and slipping it on.

"I think it best. Sybil is upstairs."

They strolled toward the study door when Damon clasped her arm and gently swung her around until her back rested against the wall. He stood close, then closer still, placing his hands flat against the wall on either side of her head. Leaning in, he nuzzled her neck, kissing it as he ground against her.

That very prominent and hard part of him rubbed against her thigh, causing heat to pool between her legs. Althea moaned, and her breathing became ragged. Oh, how he threatened her reserve. Damon cupped her breast, his thumb rubbing across her already erect nipple. Even through the layers of clothing and undergarments, every nerve ending came to life.

"Perhaps after your report," he whispered as he nibbled on her earlobe. "We can retire to my room and explore those intimacies you spoke of. Stay an hour, stay all night. The choice is yours."

Choice? As if she could say no. The duke was temptation incarnate.

Slowly, she trailed her hand along his flat stomach until she reached lower, clasped that hard thickness, and squeezed, causing a loud groan to escape him. "After the report, then." She kissed him, then slipped away, opening the study door. With a teasing smile, she buttoned his coat. "We cannot have you going out in public in that condition. You will terrify the older ladies."

"Minx."

With a brief but devastating kiss, Damon departed. Althea closed the study door and leaned against it, breathing hard.

Althea must remain firm in her resolve. They will only be involved as long as the case lasts. Afterward, they will go their separate ways.

There was no doubt of it.

She was playing with fire.

Chapter 14

NEWGATE PRISON SAT at the corner of Newgate Street and Old Bailey Street for more than seven hundred years. And it looked like it, for there have been discussions of closing it for decades. Thanks to the reformer Elizabeth Fry, who presented evidence to Parliament of the conditions women and their children had to endure within Newgate's walls, individual cells were constructed in 1858.

At one time, the authorities held public hangings outside the prison gates until 1868. All hangings were now private and done in the prison yard. Althea couldn't imagine such a thing, but those communal hangings used to attract enormous crowds.

The old, decrepit prison was filthy and dismal, with lice everywhere, so Althea would have to make this visitation brief. After paying the hansom driver, she entered the front entrance and shuddered at the sound of faraway yelling and shrieking.

A man with a large ring of keys in his hand led her down narrow hallways and through locked gates to the women's section in the right wing of the prison. There were no meeting rooms, so she would have to stand and speak to Máiréad O'Connor through the iron bars. The turnkey stood next to a wardswoman to supervise the verbal exchange.

The cell itself was tiny, with a wooden bench and a candle. The window was small and high above to let in a smattering of air or the occasional ray of sunshine—if the prisoners were lucky. The woman came to lean against the iron grates. Althea stepped in reverse, remembering it would be wise not to be so close. Máiréad O'Connor must have been beautiful once, but not now. Hard living and dire circumstances etched her face.

"Who are you, then?" Máiréad barked, pushing her tangled hair from her forehead.

A slight Irish accent. Althea introduced herself and stated her credentials. "Were you acquainted with Edward Cranston, the Duke of Chellenham?"

"Eddie? What's he done now?"

"I am here to discuss your daughter. She's the duke's, correct?"

The woman's eyes narrowed suspiciously. "Who wants to know?"

"The current duke. Edward Cranston is dead."

The woman stumbled, clasping the bars to stay upright. She wore fingerless gloves; her nails were broken and dirty. "My Chloe. What's become of her? Did Eddie find her a good home? I signed her over to him. He promised me!"

"Did the late duke pay you for your daughter's upkeep?"

Máiréad exhaled sharply. "Now and then, not much, mind. It's why I turned to thieving. And I got caught. Thirteen years I got for stealing bread for my wee girl."

"Stop your lying, O'Connor," the wardswoman yelled. "You were caught stealing women's jewelry with a man you serviced."

"Aye, aye," Máiréad muttered. "He got away and all. Left me holding the shitebag. He did a runner, yeah? I reached Silas Browning, and he told me the duke would take Chloe and see she got a good home. Poor wee mite, born on Christmas Eve, she was. I came from a good home; I wasn't always like this."

The wardswoman scoffed. The turnkey scowled at her, and she immediately quieted.

"My father was a foreman in a shoe factory. But then he died, and it all went wrong," Máiréad continued. "I met Eddie at a music hall where I served drinks to make money for my mother and me. Well, he swept me off my feet. First man I'd ever been with. I was soon pregnant, and Eddie looked after me proper. Gave me money and other gifts. But once Chloe was born, he stopped coming around. Sent his bully instead."

Máiréad started to pace. "The money trickled down to nothing. I had to make money any way I could. My mother died, and I had no one to look after Chloe. How could I get a job in a factory?"

"You have no claim on your daughter, no custody at all?" Althea asked.

"No. Browning made me sign papers. She be gone from my life, and I pray she will be better off."

"You are certain she is the late duke's daughter?"

"Aye, I was with no man before and only him then. My wee girl looks just like Eddie. She's lovely. What will happen to her?"

"I am representing the present duke. We will see her well looked after. Never fear."

"Please tell his nibs I won't come near, I promise. I want no trouble. That's if I even make it out of here in one piece." She coughed and spat.

Althea reached into her shoulder bag and held out a napkin with bread, cheese, an apple, and a couple of sugar biscuits toward the turnkey. "Can I give this to Miss O'Connor?"

"Aye. Go on."

Althea gathered the napkin into a bundle and handed the food to Máiréad, whose lower lip trembled at the sight of the food.

"Thank you," she whispered, holding the package as if it were precious cargo. "I loved Eddie. I truly did. But he left me high and dry. May God bless his troubled soul."

Troubled was one word for it. Althea didn't have the heart to tell Máiréad that she was one in a very long line of women the late duke used and tossed away. Althea thanked her for the information and was escorted outside by the wardswoman. Standing on the walkway, Althea felt the urge to cry. Poor Miss O'Connor.

Edward Cranston preyed on beautiful but vulnerable females of the lower classes, mostly of Irish background. He charmed and seduced them, got them pregnant, and abandoned them, yet still kept tabs on his illegitimate children when possible. And he used those children to turn a profit.

No wonder the duchess had asked Damon, "Are you your father's son?" because he was indeed going down a similar path. Well, not so much the reckless begetting of children, but certainly the moral bankruptcy.

Hollis Galway, her late father and once an inspector with the Metropolitan Police, used to say, "You cannot involve yourself in the private lives of your clients." But she had. Althea hadn't followed her father's advice, nor had Eleanora, though it turned out well enough for her. Perhaps it would be best to wrap up this case. What more could she possibly do? Cut it clean and continue with her agency plans, leaving Damon behind. It was plain common sense.

But when had common sense ever entered into her interactions with Damon Cranston?

GENTLEMEN'S CLUBS, or exclusive clubs for the wealthy, had existed in London for hundreds of years. Some prominent ones, like White's or Boodle's, spoke more of another age, belonging to grandfathers and great-grandfathers. Almack's closed in 1867, as did a few others from the Regency and Georgian periods. The more recent clubs were more specific, catering to those who enjoyed the arts, science, literature, graduates from certain universities, or flyfishing of all things.

Damon and his friends merged with a small club, unofficially known as The Rakes of St. Regent's Park. For several years, they met once weekly to share a drink and a few sandwiches and swap tales of their exploits. Asher, Damon, and Christian decided to have their afternoon luncheon here. It was the only place to ensure complete privacy.

Asher hosted, with his footmen setting up various dishes on the sideboard so the men could serve themselves. There was roast pork with savory potatoes, chicken fricassee over rice, watercress salad, dilled corn, stuffed cucumbers, glazed carrots, bread, rolls, cheeses, fruit, and desserts. It was a veritable feast, and Damon could not wait to fill his plate as he hadn't had a proper meal in days.

Asher dismissed his servants, asking them to return in two hours.

Once seated, Asher poured white wine to complement the pork and chicken. "Well, it has been an eventful year," Asher said, holding his glass aloft. "Though Christian and I are no longer members, here's to The Rakes, past and present."

They clinked glasses.

"Perhaps it is time to rethink the main thrust of this group, no pun intended," Damon mused. "It has grown tiresome, and I have no desire to continue with this in its present state."

"What do you propose?" Christian asked as he sliced into his chicken.

"A philanthropic bent, perhaps," Damon replied.

"You? Philanthropy?" Asher stated incredulously.

"I know. It beggars belief. We can toss the new prospective members aside if they do not want to participate. It means that you both and Gideon could rejoin. Brandon Knight as well, when he returns to London. Even our absentee friend, Huxley. I will need assistance in one particular area."

Damon told his friends of Chellenhome, what he and Althea had discovered, and his father's part in it all. Christian and Asher ceased eating and were looking at him with a mixture of shock and empathy.

"I do not know what to say. A mill and farm? A foundling home dealing in illegitimate children for profit?" Christian exclaimed. "My God, your father is worse than any of us believed. Or was—past tense."

"He was. Past tense, and good riddance. I know Gideon has joined Viscount Hawkestone's progressive group within Parliament. Do you think Hawkestone would be interested in this endeavor?"

"Tremain Hornsby, the viscount, would grant us an audience, I am certain of it. Christian and I recently attached ourselves to that liberal venture," Asher interjected. "And you will never believe this; Oliver Wollstonecraft was there alongside his grandfather, the Earl of Carnstone, and has been for months. I know you recently made Oliver a member of The Rakes. He would no doubt be interested in your plan."

Damon didn't know Wollstonecraft all that well, never bothered even to carry on a conversation with the man until he had offered Damon condolences at the duke's funeral.

"He's a prospect, not a full member," Damon muttered. "I'll certainly consider it." His friends gave him a dubious look. "I mean what I say. If Wollstonecraft is interested, why not, indeed?"

"Gideon invited you to join Tremain Hornsby's—Hawkestone's—progressive group, did he not?" Christian asked.

"Yes. But I have not given it much thought since."

Damon was not acquainted with the Hornsbys either. All he knew? They were tedious do-gooders. Didn't he hear of the Duke of Gransford, the oldest Hornsby brother, laboring underground in an abandoned train tunnel as a doctor to the poor when he was still the marquess? Harrison Hornsby. Yes, that was his name. What a peculiar family. Eccentric was a word often attached to them. Yet, grudgingly, along with the Wollstonecrafts and their many good deeds, they were to be admired. Why not emulate them?

"Well, give it some thought now. You can make a presentation regarding Chellenhome and bring on wealthy donors to improve the conditions," Christian urged. Then he took a sip of wine, took another bite of food, then swallowed. "Forgive me for blundering in and telling you what to do. You have been dealing with one revelation after another. Take your time and sort it all out. But know that we will all support you no matter what you decide. I believe I can speak for Gideon on this. He asked me to keep an eye on you and offer assistance."

"Did he, indeed?"

"Olivia was reluctant to leave you while dealing with all you have discovered, and Gideon assured her that your friends would offer support when needed. And we will, Damon. All you have to do is ask," Christian replied.

"Well. Thank you. I truly appreciate it." Was Olivia concerned? And Gideon? It gave Damon a comforting feeling to know that they were. "I will need assistance to be certain."

"Good. In fact," Asher exclaimed, "Allow me to make a fifty-pound donation here and now." He reached into his pocket and placed a roll of pound notes on the table. "Clothes, food, upkeep on the building. And if you need more, come to me. Once you decide what to do, I can arrange a large monthly stipend."

Asher was wealthier than all of them—if the truth were told. A lump formed in Damon's throat at the gesture, containing emotions he was not used to experiencing.

Gratitude. Admiration. Respect.

Christian reached into his coat, pulling folded notes in a money clip. He peeled off several. "Thirty pounds. And if you need more, I will give what I can. For as long as you need it."

"I didn't mean to turn this luncheon into a donation initiative," Damon said, his mouth quirking, "But I thank you. You are better friends than I deserve. And we *will* make a proposal to Hawkestone's group."

Christian laughed and took his seat. "That we are. Better friends than you deserve, I mean. Eat up. Our food is getting cold."

They all were silent for the next several moments while they ate.

"Where does the food go, the portions that are not eaten? I have never thought of it before," Damon said between bites.

"Well, for my part," Asher replied, "I carry on with my father's tradition. The food goes to the servants, and leftovers are taken to nearby charities and churches to distribute to the needy."

"Much the same in my households," Christian added. "We try not to waste foodstuffs, especially since I married Eleanora, as she runs things like a tight ship."

"Perhaps that could be another matter to consider," Damon murmured. "The efficient redistribution of food."

"Just who are you, and what have you done with Damon Cranston?" Asher stated incredulously.

The men laughed.

"I have another conundrum. Althea," Damon said, twirling the stem of his wine glass. "I have no idea what is happening, and it's out of my control."

Christian and Asher exchanged knowing looks.

"You think of her constantly, longing for the time you can see her again, talk to her, hold her in your arms," Christian said softly.

"She fills your thoughts, hopes, and dreams, swelling your heart to bursting. You will do anything for her, anything that will make her happy," Asher added. "Protect her, whether she needs or wants protection. All the signs of falling in love."

"Good Christ," Damon mumbled. "Then I am truly a lost cause."

"Are you?" Christian asked as he rose to take a slice of spice cake from the sideboard. "Why should the cause be lost?"

"She will never have me, not permanently. And staying faithful to one woman? Near impossible." Damon downed the rest of his wine.

"No, it is not unimaginable at all. Not if you love with your whole heart," Asher replied as he refilled Damon's glass. "And, though it may shock you to know—you have one."

"Why won't she have you?" Christian asked.

"My debauched reputation, for one. Althea proposed a short liaison, nothing more. I do not believe she would be interested in aligning her life with mine, let alone combining them, and I am not even certain I am capable of such a profound commitment."

Christian chuckled. "Eleanora proposed we have a brief affair, which led to much more. It can be with you as well. See where it goes. Embrace those perplexing emotions, for there is nothing more exhilarating."

"So you say. All I am is a chaotic mess," Damon replied. "Besides, all that talk of love can change a man? It is romantic drivel."

"No," Asher said. "It isn't. I have been rehabilitated. Did Chastity have something to do with it? Of course, she did. But I *wanted* to change. It sounds like you do as well, Damon."

"I don't know what the hell I want," Damon groused.

The men laughed and continued with other topics, but Damon could not shake his friends' words.

See where it goes. Embrace those confusing emotions.

Very well, he will give it a try.

Starting tonight.

Chapter 15

ALTHEA ARRIVED AT 10 Clarendon Place promptly at seven. The skies were overcast, and the clouds looked ominous as if a summer storm were brewing. Kingsley showed her into the study, but Damon was not there. She sat on the sofa and removed her bonnet and gloves. A bottle of sparkling white wine, two glasses, and a bowl of fresh strawberries, raspberries, and grapes sat on the table before her.

The fire crackled in the hearth, and instead of the electric lights, lit candelabras were spaced around the room, giving it an intimate glow. A room set for seduction? Well, she had suggested such, did she not?

And Damon's declaration of staying an hour or staying the night? After much internal debating, Althea decided on the staying-an-hour proposal. Remaining all night would indicate she wanted more than a brief affair. In the years of being with the investigative agency and all the men Althea had met from various walks of life, there was none Althea wished to bed. None she had yearned to be her first.

Until she met Damon Cranston.

Don't let wayward emotions carry me off.

He strolled into the room, dressed in a dark gray suit, handsome as ever. He wore his guarded expression as if not knowing what to expect.

"How was your luncheon with Asher and Christian?" she asked politely.

Damon sat opposite, not on the sofa with her. How curious. "They have contributed to Chellenhome and offered to assist." In a monotone voice, he relayed about the progressive group within Parliament and the fact that he could make a presentation to bring other donors on board.

"That is brilliant. I believe we can start to wrap up this case and finalize the investigation as soon as the safe is opened."

Damon's eyebrow cocked. "Finalize? Is this case not exciting enough for you? No grand villain for you to face as in Gideon's investigation? No opportunity for you to brandish your pistol and take down said rogue? The villain in this inquiry is dead already. How tedious for you."

Was he teasing? Being sarcastic, or a little of both? It was hard to tell as his guarded expression was still in place.

"Take down? I shot Whinstone in the knee. He deserved it. I do not relish having to use force."

Damon narrowed his eyes. "Is that so? I think you thrive on the excitement."

"Every case is exciting. So yes, I do thrive on it. What *is* the matter? You have a dour look on your face."

And he did. Damon was frowning now; the guarded expression had dissipated.

"I do not wish to discuss charitable acts or the level of exhilaration in your investigations, not tonight. I want to know what is occurring between us and where it will go."

"Go?" Althea gave him a puzzled look. "Why does it have to go anywhere? We agreed on a dalliance, and you proposed an hour. Well, here I am."

"And that is all?" he asked softly.

"I assumed that is all *you* wanted. Even though a brief liaison was all we discussed, I do take this seriously. I have had plenty of opportunities to be involved with men from all walks of life. *You* are the only one I've wanted to take to my bed."

"Technically speaking, it is *my* bed," Damon purred. "Here is irony for you, perhaps with a liberal dash of hypocrisy, but I do not wish to be used and tossed aside. Or perhaps I deserve that exact thing done to me, considering my corrupt past. Regardless, the simple fact is I do not wish to advance with this unless we agree that we both are open to—more."

"More?"

There were varying levels of more. Does Damon mean physical relations? A deeper commitment? He could not be serious.

But one glance at his tense, gorgeous face showed that Damon was deadly serious. So much for keeping his emotions behind a mask. Althea could read plenty: trepidation, vulnerability, doubt, and desire. A potent mix and one that had Althea softening all over—to a point.

The rain started to patter against the windows.

Damon reached for the bottle of wine. "We should have some before the bubbles disperse. A little wine, my Thea?"

Althea nodded, for she couldn't speak. Her mind was in a whirl.

He poured her a glass, then leaned forward to pass it to her. "I want more. My feelings for you are quite intense and evolving by the minute," Damon said, his voice deeper than usual. "Remember, I said something extraordinary was happening between us."

"Yes, but I thought you meant in that particular moment, something brief," she replied, taking a sip. The bubbles danced on her tongue, and she reached for a raspberry and popped it into her mouth. This conversation was *not* what she expected.

Damon took a sip of wine. "I wish to ban the word brief from any further conversations. Forget brief. Forget dalliance and liaison.

I am talking about an affair of the heart. We hold nothing back. And if it takes us to any permanency, we embrace it."

Althea started hacking as her wine went down the wrong way on the word permanency. He sat next to her and rubbed her back until she stopped coughing.

"Why not us?" Damon asked as he rubbed, intensifying the heat between them. "Christian and Eleanora make it work, as has Gideon and Olivia and Asher and his lovely wife. Brandon Knight, one of the most bitter men I have ever met, has embraced love and started a new life. Do you believe I am incapable of such emotions? That I am a barren husk of a man who cares not for anyone or anything?"

Althea glanced up and stared into his beautiful eyes. "Perhaps at the first meeting and a little while after, but not now. I know that you care." Without thinking, she cupped his cheek. "You are most decidedly *not* your father's son. And I am glad of it."

He rubbed his cheek against her palm, causing her insides to tumble with desire.

"That means more than you can imagine," Damon said quietly. "But I need further from you. I must hear you say you are open to exploring these powerful emotions. That you will give us a chance to discover and embrace these feelings, I cannot illustrate the change that has taken place within me, but it occurred. And is accelerating the more I am with you."

"But I have plans for the future," Althea murmured. "I have no intent to marry. That is what you mean by permanency, is it not? I can't or won't give up my agency. Not for any man, no matter how compelling."

Damon took her hand, lacing his fingers through hers. "No one is asking you to be less than you are. I would never make such demands or control your life. Do you believe me?"

"I want to, and I know Christian and Eleanora make it work. But we are not them. Oh, blast it. I don't know what to think. I did not expect this conversation tonight."

"We can discuss more when we come to it. As I said, allow us to explore first. Come with me. Upstairs. Let the investigation begin."

Althea smiled, far more tempted than she thought she would be. It is what she came here for, after all.

"Besides, it's raining," he continued. "What a fine opportunity for us to cloister ourselves away from the world and revel in each other's company."

"Very well, I will go up—"

Damon cut off the rest of her sentence with a devastating kiss. He pulled away, leaving her panting.

"I-I haven't told you of my visit to Newgate yet," Althea said breathlessly.

"Later, my Thea. Come with me now." Damon stood and held out his hand.

She followed him upstairs, and he escorted her to his room. She already liked it with its dark wood panels and gold accents, which fit him perfectly.

"I have never brought anyone here to my home or my bedroom. Until you," he murmured as he kicked the door shut with his boot.

"Oh?" Her voice shook, and Althea was far more excited than she thought she would be. And curious. She had a general idea of how this was done, for Eleanora had two very brief encounters before meeting Christian and had told her and Sybil *all* the details.

"As tempted as I am to fall on you like a wild beast, I will curb my animal instincts. For tonight. You see," he came to stand before her and slowly unhooked her cape, tossing it aside. "I've never been with a woman such as you before."

"A virgin, you mean?"

"Right to the point. Yes. We are going to take this slow. Investigate, as I said." Damon started to remove her small jacket.

"I don't know," Althea crooned. "The wild beast thing sounds intriguing."

He laughed as he tossed her jacket to the floor. Then he started in on the buttons on her starched blouse. "Are you nervous?"

"Surprisingly, no."

"That's my bold Thea." He had her blouse off and tossed it on the pile on the floor. Damon trailed his fingers across the top of her breasts. "Lovely."

His hands moved down over her hip until his fingers found the buttons of her skirt. Everywhere he touched, a heated flame ignited, settling between her thighs, where she had grown decidedly wet already.

Her wool skirt pooled at her feet, and Althea stepped out, kicking it aside. She stood before him in her chemise, corset, and stockings.

Damon's hand settled between her legs. "Naughty. No drawers."

Althea was not wearing any, knowing she was coming here for an assignation. Why burden herself with unnecessary layers?

She hadn't put on petticoats either.

With his deft fingers, he explored, caressing the most private part of her. She moaned at his touch. Then he picked her up, carrying her across the room and setting her on the table.

Damon dropped to his knees in front of her. Slowly, he unbuttoned her boots and set them aside. "I am going to taste you. Kiss you." He parted her legs. "There."

How deliciously wicked.

Before she could even form words, his head disappeared between her legs, his tongue lapping, causing intense sensations to move through her. Already her breathing was ragged when he parted her folds with his fingers. He rubbed her sensitive nub with his other hand, and the combined stimulations had her rocketing toward her peak.

"Oh, God," she gasped. "More."

Her husky demand prompted Damon onward. His tongue was like magic, tasting, caressing, and licking every part of her.

Without thinking, Althea grasped a handful of his thick hair and moaned rather loudly with her head thrown back. Then, without any warning, the climax slammed her. More breathtaking and forceful than any time she had touched herself.

Damon gazed up at her, his eyes alive with desire. "Yes. Passionate. I *knew* it." Then he stood. "When you catch your breath, undress me, as much or as little as you wish."

"Yes," she said with bated breath. "Give me a minute. Oh, that was astonishing."

"Why, thank you."

"Do you wish me to do the same to you? It is called oral pleasure, correct?"

"Oh, I want that above all things," Damon whispered huskily. "But not tonight. This is about you. Your pleasure. Your desire. Your needs."

Exhaling, Althea jumped off the table and came to stand before him, despite her shaking legs. "You are quite a specimen, but you are well aware of that, aren't you?"

"I am. If my looks and build please you and heighten your desire, I am glad of it."

Althea laughed as she removed his coat and added it to the growing mound of garments. She did the same with his waistcoat, then attacked the silk-covered buttons of his shirt. No going slow for her. She wanted to see him.

All of him. Naked.

In her haste, one button popped and flew across the room. A rumble of laughter left his throat.

"My eager darling."

Althea had no idea this could be—fun. That teasing and lightheartedness would be involved. She gave him a brilliant smile as she clasped the ends of his shirt and pulled with all her might. The last two buttons pinged and skittered across the floor. She quickly divested him of the shirt, casting it aside, then stood back to admire the view.

He was lean but muscled, nonetheless. His chest was dusted with golden hair, narrowing to a straight line and disappearing under the waistline of his trousers. As if sculpted in marble. What a cliché, but it was true.

Yes, his trousers.

They were the next to go.

Once undone, she pushed them and his drawers past his hips. He kicked the clothing aside. Oh, he was astonishing. Althea had no idea men, when erect, could be so formidable. How many virgins whimpered at the sight of a naked man, wondering how on earth was *that* going to fit inside her?

Not Althea.

She could not wait to take all of him. Sighing at the glorious sight, Althea trailed the tips of her fingers across his flawless skin, down his muscled arms, and across his hip. Then she grasped him. So thick, so potent. The temptation was too great. She had to taste him. Dropping to her knees, she trailed her tongue along his length before he protested. Such a musky, earthy experience heightened her interest in exploring further.

Damon's only response was a tortured groan.

Althea then placed the head of his shaft in her mouth and licked enthusiastically.

After several minutes, he grasped her arms and brought her to her feet. "We will explore this later, I promise. I will lose all control if my cock is in your luscious mouth one second more."

"I will hold you to that promise. I want this—inside me now."

Damon moaned at her words. "Then you shall have what you want." Damon kissed her soundly, then backed her up until they reached the bed. Althea laid upon it, her entire body thrumming with need. Damon brought out a small case from the side table drawer. "Sheaths."

Althea watched as he deftly fitted one on his erect shaft. He climbed on the bed and spread her legs.

"I cannot wait, either." He inserted two fingers inside her, and she gasped. "So deliciously wet, still. You tasted so blasted sweet. Better than the wine." The head of his cock—as he called it—replaced his fingers, and with deliberate care, he pushed inside her. Inch by inch. "If I am hurting you, tell me. But I know you will."

Not hurt exactly, a slight pinch, but that feeling of fullness, as if he had taken complete possession of her body, was not something she had ever experienced.

Oh, it is lovely.

He was wholly seated, but he stayed still. Impatient, Althea lifted her hips.

"Wait. Just stay like this. For a moment," Damon rasped.

DAMON HAD TO SAVOR this and commit it to memory. Being joined with Althea was a moment of clarity when everything in the world finally made sense to him. This is what he was brought into the world for. To be joined with this lovely lady until the end of his days.

He had heard the talk amongst the elites that when rakish rogues fell, they fell hard. In the past, Damon derided such declarations. But he need only look at the members of The Rakes to see the proof. First Christian, then Asher, Brandon, Gideon, and now—him?

Oh, yes. Even the infamous rake, Damon Cranston.

"Um, Damon?" Althea whispered.

"A moment longer," he replied huskily. He took that minute, then pulled out and thrust back in, bringing about a series of gasps from Althea.

"More?" he asked.

"Oh, yes. More."

Damon started slow, with long, even strokes, rising above her so that he rubbed against her clit. Her gasps turned to moans, ending with a loud mewling. Those sounds of passion urged him on, increasing the pace until he was pounding into her with wild abandon. How much time passed, he hardly cared. Damon silently thanked providence for his stamina, for he needed it now more than ever.

Althea tilted her hips upward, crossing her legs across his back as they rocked and bucked. Their mingling moans and whispers, the scent of their lovemaking, and the sounds of their bodies coming together were not something he would soon forget.

Damon was past the point of no return and close to his climax. But he held back, waiting for Althea to reach her peak first.

"Come for me, now," he demanded.

She did precisely that with a loud, piercing cry, and Damon reveled in her inner muscles clutching him tightly.

Throwing back his head and grimacing, his climax tore him asunder.

Intense, all-consuming.

He moaned and collapsed at her side, pulling her into his embrace, breathing hard.

He kissed her forehead. "Stay with me a while longer?"

"Yes."

Chapter 16

THE SUN SHONE LATER in the morning when Damon picked Althea up at Cleveland Street. It took all his inner restraint not to tumble her in the carriage as they headed to the East End to collect Doctor Buchanan, for the sensual doings of last night still saturated his thoughts, mainly since she stayed beyond the stipulated one hour.

Besides the robust and earth-shattering lovemaking, what he enjoyed almost as much? Althea cuddled in his embrace, telling him of her day, the discovery of Chloe's mother at Newgate, and the conversation that had transpired. Damon also spoke of his luncheon with his friends. He relayed part of their discussion but kept their conversation regarding love to himself. By God, his friends were correct. He experienced everything that they had spoken of.

"How are you?" he asked, staring at her fixedly from the opposite side of the carriage. "Hopefully, not too sore."

Althea blushed prettily. "Perhaps a little, but happily so. It was a night to remember."

"And the first of many. There is much to share and explore, and it will only get better; I know it."

"I don't see how it could get better," Althea smiled teasingly. "You are very thorough. Skilled would be the appropriate word."

"Thank you. These are just the words a man longs to hear. When can we arrange more time together?"

"I am not certain. There is not much more I can pursue regarding your case. I suppose we should wait until we open the safe. I should have word from Archie later this afternoon."

"Althea," Damon smiled. "I was *not* speaking of time together on my case."

"Oh, of course. Soon? In a day or two?"

They came to a stop in front of the Bethnal Green Police Station. Before Damon could even respond, the door opened, and Corbett Buchanan climbed in, sitting next to Damon. Grunting, Damon slid down on the cushioned seat to make room.

The doctor set his kit at his feet, along with another parcel. "Some treats for the children, as it assists with smooth examinations if there are delicacies as an inducement."

"Is that how you court Miss Sybil Norton, Doctor?" Damon asked sardonically.

Buchanan laughed, taking it in good spirits, which had Damon liking the man all the more. "Perhaps. How many children are there, Your Grace?"

"Chellenham is fine. There are seventeen," Damon replied. "And you must examine Mrs. Seddon as well. She was deprived of decent food for months, and a bully attacked her." Damon explained about Silas Browning.

"The man escaped?" Buchanan asked.

"To points unknown. Hopefully, Browning stays gone." Damon caught Althea's gaze. "But I have Miss Galway and her trusty revolver to protect me."

"That you do," Althea responded, giving him a sly smile. "I have it with me now."

"Completely ferocious. I truly admire that." Damon gave her a heated look. "To change the subject, my man, MacClery, traveled to the home yesterday to start an assessment of the place and its viability. I already have donors lined up."

"This may become a permanent venture?" Buchanan asked. "I hope so, for there are more children in need than there are facilities to accommodate them."

"It may well become that. I should give you a little more information regarding Chellenhome." Damon briefly narrated the discoveries and his father's part in the scheme.

"The former duke? Your father? My God," Buchanan muttered.

Althea reached into her satchel and passed Damon a folded piece of paper. "A list of the children currently at Chellenhome with the initials EC next to their names."

He took the note. "My half-siblings, at least, are the ones we know of now."

"My God," Buchanan stated, still clearly shocked.

Damon unfolded the stationary.

Chloe O'Connor age 5

Byron Holloway age 8

Adina Desmond age 12

Hugh Crossingham age 13

Jack Benton age 6

My God, indeed.

These poor foundlings were of his blood, which meant something to Damon. But how does he single out these children over the others? What a damned jumble.

As if reading his mind, Althea said, "I believe we should speak to these children and hear their stories, at least what they remember. Some have been at the home a long time, others, like Chloe, a matter of months."

"Yes, we will. Buchanan, perhaps you can look at these children first, then allow Miss Galway to ask a few questions."

The doctor nodded. "Of course."

They arrived at the home, and what a complete difference from a few days ago. The younger children were playing in the yard, some of the older ones sitting on chairs, reading.

Mrs. Seddon came to greet them, wiping her hands on a clean apron, with MacClery right behind her, carrying one of the younger girls.

"Your Grace, and Miss Galway. How wonderful to see you," Mrs. Seddon smiled warmly.

Damon was not used to people being happy to see him, and all the youngsters seemed to be as well, bowing and giving him curtseys or casting shy glances his way. It was a strange feeling.

"This is Doctor Buchanan; he will be examining everyone. MacClery, you seem to be fitting in," Damon said.

"That I am, Your Grace. I have much to tell you."

Damon waved his arm. "Later. I—"

"Mr. Duke!" a young female voice squealed with delight. Chloe ran toward him, and he scooped her up into his arms. She hugged him tight, and Damon's heart squeezed in response. This pint-sized darling had stolen his heart. What a discovery to find that he even had one. Well, Althea had stolen it months ago. He could admit that now.

"Chloe, you say, 'Your Grace,'" Mrs. Seddon chided gently.

"It doesn't matter," Damon replied, reveling in the warmth offered by the little girl. "Can you show the good doctor to a room where he can examine the children? Miss Galway and I want to speak to Hugh and Adina after the doctor." He passed Chloe to Mrs. Seddon.

A flurry of activity ensued as the adults herded the children inside, and Damon and Althea headed to Mrs. Seddon's small office. MacClery also stepped into the room, making the area cramped indeed.

"Beneath the neglect, the building is solid, Your Grace, in need of general maintenance, perhaps new windows. The farmer abandoned the mill a few months ago; so we could quickly make it functional again. Chellenhome could be a solid and ongoing concern," MacClery stated firmly.

"Good to know. It will assist with my decision."

"Your Grace, allow me to put in a word to convince you," Mrs. Seddon interrupted. "I am not married, never have been. I took on the missus mantle as it denotes respect and seniority. I was brought up in a workhouse. It is not a life for any child. I know there have been improvements, but it is still not enough. I was raped in the workhouse by one of the guards there. He took me to some back-alley abortionist who botched the job so badly I nearly died. I was thrown to the cobbles to fend for myself at fifteen."

Mrs. Seddon shook her head. "You haven't lived until you find yourself digging through rubbish bins to find a morsel of food. I won't continue with my tale of woe, only to say that if we can improve things for a group of children, we should take it. We can't save them all as there are too many. But to give some a chance at a better life? There is nothing more rewarding, Your Grace. Take my word for it."

Mrs. Seddon's emotionally spoken words took hold.

Give some a chance at a better life.

"You have given much to contemplate, Mrs. Seddon. I haven't opened the safe yet, but I will make an informed and swift decision when I do."

"The five children with the initials EC after their name," Althea stated. "What can you tell us about them?" She reached into her satchel and pulled out the ledger. "For example, Adina Desmond has no parent listed. The girl has been here four years, which means she came here when she was eight."

"EC?" MacClery said, a puzzled look on his face.

"MacClery, this place acted as a mill, a hiding place for illegitimate children of my father and his wealthy associates. The children were sold for a profit," Damon stated. "EC is the late duke's initials, and he fathered these children on the list."

"Bloody hell!" MacClery explained. "My pardon, ladies, Your Grace."

"Bloody hell, indeed," Damon muttered.

"As to Adina, Browning brought her here in hysterics," Mrs. Seddon replied. "It took months for me to earn her trust, enough that she revealed that Mr. Browning took her from her mother by force and brought her here. It was hard to figure out where she lived, but she told me a name of a village by the sea, and I managed to locate it in Cornwall."

"Good God," Damon exclaimed.

"I wrote to the local constabulary hoping they could locate Adina's mother, Your Grace, but they told me she had moved to London to find her daughter. But that was four years ago. Perhaps Adina's mother has returned to the village."

Damon rubbed his temple. "It appears, Miss Galway, this investigation is far from over."

Doctor Buchanan opened the door. He had a young lad at his side. A blond-haired, blue-eyed one. "This is Hugh Crossingham. You wished to speak with him."

The boy was gangly as a lad of thirteen often is, and he eyed Damon warily.

Mrs. Seddon pulled on MacClery's sleeve. "We will leave you to it, Your Grace."

Damon and Althea were left alone with Hugh, who stood with shoulders back and fists defiantly clenched. Althea turned to a page in the ledger and passed it to Damon.

"It says here your mother is deceased, that you came here three years ago," Damon began.

"Aye, sir. I don't remember much. She died long ago. I was in an orphanage when that brute took me out of there, and he brought me here. Browning, his name."

Damon would not correct any of the children about how to address him. Who cared, except for the upper echelons of society?

"Do you know why you were brought here?" Althea questioned.

"I think to sell me to a factory. Browning always yelled at Mrs. Seddon to see it done, but she came up with excuses. I was fixing to run away because that bully said he would take me to a factory the next time he came here. I thought he had come for me when he showed up here the other day."

"Do you know who your father is?" Althea asked.

"No. Some nob, my mother said once." The boy looked Damon square in the eye. "Is it you? Is that why you're here, sir?"

And here it was. There was no use denying the blood ties.

"I could be since I was eighteen when you were born. But no, Hugh, I am not your father. I am, however, your half-brother."

"Half-brother. Blimey," the boy whispered. "What now?"

"That is a good question. Would you like to stay here until we work out the details? I want to assist you with schooling and whatnot. We can visit, get to know each other better, and go from there if you like. Think about it."

Hugh remained quiet, his brows furrowing as if deep in thought. "I'll stay here for now, sir. I need to think about things."

"You do that."

"Is it a secret?"

Damon looked at Althea. She gave a slight nod.

"Yes, until I speak with the others," Damon replied.

Hugh's eyes widened. "There's more?"

"Oh yes," Damon murmured, "You have no idea."

"What do I call you—Duke?"

"My name is Damon, but you can call me that when you feel comfortable. In the meantime, refer to me as Duke or Chellenham." Damon stood and held out his hand. "There is no need to run. If you decide you want a brother, we will go from there. Regardless, I will see that you have a future. Pact?"

Hugh looked at the hand, then shook it. "Pact. Chellenham."

The corner of Damon's mouth quirked with amusement. He liked the boy already. Hugh turned and left the room, closing the door behind him.

Damon exhaled and plopped onto the chair. "God."

"You handled that well. You were kind but not assertive. You gave Hugh options and plenty to think about. He will be a handsome man one day. But then, how could he not?"

Before Damon could reply, Buchanan was at the door with a young girl who was sniffling and clearly frightened. "Adina Desmond."

Althea immediately stood and went to the girl, gently placing her arm around her shoulder. "There, there. No need to be alarmed. The duke and I wish to ask you a few questions, that's all." Althea steered the girl to the chair.

"All I want is my mother!" she wailed.

Althea handed her a handkerchief. "Calm yourself, Adina. And wipe your tears."

The girl did but was still clearly distressed.

"We are going to try and locate your mother. What is her name?" Althea took out her notebook and pencil.

"Sarah Desmond," she whimpered as she wiped her nose. "We lived in Downderry, a cottage across from the beach. It was a small cottage with only a couple of rooms. But we were warm enough."

"Do you remember your father?" Althea questioned.

Damon thought it best to stay quiet so the girl would not be upset further.

"No. My mother said he was dead and was a well-to-do gent."

"Is there anyone in the town you and your mother used to visit? I know it was many years ago, but anything you can recall will help us find your mother," Althea asked.

Adina had black hair, but the blue eyes were Cranston through and through. Damon recalled his mother saying that only some children may be blond. The girl was so distressed, and this was not the time to mention any blood connection.

"There was a woman who lived on the road to Seaton. My mother called her Aunt Fiona. I don't know her last name." Adina dabbed at her eyes, tears still welling in them. "Same as mine, maybe."

"Adina," Damon said gently. "Miss Galway is a top-notch investigator. Her agency will find your mother. Meanwhile, do you want to stay here with the others? Mrs. Seddon could use your assistance in looking after the younger children. Do you think you could do that?"

She finally met Damon's gaze. His heart skipped a beat, for there was a resemblance in the color and shape of the eyes—along with the sharp cheekbones.

"Yes, sir. I will help Mrs. Seddon. She's been good to me, to all of us."

"That's the good girl. Things will be better here from now on, I promise. Dry your tears and find Mrs. Seddon."

Adina nodded and left the room.

"You were wise not to mention your familial ties," Althea said in a low voice. "Perhaps we should forgo speaking to the two younger boys, Jack and Byron, ages six and eight. I doubt they could add anything. They have been here for nearly four years, and they would have no memory of their mothers," Althea flipped to another page in the ledger. "I wanted to wait to bring this to your attention. The boys arrived at Chellenhome the same day. No mother was mentioned for either one. They could be brothers."

A knock sounded at the door, and Buchanan stepped in. "I finished the examinations. There are signs of malnutrition all around, but a few weeks of healthy meals will reverse that soon enough. As for Mrs. Seddon, there is bruising where the bully kicked her, but she is recovering nicely. I have Jack and Byron outside. You should say hello, at least."

"Fine, show them in."

When the two boys entered the room, Damon felt like he had been kicked hard in the midsection. It was as if looking at a portrait that had been done of him when he was that age. Damon always hated the artwork. The artist completed it soon after his mother was banished. His mother had commissioned the blasted thing, and the portrait sat in a dusty corner of the attic for decades. His contemptible father never hung it on the wall.

The boys were unmistakably brothers and were holding hands. Yet, they had different last names. Both looked wary but not afraid.

"Do you remember your mother, know of your father?" Damon asked.

The taller of the two, no doubt the oldest, Byron, shook his head. "No, sir. Nothing. All we remember is here."

"We believe we know who your father is. I will tell you about it later. Do you wish to stay here with the other children for now? Things are going to be better; I will see to it."

"Yes, sir."

"Good lads. Go and find MacClery."

Once the door closed, Damon sat forward, his head in his hands. "This was harder than I thought it would be," he said, his voice muffled.

Althea stood and laid her hand on his shoulder. He took her hand and kissed it, holding it tight. "I know, Damon. There is nothing to investigate concerning those boys unless we find Browning and ask where he collected them. As for Chloe, we know of her situation. Of the five, Adina wants to be reunited with her mother. That leaves four children for you to—consider."

Damon looked up at her. "Consider what?"

"If you want them to be your siblings. You can maintain a polite distance, pay for any education, and see them placed in good jobs. Or even taken into suitable homes. Or you can bring them into *your* home and become a family."

"Four children, aged five to thirteen? What do I know about the care and feeding of demanding tots?" he cried incredulously.

Another knock sounded at the door. MacClery stepped in. "Mrs. Seddon wishes to know if you are staying for lunch, Your Grace, Miss Galway. The doctor, too."

It was all too much to take in. Damon could not handle any more revelations today, let alone sit with the children and share a meal. "No, but thank her. MacClery, if you believe the building is sound, we shall start with repairs. Put together a detailed list of what needs to be done.

Damon reached into his pocket and hauled out Christian's folded bills. "Meanwhile, here is thirty pounds. Buy clothes, shoes, books, food, whatever is needed. I want an accounting of every last penny. I will return in a few days."

"Yes, Your Grace, I will see it done. I will start by buying a horse and a small wagon. The few animals that were on the farm were sold long ago."

"Fine. We will discuss the homestead at another time."

Damon and Althea moved outside. His head was swimming and starting to ache as it often did when overwhelmed. The children milled about, looking at him curiously as if trying to ascertain his intentions. He could not blame them.

One small child accepted him wholeheartedly. Chloe waved and gave him a sunny smile. "Mr. Duke!"

As she ran toward him, Chloe tripped, fell to the ground, and promptly wailed. Althea immediately sprang into action, picking up her skirt and dashing toward the injured child, but then, she tumbled. Damon's heart literally stopped at seeing Althea sprawled on the ground.

She had fallen. Again.

What in hell is going on?

Chapter 17

"THAT'S IT," DAMON EXCLAIMED. "Buchanan, you must examine Althea immediately. She has stumbled and fallen more than once in my presence."

Damon rushed to Althea's side as Mrs. Seddon attended to Chloe.

"I'm perfectly fine," Althea sputtered as he scooped her up.

"I agree about the perfect, but not the fine part. Follow me, Doctor." Damon marched into Mrs. Seddon's office, then placed Althea on the chair. "The left leg. When she slipped about ten days ago, I checked for a sprain and felt a lump on the lower leg."

"It's nothing," Althea murmured.

"We'll see," Buchanan replied. He swiftly lifted Althea's skirt above her knee and explored the lower part of her leg. "Allow me to remove your boot." He tossed it aside. "There. Does it pain you when I press on it?"

"No. There was never any pain," Althea responded.

"When did it first appear?" Buchanan was using his medical-professional voice, or one Damon imagined all doctors used when examining a patient, and it was hard to read him.

"Several months ago. It has not grown any larger, and it doesn't hurt. I thought it would go away on its own."

"It very well could. However, the cyst could be pressing against bone and nerve tissue, causing you to become unsteady. I would like to have another doctor look at it. If that is agreeable."

An alarm bell began to peal deep inside Damon. "What kind of doctor?" he asked warily.

"One who specializes in growths on bone."

"First, it is a cyst; now it's a growth. Come, Buchanan, speak plainly. What do you suspect?" Damon demanded.

"Yes, Corbett; what about his specialty?" Althea interjected.

"He specializes in—tumors."

ALTHEA'S BLOOD RAN cold.

Tumor.

No one wanted to hear that word—especially after her father's cancer diagnosis. Tumors were often malignant. They spread and leeched the very life from a person until death mercifully took them as it had her strong, vibrant father.

A buzzing sound took hold in her head, blocking out the voices. A few words drifted through her hearing, like 'most likely benign' and 'must rule it out,' but otherwise, Althea became lost in a fog.

I mustn't think the worst.

But how could she not?

"Althea!"

She started and stared in the direction of the worried voice.

Damon.

He had mentioned months ago that she should see about her stumbling. Why didn't she listen? Because she could not stand any man telling her what to do? Or because it came from him, an arrogant peer? He didn't look arrogant now. Damon displayed genuine concern for her. How mistaken she had been about him. In so many ways.

"Yes. Bring the doctor tomorrow at Cleveland Street if he's available. I want Eleanora and Christian to be there. And Sybil." Her voice sounded flat to her own ears. Althea was stunned, absolutely numb.

"I believe we should leave immediately," Damon said.

"First, see about Chloe. The poor child took quite a tumble," Althea said.

Corbett retrieved her boot and handed it to Damon. "I will examine the child and tell the driver we will depart shortly thereafter."

She was left alone with Damon.

He fell on one knee and slipped on her boot, slowly buttoning it. "So, you do not want me there tomorrow," he said low enough that only she could hear, not that there was anyone else in the room.

"Just my family."

"I care about your well-being as much as your family. More so, even."

Tears welled in her eyes at his serious but heartfelt tone. "It's probably nothing. There is no need to concern yourself."

Damon glanced up at her, and Althea could see the shutters come down as he deftly tucked away his emotions. "So be it. We had best depart." Damon stood. "Take my arm, and I will escort you to the carriage."

"I can walk to it myself," she muttered stubbornly.

Oh, why was she acting this way? Althea had no explanation except shock and obstinacy.

Once in the carriage, they were off. No one spoke the entire way to Cleveland Street. Once they arrived, Corbett helped her down.

"I will make arrangements and send word as to the time. Hopefully, Doctor Stevenson will be available," Corbett said gently.

Althea nodded.

No words of goodbye, for Damon was staring out the opposite window. The carriage pulled away, and Althea unlocked the door and stepped into the vestibule. All she wanted was to go to her room and have a good cry.

All her plans, her hopes for the agency—gone.

"BUCHANAN, IT WOULD have been expedient to drop you at Bethnal Green police station, but I wanted a private word."

"So I surmised."

"Don't spare any detail. I saw that slight arch in your eyebrow when you felt the lump. You already know that it is a tumor, correct?"

"That is something I should be discussing with Althea and her family—"

"Fuck patient confidentiality. What do you know about this growth?" Damon barked. But he was worried too. His hands were shaking.

"Not much," Buchanan sighed. "That's why I am bringing in Stevenson. It may *not* be cancer."

"Oh, God," Damon moaned.

"I have heard of these growths on the lower leg before. From my understanding, they rarely spread elsewhere in the body. If it is even cancer at all. We are getting ahead of ourselves, and do not repeat this to Althea."

"No," Damon replied, plowing his fingers through his hair in agitation. "What is the treatment?"

"I am not going to discuss it, Chellenham." Buchanan folded his arms in defiance.

But Damon was not going to have it. "To hell you're not. I will find this Stevenson myself and shake it out of him. Tell. Me. Or I will shake it out of *you*," Damon hissed through his clenched teeth.

"One common way is—amputation. It stops the growth and eliminates any possible reoccurrence. But again, this is the worst-case scenario. Cancer is not easy to diagnose, let alone treat. Throughout this century, there have been wild treatments from using sulfur to electricity and everything in between."

The doctor sighed. "We are no closer to curing cancer than we were one hundred years ago. We can postpone death, relieve some suffering, and make life more tolerable. Ultimately, the knife removes the disease permanently, as would be the case for Althea. As I said, *if* it is even cancer at all. Is that enough information for you?"

Damon shook his head. "How in hell can you do this for a living? Surrounded by suffering and death."

"It is why I turned to drink, that, and my time in the Canadian North-West Mounted Police during the Riel Rebellion. It is why I do not have a medical practice. I mostly do autopsies and forensic investigations. It's easier to deal with the dead. I have plenty of training in *that* regard."

"Do you drink to excess now?"

Buchanan shook his head. "Not for almost a year, and it is a struggle. But I want a future with Sybil, and I must prove to her that I am worth the investment. But more importantly, I have to prove it to myself."

"Yes, I know of what you speak. Only for me, it wasn't drinking, but anonymous sex with strangers."

And why Damon revealed that private part of his life, he had no idea. Perhaps because the doctor was being forthright about his.

Buchanan shrugged. "We all deal with traumatic situations in different ways."

Traumatic? What was he on about?

Damon scoffed. "I was hardly taking part in violent insurgencies on the untamed Canadian prairies as you were."

"No, but there are other levels of trauma one deals with. Regardless, this isn't about us."

"No, it is not."

The men grew quiet and reflective, and Asher's words at their luncheon entered his mind.

"Protect her, whether she needs or wants protection. All the signs of falling in love."

Protect. Hang it all.

As soon as Damon dropped off the doctor, he was returning to Cleveland Street. Damon wanted to be there for Althea. As strong as she was, he would offer his support.

Once he saw Buchanan off, he banged on the roof, and the window slid open. "Back to Cleveland Street, Dawson. And be swift about it."

"Right away, Your Grace."

The whole way there, Damon recalled his conversation with the doctor. It was entirely possible Althea would turn him away, which would be her right. But he wanted at least to offer comfort and sympathy. Emotions that, in the not-so-distant past, were utterly foreign. But not as far as Althea was concerned.

When he arrived at Althea's, Mrs. Bartle answered the door.

"Miss Althea Galway."

"She's in her room; she said she's not feeling well, Your Grace."

"And I know why she said that. I am going upstairs to her room. I hope you will not stop me. I have no nefarious purpose except to offer my support," Damon declared in an empathetic voice.

The housekeeper was grappling with what to do.

"You have my permission to bash me about the head with your trusty broom if I act the cad," he added, giving her his best charming smile.

"I will follow you upstairs, and if Miss Althea agrees to see you, you can stay." Mrs. Bartle stepped aside to allow him to enter.

"Stay put, Dawson," Damon called over his shoulder.

They climbed the stairs, and Mrs. Bartle knocked on the closed door. "His Grace, the Duke of Chellenham, to see you. Do you want me to send him away?"

Damon could hear sniffling behind the door, and his heart ached at Althea's anguish.

"It's all right, Mrs. Bartle. He can come in. The door is unlocked."

Damon turned to the housekeeper. "Can you fix a tea tray?"

"Yes, Your Grace."

Damon waited until the housekeeper descended the stairs, turned the handle, and entered. Althea was lying on her stomach across the bed, her eyes red, holding a handkerchief clutched in her trembling hand.

"Oh, Damon," she cried.

He ran to her side, gathering her up into his arms. "My sweet, not all is lost, and it may not be as bad as you think."

Althea grabbed his coat lapel and buried her face into his cravat, her shoulders heaving.

Damon held her closer, smoothing her hair. "Cry it out, love."

"H-h-hold me?"

"For as long as you need and longer. For the rest of my life."

Althea cried, and he rocked her slightly, whispering words of encouragement. A knock sounded at the door.

"It is Mrs. Bartle with a tea tray. Do you want her to come in?" Damon asked, his voice soft.

Althea shook her head. "Not now."

He stood, reached into his pocket, and handed her a fresh handkerchief.

"Yours is positively drenched, my darling. Here, dry your eyes, and I will fetch the tea."

He opened the door partway and held out his hands to take the tray. Mrs. Bartle looked worried. "It will be fine, Mrs. Bartle. Althea has had a shock. She will tell you when she is ready."

Damon took the tray and kicked the door shut as Mrs. Bartle moved away to head downstairs. "Is your cousin here?" Damon asked.

Althea sat upright and wiped her nose. "No, she is out on a divorce case."

"A cup of tea? I will even pour it for you," he teased, hoping to get at least a fragment of a smile.

"I can't drink it right now. All I want is for you to hold me again."

"Say no more." Damon sat the tray on the side table, then removed his coat and tossed it aside. He sat upright on the bed, his back against the headboard. "Come, let me hold you."

Althea crawled up to sit next to him, and he slipped his arm about her shoulders, bringing her in close enough that her head rested against him.

"All I can think of is part of that conversation last year regarding Christian's case," she whispered miserably. "You said, 'You seem a little too curious about my private sex life, Miss Galway. What do you believe—that I have a deviant bent along the lines of engaging in sex with those with limbs missing?' That may be me: a limb gone. How ironic that the Galway Agency's first major case involved a sawed-off leg."

"A caustic observation. Please listen to me. We are friends, are we not?" Althea nodded. "Then I shall speak frankly, as a good friend would do. Suppose the worst occurs, and the doctors determine that they must remove part of your lower leg. You will still be alive, and you can still live a full life."

Althea sniffled quietly. "I know this is self-indulgent, but my life will never be the same. All my plans for the agency—"

"Can continue onward. Chasing a villain down an alleyway brandishing your pistol may be out of the question, but everything else? You can still do it. Interviews, the general management of the agency, and taking on clients. You told me you would hire more people to do the legwork, no pun intended."

Althea laughed shakily.

"There, see? Not all is as terrible as you believe. I told you last night I am falling for you, Althea. Do you think I care if part of your leg is removed? If it saves your life, then so be it. If you had to have both legs removed, I would carry you around until I am too old and weak to do so."

"Oh, Damon. You say that now."

He turned slightly to look into her eyes. "Do you believe I am so shallow, so devoid of feeling, that I would turn from you in your hour of need? That I would reject you?" He took the handkerchief from her and gently dabbed at the tears trickling down her cheek. "Never. All I care about is your well-being. Quite the confession from such a deviant rogue, but it is true. For once in my selfish life, I will put others before my needs. But the person I most wish to support, care for—and love? You, my Thea. Only *you*."

Althea burst into tears.

Damon's heart tumbled seeing her in such distress. But he held her close until she had no more tears to shed. How long they stayed like this, Damon had no idea. How right she felt in his arms. How absolutely perfect.

Sniffling, Althea sat upright, wiping her eyes. "I feel foolish, carrying on so," she whispered. "I usually do not act this way."

"See that closed door? What goes on behind it when we are alone is no one's business. All that matters is—us. Together. We shut out the outside world."

"You are speaking as if we are a couple," Althea murmured.

"And why not? Why shouldn't we give it a go? Unless your feelings for me are not serious at all. You should tell me now to avoid smashing my little-used heart to complete bits."

She stared at him, sadness swimming in her red-rimmed eyes. "Oh, Damon. I didn't count on you coming into my life and making such an impact. My feelings are in complete disarray. Despite my initial horror, I was attracted to you from the first."

"Oh, thank you very much," Damon said sarcastically.

"You were not likable at all. Not at the beginning. Yet, I wanted to know more about you, to scratch below the handsome perfection to see if a human being resided there."

"And what have you discovered?"

"That you are human after all, complicated, a bit egotistical, somewhat arrogant, but also a little damaged, as we all are from life. You care about people far more than you let on. We've become friends against all the odds. You have a heart, Damon. And I could fall for you very easily."

A feeling of dread settled deep inside him. "But?"

"I am a mess and cannot explore my feelings for you until other issues become more settled. Is that horribly selfish? It sounds it to my ears. I need order in my life, and everything is upended, a complete jumble."

Althea turned to face him, cupping his cheek as she often did. Her touch seared, heating his skin, and that intense warmth traveled deep within him.

Regardless of his physical reaction, he did not like the sound of this. It appeared she did not care for him as much as he did for her. It would be an apt reward for all his haughty dalliances to finally fall in love with a woman and have her soundly reject him. Damon had the distinct notion that a broken heart would not be something he would snap back from any time soon.

"Oh, when you look at me like that," she sighed. "The mask removed, showing the conflicting emotions. I'm not saying we can never be. Not at all. I need—time. Just a little. Please?" She kissed him gently on the lips.

Tempted as he was to take the kiss deeper, this wasn't the time.

The doorknob rattled. "Althea? Open this door!"

It was Sybil Norton, obviously home from her investigative case. And no doubt Mrs. Bartle filled her in on the doings. "I have a note from Corbett; what's going on?" Sybil called out in a worried voice.

Althea sighed once again. "The outside world beckons."

Damon gently grasped her hand. How to say this without sounding so damned needy? "So, I am to have hope?"

"There is always hope, and I need to remember it," she mumbled. Then she gave Damon a wobbly smile. "Just a little time. I promise."

Althea got to her feet slowly and made her way to the door. Turning the key, she unlocked it and opened it. Damon stood just as Miss Norton peered into the room.

"Is this the note?" Althea pointed to the slip of paper her cousin clasped tightly.

"Oh, yes." She passed it to Althea.

"Corbett will be bringing Doctor Stevenson tomorrow at one o'clock," she said, folding the note and placing it in her skirt pocket. "I will need Eleanora and Christian to be here, and you as well, Sybil. It's to examine my leg. There is a cyst on it that is pressing against nerves, causing me to stumble."

Althea spoke steadily, hiding her anguish away to not alarm her family. By God, he was proud of her.

"Damon was with me when I fell. He called in to check on me," she continued. "I am fine, as you see. We shared a little tea and conversation, Sybil, nothing nefarious." Althea turned toward him. "You will be here tomorrow afternoon at one?"

"Of course, if you wish it," he replied, his heart soaring that she had asked.

She took his arm, escorting him into the hallway. "I do wish it very much," Althea said softly enough that only he could hear. "Thank you for coming to comfort me. It meant the world."

In other words, it was time for him to depart. Damon could take a hint. Miss Norton followed them into the hallway.

"Now, I am exhausted and going to try and sleep for a while." Althea gave them a wobbly smile, entered her room, and closed the door.

Damon turned and trotted down the stairs, Miss Norton hot on his heels.

"What's going on?" she whispered furiously.

Once at the bottom of the stairs, he turned to face her. "Is Mrs. Bartle still here?"

"Yes, she's in the kitchen."

"Please take me to her."

Miss Norton escorted him to the kitchen area, and Mrs. Bartle started at his presence. "God above!" she exclaimed, wiping her hands on a tea towel.

"Could you make Miss Althea toasted cheese and bacon and a fresh cup of tea? I think she would appreciate it, Mrs. Bartle."

"At once, Your Grace."

Miss Norton grabbed his coat sleeve once they stepped into the hall. "I ask again, what is happening here?"

"The cyst on her leg may be serious or not. That is why Buchanan is consulting someone with expertise in growths on bone. Althea is afraid it will impede her walking and thus impede her investigations. She is afraid her dreams will all be for naught."

Not the complete truth, but enough to appease Althea's cousin.

Miss Norton deflated. "Oh. No wonder, then. The Galway Agency is Althea's entire life. Nothing else matters. I can see why she was upset."

Those words cut through him like a thousand slices from a serrated blade. His fear, his particular vulnerability when it came to Althea, was that she would choose her career over him. How could he make her understand that he would never oppose her ambitions and dreams?

By telling her, you dolt.

As soon as the doctors addressed Althea's health crisis.

Chapter 18

ALTHEA AWOKE TO FIND that complete darkness had filled the room. "Damon?"

She thought he was still in her room, holding her in his arms, comforting her. For his alluring scent still clung to her pillow and quilt.

But she was alone.

When Mrs. Bartle arrived with a fresh mug of tea and her favorite sandwich—ordered by Damon, the housekeeper had told her—she had welcomed the distraction. The food assisted in relaxing her. It had taken her a long time to fall asleep.

The complicated duke cared for her; it was evident—by word and deed. Damon was falling for her; he had said so. But she had spoken the truth. Althea could not sift through her confused emotions right now. That brief but intense encounter in his bedroom only mixed-up things more. Althea believed she could act on her desire without it touching her feelings.

But she had been dead wrong.

It only heightened and enhanced them.

It was not what she expected; it had been more than she could have dreamed.

Althea turned over and pulled the quilt up to her chin. Damon Cranston looked the part of a fairytale prince with his golden perfection. But he was *not* perfect—and Althea found she was glad of it. The future was so uncertain in many ways. And until Althea cleared up some of that ambiguity, she could not make any personal plans.

Especially regarding her not-so-perfect duke.

A KNOCK AT THE DOOR woke her this time, and sunshine poured through the gap in the draperies.

"Althea, we have a late breakfast ready. Please come and join me," Sybil asked pleadingly through the closed door.

Rubbing her eyes, she glanced at the clock. Good Lord, it was past ten. "Yes, I will be down directly," she called out.

Althea took her time dressing, aware of her sporadic shakiness, then made her way downstairs. In the dining room sat Sybil, Eleanora, and Christian.

"Come and sit, Sister," Eleanora said soothingly, which was *not* like her at all. "Mrs. Bartle made your favorite. Plenty of bacon and scrambled eggs with cheese and chives. Christian? If you will pour her tea?"

"I am not an invalid," Althea snapped. Then she sighed. "I'm sorry. Please, no hovering, Ellie."

Despite her worry, Althea was hungry. Christian poured her tea and passed her the cup and saucer. Mrs. Bartle entered and set the plate in front of her. Mrs. Bartle departed, leaving them alone.

"I am sure Sybil told you of the growth on my leg. Corbett is bringing a doctor who is skilled in bone tumors."

Eleanora gasped.

"Call it what it is," Althea continued. "It could be something, or it could be nothing at all. Come, let us eat and change the subject. How is the railway case coming?"

"At its conclusion," Christian replied, cutting into his ham. "It appears the scheme involves two members from the board. You would think people would have learned from the railway mania boom and bust of the mid-forties, but then, that was fifty years ago. Today's young investors would know next to nothing about it. We have recovered the money invested by our clients, and it is up to them if they wish to press fraud charges."

"Well done," Althea smiled as she bit into a piece of crisp bacon. "And you secured payment for services rendered?"

"Absolutely," Eleanora replied. "Took it out of the recovered money. So, we are available to help with Chellenham's case."

Althea's smile disappeared. "Yes. I think I will need assistance. Have we heard from Archie about opening the safe?"

"I saw him this morning," Christian stated. Archie stayed in a small guest house at the rear of Christian's town house. "He was heading to the East End to speak again with the person in question. We will know more later this afternoon."

"We have been tasked to find one of the children's mothers," Althea told them about Adina Desmond and her predicament.

"Five of the children are possible half-siblings?" Sybil stated with shock in her tone.

"Damon thinks there are multiple dozens, and I think he realizes it will be impossible to track them all or assist them as he originally hoped," Althea replied between bites.

At least she was able to eat. Perhaps she was over the worst of the shock.

Right. Sure I am.

They spoke more of Damon's case, with Eleanora going to the study to retrieve paper and ink once Althea cleared the dishes. Mrs. Bartle brought fresh tea, then departed for the day.

"Downderry, Cornwall? That is a fair distance. Whom should we send?" Christian asked.

"Well, the family cannot go. I am not leaving Althea," Eleanora stated firmly.

"There is the newest employee. Edwina Callen," Sybil suggested.

"That is quite a journey for a novice," Althea replied. "Can we rely on her to take this on?"

"Well, she has been efficient with the duties given to her so far. Why not?" Eleanora said. "I say we send her immediately. We must hire another investigator, as we have more cases than we can handle."

A spark of an idea flared in Althea's mind. "Olivia told me of a woman who had come to her rescue when those bullies abducted her. The brave lady held off those two tyrants with a knife. We need someone besides Archie who knows the streets, is tough, and is handy with a blade."

"Wait, isn't this woman a prostitute?" Eleanora asked.

"What does it matter if she is?" Althea replied. "Think of the undercover work she could do, and no, I do not mean that sarcastically or literally. Her name is Mary O'Toole, though Olivia is not sure that is her true name."

"Of course, it doesn't matter," Eleanora stated firmly. "By all means, look into it."

"I will write to Olivia about it directly, and she can give us information on contacting Mary." Should she mention her health crisis in the correspondence? Best to wait until there was news before crafting a letter to her new friend.

They talked some more, and the bell sounded at the front entrance before they knew it.

Christian jumped up. "I'll see to it."

Her brother-in-law reentered the dining room, with Damon following close behind. At the sight of her golden duke, Althea nearly burst into tears as she was so relieved and happy to see him. It took all her restraint not to leap to her feet and throw herself into Damon's strong, warm, and comforting embrace.

Oh, dear.

Her feelings were much more engaged than first surmised and intense than she had verbalized to Damon. They were moving beyond friendship—and at a swift pace. So much for taking the time to work through the emotions. Nothing like a crisis to bring one's feelings into sharp focus.

Damon took off his hat and ran his fingers through his hair. "I am early. I couldn't stay away." He placed his hat on the side table, removed his coat, and hung it on the hook. "What are you all talking about?"

"You. Or more specifically, your case," Althea replied, giving him a shy smile.

Smiling, he sat beside her, took her hand, and kissed it. Oh, how she loved it when he did that. Her cheeks grew hot and hang it if everyone saw how he affected her.

"We will be sending Miss Callen to Cornwall with all haste," Sybil replied. "And Archie is in the East End procuring a cracker for the safe. Things are moving along."

"I never doubted it," Damon replied, not taking his eyes off Althea.

In response to his heated regard, her blush deepened. He still held her hand, and she laced her fingers through his.

"Have things progressed between you?" Eleanora demanded.

"El," Christian admonished.

"It's fine, Christian," Damon replied. "I would like to think things are progressing, but that is entirely up to Althea." He kissed her hand again, then released it.

And Althea missed the warmth of his touch. All she wanted to do was crawl into his lap. Could it be her health predicament fueling this need? Would the fever dissipate once the doctors gave her a clean bill of health? Or has this emergency solidified her unruly and chaotic emotions, as she had deduced earlier?

There was no time to contemplate it further, for Corbett arrived with Doctor Stevenson. He was an older man with white hair and kindly brown eyes.

After introductions, the older doctor asked, "Is there a private place we can examine Miss Althea?"

Eleanora escorted them to the study, then left them alone.

"Can we clear this desk?" Stevenson asked. Corbett immediately snapped into action. "Now, Miss Althea, sit on the desk with your legs straight before you. Doctor Buchanan will assist you. There. Perfect. Now, Corbett, remove the boots and stockings."

It was challenging to remember to breathe as the doctor examined the growth. "And it doesn't hurt when I squeeze it?" he asked.

"No, a little pressure, but no pain," Althea replied.

"I believe we will need to do a biopsy. Do you know what that is?" Doctor Stevenson asked.

"No. Not really."

"We have the choice of two options. The image-guided biopsy is very new. We use a shadowgram or x-ray of your leg. It shows the bone beneath the skin and gives us a picture of the growth. Then there is the needle biopsy, where we collect tissue from the growth to study it under a microscope."

Corbett shook his head. "I have heard stories of this new x-ray, or Röntgen rays, and how it causes burns on the skin and hair loss."

"I have heard such as well," Doctor Stevenson replied. "Thomas Edison is working on a similar apparatus. Hopefully, he will make needed improvements."

"Burns on the skin?" Althea shook her head. "I will forgo the image biopsy."

"As you wish. I want to be upfront with you, Miss Althea. Doctor Buchanan told me you are strong and have the courage to spare. So, I will tell you my experience regarding the growth of this type on the lower leg. They *can* be malignant. Not always, but possibly, yes. Most are benign. If it is malignant, the good news is this specific tumor does not spread to other parts of the body."

"This could be cancer, then," Althea murmured, her insides tumbling.

"Right to the point. Yes, it *could* be, but possibly not. Probably not. Malignant tumors generally are painful. But for some reason, these on the lower leg often are not. Malignant tumors invade surrounding muscles and nerves. Generally, they are fixed and firm like this one. But as I said, it could also be benign. There is no way to diagnose properly, for these growths are different for every person. It is why curing cancer has been elusive and undoubtedly will continue to be in the future."

"Is there a way to be rid of it? You see, my father died of cancer. Is it passed on?" Her voice shook. And her hands trembled as well.

"Doctor Buchanan told me about your father. We cannot know if cancer passes on to family members. That is something for future generations to determine. The best cancer treatment—to eliminate it—is the knife. But it may not come to that. It will probably not come to that. Yet, you should prepare for that possibility." The older doctor spoke plainly, but kindly.

"Amputation," she whispered.

"An absolute worst-case scenario," Corbett stated. "Even so, the cancer will be gone and rarely returns. Is that not correct, Doctor Stevenson?"

"With these types of tumors on the lower leg? Yes, that has been my experience. Scientists gave it a name in '85, and it is called Adamantinoma. It is rare, but in the patients that had it, twenty or more years on, they live healthy lives."

"But without a lower leg," Althea said in a low voice. "Can you not just remove the growth?"

"It is difficult but not impossible. As I said, it can invade surrounding tissue and muscle," the older doctor replied. "First, the biopsy. I will immediately schedule an appointment at St. Thomas's and send word through Doctor Buchanan. Should be within a few days or a week at most." He snapped his case shut. "In the meantime, no unnecessary pressure on the leg. Take care when walking. No running, of course. Would you like me to go into the other room and tell your family everything I relayed to you?"

Althea nodded, unable to speak. Doctor Stevenson's words were tumbling about in her mind.

Words like *malignant, biopsy,* and *cancer. Amputation.*

Doctor Stevenson left the room and closed the door behind him.

Corbett passed her the stockings. "Althea," he said softly. "If it *is* cancer, I read the study that Stevenson mentioned. One patient is healthy well into his seventies, and the cancer never returned—not since his amputation at age twenty-five. I know that is no comfort to you. All I ask is that you do not dwell on this until we know for certain. Easy for me to say. Your family and friends love you and will support you, no matter what."

An anguished cry came from the dining room—it was Eleanora. And that mournful sound ripped Althea's heart afresh. Try as she might, as hard as it may be, Althea decided then and there to remain positive. The doctor said most of the tumors are benign. Last night would be her moment of grieving and lamenting her fate. Why dwell? Her fate was *not* sealed, not as yet.

"Thank you, Corbett. You have been a real friend. And I hope that someday you will be part of the family."

He gave her a warm smile. Corbett was a good-looking man with his closely cropped beard and longish brown hair. Althea could see what attracted Sybil initially.

"I hope the same—if Sybil agrees. I intend to ask for her hand—and the rest of her—very soon."

Althea chuckled. Then she sobered. "Will you be there for the biopsy?"

"Of course. Whatever you need. Are you going to tell your uncle?"

Oh. Uncle Reece.

How could she forget her beloved uncle?

"Yes. I assume you are heading to Bethnal Green station?" Corbett nodded. "Could you ask him to stop by when he finishes his shift?"

"Of course I will."

She gathered her courage, took Corbett's offered arm, and headed into the dining room. Everyone swung about to look at her. Eleanora dabbed her eyes with a handkerchief as Christian slipped his arm about her shoulder.

When Althea's gaze turned to Damon, he looked not at her with empathy or pity but with admiration. And love. Yes, she could see it. And nothing could stop her from hurrying to his arms. Damon held her close, and she laid her head against his chest; the comforting beat of his heart calmed her. Althea did not cry. Honestly, she was all cried out. Nor did she care that everyone stood about watching.

All she wanted—and needed—was Damon to hold her.

"Doctor Stevenson and I will be off. I will send word when I set up the appointment," Corbett called out.

Althea turned to face the doctors as Damon stood behind, his hands gently rubbing her upper arms in comforting support. "Thank you for everything—both of you. I especially thank you for your honesty in laying out the possibilities. I will endeavor to remain positive about this," Althea stated steadily.

"My dear Miss Althea," Doctor Stevenson said gently. "Positivity does the world of good, even in medicine. Good day."

Corbett squeezed Sybil's hand in farewell, and the doctors departed.

"Ellie, I mean it; we must remain positive—all of us. Or I will fall to pieces, I swear it," Althea said firmly.

Eleanora tucked her handkerchief under the sleeve of her blouse. "Quite right. Only optimistic thinking from now on."

Althea strode toward Eleanora and pulled her into an affectionate embrace. "Dear sister."

The bell sounded at the front door.

"I will see to it," Sybil replied, already partway out of the room. "Then I have a follow-up on the banker divorce case, but I can postpone the appointment. The meeting is at a friend of the client's home."

"No, you go, Sybil. I want us all to carry on as normal," Althea said adamantly.

Her cousin soon returned, showed the men into the room, then departed. Archie was with a dubious-looking man whose gaze darted about the room. Either he was sizing it up for a future robbery, or he was uneasy with the people and the surroundings. Or it could be a little of both. The man wore a tattered coat, patched trousers, and a frayed cap and wasn't much taller than Althea.

"This here is Nigel Cleve; he will open the safe for a price," Archie announced.

Nigel was in his late thirties, early fifties, or somewhere between. It was hard to tell. The man took off his battered cap and twisted it in his hands, clearly uncomfortable. "Ladies, milords," Nigel murmured.

"They're dukes, Cleve. Remember? It's 'Your Graces,'" Archie corrected.

"Oh. Right you are." He rubbed his whiskered chin. "Beggin' your pardon. My Graces."

Althea couldn't help but smile. Although his clothes were worn, he was clean and presentable enough. She made the introductions. "Now, Mr. Cleve, how much do you charge for opening the safe?"

"Well, Miss Galway. I be wantin' ten pound. That's me duke rates if you please."

Althea could hear Damon mutter 'extortion' under his breath, but he nodded in agreement.

"Then it is settled." She headed to the corner of the room. Lifting a vase in one arm, she swiftly pulled on the long tablecloth with her free hand and revealed the safe hidden beneath. "And here it is."

"Hiding in plain sight, well done," Damon grinned.

Nigel stuffed his cap in his pocket, then cracked his knuckles not once but twice. "Right you are. Stand aside, ladies and dukes, and be very quiet. A Chubb safe with a single-dial rotary lock. No worries, yeah?" He got to his knees, leaned close to the dial lock, and turned it as he listened. "And if this don't work, I've got me tools outside, yeah? Crowbars and such. This will take a while."

"I'll stay with Nigel," Archie offered.

"Perhaps we should locate Edwina Callen and put the journey to Cornwall plan in motion," Althea suggested to Eleanora. "Let's head into the study." They all made their way down the hall to the office study.

"I concur," Eleanora said. "Edwina's rooms are not far. Christian and I will fetch her and bring her here."

"Take my carriage," Damon suggested. "Just inform Dawson where you wish to go."

With a nod and wave, they were off.

Damon sat on the sofa and patted the cushion next to him. "You know, it's very telling."

She sat next to him and gave him a puzzled look. "What do you mean?"

"After the examination, you came straight to my arms, not to your family, but to *me*. I confess that the egomaniac inside me is crowing loudly. But more importantly, it told me that your feelings for me are more serious than you have let on."

Althea sighed resignedly. "I cannot deny it. I tried to be practical and analytical about it all. Our different backgrounds and our status in society. It couldn't be possible. It *shouldn't* be possible." She gave him a tremulous smile. "But I am falling for you. Tumbling, in fact."

"My Thea, I am quite besotted. Whatever the future brings, we will see it through together. I want no other woman but you. Make of that what you will. And I want you to hear me on this. I will never try to rule your life or try to change you. Not ever."

Tears beaded on her eyelashes.

"I am not a good man," he continued. "I am not used to all this drama. I glided through life, not caring for so long. I am finding it all rather overwhelming."

"Yes. It is called life, and it is messy," Althea said gravely. "And messy quite frequently. And a health crisis is just one part of that chaos. There could be more upheavals, and I am sorry to cause you any anguish."

Althea was not condescending, as she understood what Damon had been through these past weeks—the death of his miserable father. The revelations of the dukedom and all his father had done. His feelings concerning her. And now, this predicament of her health.

"And I want to face this swirling chaos with no one but you, my Thea."

She threw herself into his arms, kissing him soundly.

Damon took the kiss deeper. It spoke of desire, hunger, and an unfettered passion. Then he broke it and pulled back, giving her such an intense gaze that a soft moan escaped her lips. "This is quite the admission from both of us," Damon whispered. "I also noticed we are dancing around a particular word. Falling for, besotted—"

"We are. Until I know how the present resolves, I cannot look to the future, not yet." She stroked his cheek with the back of her fingers. "Can you be patient with me a while longer? There is still much to work out in my mind."

He gently clasped her fingers in mid-stroke, then kissed them. "No matter the diagnosis, I will still want you. I want you now. Come to me tonight."

"Oh, how you tempt me. I foolishly thought I could indulge in a brief affair and remain detached from it all."

"Take my word for it. It can be accomplished. I am living proof, considering my past. I had no inkling of what love could entail." He released her hand and put a finger to his lips. "I said the word, but I *am* speaking of my past. My father never showed me any affection. I concluded at an early age that it is best not to feel. That way, you are not hurt. It was a code I lived by—until I met you."

Damon's stark words touched her. Revealing such a profound susceptibility caused her protective instinct to burst the surface once again.

With a resigned sigh, he took her hand. "When I was seven, my mother tried to leave my father. My father's cold, cruel ways made our lives miserable. He flung his numerous infidelities in my mother's face. With a few bags packed, we traveled as far as Euston Station before Silas Browning, and a couple of footmen dragged us back to stand before the duke. It was the only time my father beat me. He used his fists and a log from the fire."

"Oh, my God," Althea cried.

"That was not the worst of it. The duke made me stand there, bruised and bleeding, and made me watch while he did the same to my mother. And worse. And by worse, I mean he violated her right in front of me. He would not let me turn away. 'This is how you treat a woman when she disobeys. Show her who is the ruler and master,' he screamed at me. I never followed my father's dictum in that regard. I never forced or humiliated a woman—or anyone."

Damon laughed brokenly. "Is it any wonder I turned out the way I did? I sought meaningless encounters, hoping to feel anything, for my father killed something within me that day. I have never told anyone this. I am not looking for pity or making excuses. Or perhaps I am."

Althea stroked his cheek once again. "I know. That is horrendous. Your father was a terrible, amoral beast, and I am glad he's dead."

"As am I. I have been alone and lonely my entire life. Is that why I am seeking a family? To try and repair the trauma done to me? Buchanan astutely observed that I must have suffered a deep-rooted trauma earlier in my life. I scoffed at that. But it is a valid point, isn't it?"

Althea hugged him tightly, her eyes filling with tears. "Yes, my dear. But now that you are aware, you can move past it. Be absolutely certain you want those children or any other half-siblings in your life because you truly wish it, and not to heal past hurt."

"I agree. And before the thought crosses your very sharp mind, that is *not* why I want *you* in my life. To heal past hurts. Well, perhaps a little. As you have done much to bring me some semblance of peace. And humanity. Basic decency and humanity. That is what my father killed in me on that terrible day. I see it now."

Before she could reply, the bell sounded from the front door. Reluctantly, they broke apart, and Damon reached out to dash away a tear that had escaped the corner of her eye. Then the pad of his thumb brushed across her lips.

"I have to answer the door," she murmured, reluctant to leave him. Oh, how he made her insides turn to jelly with the slightest touch.

"Perhaps if we ignore them, they might go away," Damon replied huskily, kissing her chin.

"We really must get the telephone installed," Althea sighed, getting to her feet.

"And have people ringing you at all hours of the day or night? Bad enough they are bashing on the front bell," Damon barked, exasperated.

"Quite right. I should wait until I have the office."

If I ever get an office.

Althea admonished herself all the way downstairs. Enough of such thoughts. One thing at a time. She opened the door to find a tall, dark-haired man who, she must admit, was rather good-looking. His eyes were a prodigious mix of light gray and green.

He removed his hat. "Good day, miss. I was told that the Duke of Chellenham is here. Could I please speak to him? I am Oliver Wollstonecraft."

"Wollstonecraft? Like Mary Shelley? And her mother, Mary?" Althea greatly admired both women.

"Very distantly related, a branch so far removed from our family tree, it is hardly any connection at all," Mr. Wollstonecraft replied pleasantly, a twinkle in his eye.

"Come in, sir. The duke is upstairs. I am Althea Galway."

"A pleasure, miss."

She led him upstairs and down the hall, then into the study.

"Mr. Oliver Wollstonecraft to see you, Your Grace," she said, giving Damon a teasing wink.

Mr. Wollstonecraft stepped into the room. "Your butler said I would find you here. The club has been burgled, completely sacked."

Chapter 19

"SACKED? WHAT ARE YOU on about?" Damon said. "This is Miss Althea Galway of The Galway Investigative Agency. Miss Galway, Mr. Oliver Wollstonecraft. His grandfather is the Earl of Carnstone."

Wollstonecraft took Althea's hand. "We met downstairs."

Damon snarled low in his throat. Another man touching Althea? Possessiveness gripped him tight, and it was rather disturbing as he had never experienced such with any other woman.

"A distinct pleasure, once again," Wollstonecraft kissed her hand, and Damon's voice rumbled in response. Doing the man bodily harm became more appealing at the moment. "Never knew you to be predatory, Chellenham." The wretched man had the audacity to grin at him.

Blast Wollstonecraft for his dark good looks, coming here to interrupt their serious and private conversation.

"Please, take a seat, Mr. Wollstonecraft. And tell us about the club," Althea said politely.

"I stopped by to see if the liquor needed replenishing before our next meeting. I found the door unlocked, which isn't common as we are all diligent in locking up. With a closer inspection, I could see that the doorframe had been jimmied, as it were, with a crowbar. Well, I immediately headed upstairs to find the place in shambles."

"Was anything taken? Not that we have much value," Damon asked, trying to keep his voice calm. These volatile emotions were going to be the death of him.

"Not that I observed. But everything was tossed every which way as if the person were looking for something. All the liquor was still there. And some of our expensive whiskey blends would fetch a pretty penny on the streets. The silver coffee and tea service is still there as well. Robbery could not have been the motive."

Althea laughed lightly. "A fine deduction, Mr. Wollstonecraft. I should hire you for my agency."

Damon's insides twisted when Althea smiled warmly at Oliver Wollstonecraft. Yes, Damon acted in a predatory manner—not like him at all—further proof he was utterly smitten with the lovely lady detective.

"I'm flattered, thank you," Wollstonecraft grinned, showing his straight white teeth. "I came here from your town house since you are the leader of our group."

"As if someone was looking for something," Althea mused. "Could it be Browning looking for the safe?"

"It could be," Damon replied. "Why didn't he look for the safe before now?"

"When I interviewed the staff, they informed me Browning never showed up to Queen Anne's Gate until days after the funeral. He was unaware your father had passed and, when he learned of it, traveled straight to Chellenhome." Althea rubbed her chin. "As to what he has been doing after that, I am uncertain—perhaps watching us all? Waiting for an opportunity to search for the safe unencumbered? Is he a threat?"

"Who is Browning?" Wollstonecraft asked.

"An employee of my late father. It's a long story," Damon replied. "As to if he is a threat, perhaps he is. He always carried out my father's dirty work and, I recently discovered, bullied the staff."

Christian and Eleanora entered the room with a young woman following close behind. Edwina Callen was attractive, with golden brown ringlets peeking under her bonnet.

So, this is the new employee.

Oliver Wollstonecraft immediately stood, his gaze firm on Miss Callen. It took all of Damon's restraint not to grin, for the look on Wollstonecraft's face no doubt matched Damon's own when he first clapped eyes on Althea.

Interest. Attraction. A hint of it, anyway.

Damon made the introductions, and Wollstonecraft came to stand by the young lady, taking her hand and bowing over it. "A pleasure to meet you, Miss Callen. You work for the investigative agency?"

"I do, Mr. Wollstonecraft." Miss Callen replied. Her voice was throaty, and her cheeks slightly flushed.

How interesting, Miss Callen was affected by the meeting. Damon supposed most women would find the tall, dark, handsome heir to an earl a fine catch.

"Fascinating," Wollstonecraft murmured, then in a louder voice, he said, "I must dash. You no doubt have plenty to discuss." Then he met Miss Callen's gaze. "Until we meet again."

"I will show you out," Damon announced. The two men headed into the main hallway.

Damon held out his hand. "Oliver, I wish to apologize for acting as such a bastard since you joined the club." And he meant it. It was past time to make amends for boorish behavior and acting jealous mere moments ago.

"You acted as any heir to a duke would act, at least in my experience. I took no offense—Damon." Oliver shook his hand.

"Well, again, thank you for your condolences at the funeral. And for coming here today. I will see the club's door is repaired forthwith and contact you when the next meeting is. I have ideas about a new direction with more to do with philanthropy than our egotistic needs. But you know of what I speak, seeing you are already involved in Hawkestone's group."

"I welcome the change."

The men said their goodbyes, and Damon rejoined the others in the study.

"What is this? The club has been burgled?" Christian stated, shock in his voice.

Damon repeated what Oliver had relayed. "Althea thinks it might be Browning."

Eleanora stuck her head in the door. "I have tea and scones ready in the dining room. I already served Archie and Mr. Cleve. He is making progress."

"We will be there directly," Althea called out. Then she turned to Miss Callen. "We require you to take a train to Cornwall right away. I will fetch the money for the ticket and your accommodations and fill you in on the details. I will join the rest of you later."

"Miss Callen, please make use of my carriage. Dawson can take you back to your place, wait for you to pack, and drive you to the station," Damon suggested.

"Thank you, Your Grace."

Christian, Damon, and Eleanora headed toward the dining room.

"Well, one good thing about all this activity. It is keeping Althea occupied and not allowing her to dwell on her health predicament," Eleanora whispered.

"Althea is going to come through this. I am certain of it. She is stronger than we think," Damon said.

Eleanora stopped in mid-step and faced him. "You act as if you know her. You know nothing, Chellenham."

Damon took a step closer, firmly meeting Eleanora's intimidating gaze. "I know that Althea has courage to spare. I held her as she cried.

Now she is ready to face what comes, and I will be there to support her."

"Sweet Mother," Eleanora whispered. "You are in love with her."

"That is between Althea and me," Damon retorted.

Christian took Eleanora's arm. "Come, El—Damon's right. Stay out of it. It's their personal business."

"Yes, Chris. You are correct," she capitulated. "Do forgive me, Chellenham."

What a fascinating glimpse into their marriage. Damon assumed Eleanora ran everything and dictated all aspects of their lives, personal and business. But it was clear Christian had his say as well. How surprising to find that he longed for the same? A true partnership.

They entered the dining room just as Mr. Cleve opened the safe door.

"Bloody hell, that took some doin'. Beggin' My Graces and ladies' pardon," Mr. Cleve stated, wiping his brow with his coat sleeve. He then reached for the teacup and slurped it. "It's open. Have a gander."

Damon stepped forward, then sunk to his haunches. "Several ledgers. And a strong box."

"I can get that box open for you, quick as spit," Mr. Cleve crowed, obviously pleased with himself over cracking open the safe.

Damon stood, reaching in his pocket. "No, I think we can manage from here, Mr. Cleve. You are not to repeat to anyone about this job."

"Me lips are sealed," Mr. Cleve replied firmly.

Damon thrust the pound notes into the man's hand. "Paid in full. Take a couple of scones with you, my good man. And thank you. Archie, do you need money to escort Mr. Cleve home?"

"No, Your Grace, I'm fine," the lad answered. "Come, Cleve. Let's catch a hansom."

Mr. Cleve stuffed the money in his tattered coat's pocket. Then he quickly gathered up four scones and grabbed his tool bag. "You ever need a safe open again, Cleve's your cracksman."

Archie tugged on the man's arm, pulling him toward the exit.

"Tell your nob friends!" Cleve shouted as Archie closed the door.

Eleanora smiled. "Good to have a safe cracker on our list of contacts. Quick, pull everything out."

Christian and Damon made room on the table, laying everything on it.

There were numerous ledgers. The listings showed a strange cross-section of monetary dealings and numbers and initials. At least now, they understood that the numerical code next to each child's name corresponded with the transactions in a different ledger.

"Try and find a list of the donors so that we can match with the initials in the entries," Damon suggested.

"What about the strongbox?" Eleanora asked.

"I have just the thing for that," Althea answered.

ALTHEA LEANED AGAINST the doorframe, holding up a velvet bag. She had fetched it from her room after Edwina departed. "My tools of the trade."

"Oh, good. Your lock-picking tools," Eleanora enthused. "Bring them here."

Althea speedily worked the small lock, and it popped open. Inside were numerous loose pound notes and sovereigns with ten bundles of pound notes tied with string. "Look, there are initials carved on the underside of the lid. SDB. Silas Browning. I would guess that this is his hidden savings. No wonder he was trying to locate the safe."

Eleanora took the case and sat at the table. "I'll count it; meanwhile, keep searching for the list of donors."

The rest searched through the ledgers, going page by page.

"It's not here," Christian replied, disappointed.

"Wait," Eleanora cried. "Look! Folded papers in between the pound notes in this bundle."

Eleanora handed them to Althea. The list started in 1863, and many names had lines through them. The men were probably deceased or no longer part of the scheme for one reason or another, with enfeeblement as the prime indicator.

Edward Cranston's organization had fallen through, though he tried to recruit new blood. His plan must have failed. No doubt the reason he abandoned Chellenhome in the last few months before his death—callous, cruel man.

Althea scoffed. "Whinstone is on the list. Why am I not surprised?" She handed the papers to Damon.

As he examined the documents, he whistled low in his throat. "Some prominent names here, and not just peers. Men of industry, bankers, and a few others that I do not recognize. Many are dead. Here is Sir Anthony Crossley, baronet. Remember, the friend of the late Earl of Oakby? Crossley died in an asylum from syphilis. There were always salacious rumors about Crossley and Oakby. And two Earls of Southen, no doubt father and son, twenty-odd years apart. Baron Stonecliff? Wasn't he an original member of The Rakes?"

Christian came to stand by Damon and looked at the papers. "Jonathan," Christian said. "Must be the father. Simon Wolstenholme was an original member of The Rakes of St. Regent's Park. Gideon said that Simon was only a member for less than two years. He went to war and became horribly scarred in a battle. Cloistered himself away, though Gideon said he's been happily married for several years now."

"Look. Baron Addington. Hayes's father. That is a surprise, as the baron always acts as a prig. Well, there will be no contacting these reprobates to give donations to Chellenhome. Most are deceased," Damon frowned. "What a blasted tangle this all is."

"Addington isn't dead—yet, though I hear he is seriously ill," Christian said. "I say confront him on this and make him leave a legacy to Chellenhome. It is the least the bastard can do."

"I will. Perhaps a few others, as well," Damon replied.

"I have the feeling most wouldn't give a toss," Althea said quietly. "These men of means wouldn't care where these children ended up. And I doubt they would be concerned if you publicly exposed their doings. Isn't this how things are done? And have been, for centuries? Although, centuries ago, people often dropped unwanted children down a mine shaft."

Yes, she was getting angry now. The injustice of it all cut deep.

"If we took this to the newspapers, most wouldn't print it," she continued, her ire rising. "And if they did, it would be swept away as so many other scandals have concerning peers and wealthy men of means!" Althea cried. "I am sick to death of it. No consequences for corrupt behavior and doings."

"You have the right of it, unfortunately. Why pay to have the unwanted children sent to Chellenhome in the first place? Why not abandon them as many had done in the past?" Eleanora asked.

"A valid point," Althea replied. "And I will wager we find the answer within these ledgers."

"So, what will you do, Damon?" Christian asked.

He sank into a nearby chair, deflated. "I have not the foggiest idea. This scheme is far bigger than I originally imagined. I believed it was a list of seven or eight names and concerned my father only. But this? It is a scandal, a conspiracy. But it is not illegal. Althea is right. There will be no consequences, legal ones at least. Or societal. Most would read this in the paper, shrug, and turn the page. For decades, workhouses, orphanages, and the streets of London have overflowed with unwanted children."

"All true, but what about Browning?" Eleanora held up a bundle of notes. "There are five hundred and twenty-two pounds here, along with a few shillings and florins. Some of the notes are the old issue, and most are in five-pound denominations. This money is Browning's savings. At least, we can surmise that."

"Savings from buying and selling children?" Damon spat.

"Yet, he earned this, nonetheless. It *is* his property, and he wants it. Where will he break into next?" Eleanora observed.

"I say we give it to him in exchange for information," Althea suggested.

"What good is information? We can do nothing with it," Damon replied, clearly exasperated.

"And I think, Eleanora, we should depart and allow Althea and Damon to review the records. If you need us, we will be at home," Christian stated.

Eleanora embraced Althea. "Anytime you wish to talk, I will listen. I love you, Sister. And I am here for you."

The rare declaration of affection caused Althea's heart to tighten. "I love you, too."

The sisters parted, and Eleanora and Christian turned to leave.

"Tell Dawson to run you home if he has returned," Damon declared.

Christian grinned. "We will. If not, we can catch a hansom quickly enough. We should remain vigilant. That is a lot of money, and Browning might be desperate enough to break into any of our residences."

"Wise advice. Although I do not know the man well, I cannot see him jeopardizing his freedom or savings by burglarizing our homes while we are there," Damon stated. "But who knows what a desperate man might do?"

"Exactly, stay cautious," Christian replied. With a wave, they were gone. And Althea and Damon were alone.

"When the carriage returns, I will depart. That is if you wish it."

No, she didn't wish it. Not at all. Althea stepped close and grabbed his lapels. Standing on the tips of her toes, she kissed him hard. "Come upstairs."

Damon took her hands and stepped back. "I cannot believe I am about to say this, but I should head home."

"For God's sake, why?" His gentle rebuff hurt Althea, but she was more curious than anything.

"You said it yourself; you have much to work out."

"And *you* made the invitation. You said, 'Come to me tonight,' remember?"

"It appears that I also have matters to work out." Damon caressed her cheek. "You are so incredibly wise, Althea. And brave. Will you let me know when your hospital appointment is? And allow me to accompany you?"

"Yes, of course. I don't understand this."

"For once in my life, I am thinking of someone else before my self-seeking needs. You asked for time, and I wish to give it." He leaned in to kiss her forehead, then turned toward the table and picked up one of the ledgers. "Mrs. Seddon's copy. I will take this with me. As far as the money, I will take that and put it in my safe at Clarendon Place. I leave the other ledgers with you. Please write me a report about the donors, how many children, and how much money exchanged hands. That sort of thing."

"Very well." Althea's emotions were in a swirl. She understood what Damon was saying but was disappointed, nonetheless.

"Lock the door behind me. I doubt Browning would be brazen enough to break into our homes, but we must remain alert."

"I agree."

Damon looped his arm around her waist and brought her close, causing her to squeak at the suddenness. "Remember all I said," he whispered huskily. "About wanting you in my life. I meant every word. I want you in my arms. In my bed. But only when we can discuss and accept what is happening between us. No other woman. Ever. Only—you."

And with that, he picked up the strong box, turned, and exited the room.

Althea ran to the window and watched as he stepped onto the sidewalk as his carriage drew near. Damon stopped and looked up as if knowing she was standing in the window. He smiled at her, then blew her a kiss.

Without thinking, she made a gesture as if catching it, then held her fist to her heart. Oh, yes, she was tumbling head over ears, heels, or whatever body part was involved in whatever idiom fit the situation.

Say the word, Althea.

"Love," she murmured as the carriage pulled away. "I love him."

Admitting to herself was hard enough.

Would she be brave enough to say it to Damon?

Chapter 20

LEAVING ALTHEA WAS one of the hardest things Damon had ever done. However, there was too much going on—particularly with her health emergency—to complicate it with powerful emotions and the subsequent discussion, at least for a short while.

When he stepped onto the sidewalk, he said inwardly: *When I turn around, look at me.*

And Althea was watching him intently from the window above.

His heart soared, and it was still spiraling.

They all but said the word. *Love.* His heart was in his hand, all but offering it to Althea. But the admission of intense feelings was enough—for now.

Althea asked for time.

And frankly, he should take that time to come to terms with his various issues before committing to anything permanent with Althea. It wasn't as if he doubted his feelings for her, far from it. Damon was falling in love, no question.

But no one rushed Althea into anything, and he respected her for it. Truthfully, he rarely acted impulsively, at least when it comes to emotions. The first time he saw Althea, it was as if a thunderbolt had struck him. His feelings toward her simmered for months, growing in intensity with each encounter. It was more than physical—much more. Too much had transpired to deny or ignore this strange but not unwelcome transformation taking place inside of him.

But beyond all that, and considering he could be pessimistic with the best of them, Damon had the distinct feeling Althea's health dilemma would work out satisfactorily. Whatever the consequence, he would love and support her.

They could have a future; why not indeed?

The carriage pulled up in front of Clarendon Place, and he hopped out, the ledger and strong box tucked under his arm.

Kingsley greeted him at the door. "Your Grace, there is a police detective here to see you. He insisted on waiting. Detective Evercreech from B Division. I placed him in your study with a tea tray."

Evercreech?

Funny about fate, for Damon had been planning to go and see the detective tomorrow. It's the reason he had taken the ledger. "How long has he been here?"

"Close to an hour, Your Grace."

"I will see him alone."

"There are several correspondences on your desk, including a letter from the duchess."

Damon handed Kingsley the iron case. "Thank you. I am not to be disturbed. Take this strong box and place it in my safe after the detective departs. Do not allow it to leave your sight."

"Of course, Your Grace."

After inhaling deeply, Damon entered the study, closing the door behind him. Evercreech, holding a teacup in his hand, started to stand.

"Please, stay seated." Damon strode over to the tea tray on the sideboard, placed the ledger next to it, then poured himself a cup of tea. The pot sat on a candle warmer, so the beverage was at least tepid. "What do I owe this pleasure?"

"You are a hard man to pin down, Your Grace. I have been by a few times the past ten days."

"No one told me." Damon came to sit opposite Evercreech.

"I didn't leave my name." Evercreech reached into his side coat pocket and pulled out an envelope. "Your father's personal belongings."

How can that be?

Damon placed his cup on the table and reached across to take the envelope. He tore it open. His father's signet ring—or more specifically, his now. It had been in the family for generations. Gold with black onyx in the center, the Latin words *gloria honos* etched beneath the jewel, which meant honor and dignity. He ran the tip of his finger across the surface.

Those words never applied to his father. Or himself, for that matter.

Time that changed.

Turning the ring over in his palm, he noticed the initials CH etched on each side. It stood for Chellenham. He had forgotten all about this ring.

"I suppose it was the only thing my father had on him, considering his naked state. Thank you for returning it," Damon said in a low voice as he slipped it on his pinkie finger.

"The cause of death; I have the report here." Evercreech retrieved another envelope and placed it on the table between them. "A diseased heart."

"In more ways than one. I had planned to come and see you on a matter that concerns my wretched late father. I'm not sure where to begin. As you no doubt construed from how you found the duke, he was a debauched, unfeeling son of a bitch who left illegitimate children across London and beyond because of his recklessness. I had only recently discovered it, but in hiring an investigative agency, I have uncovered a conspiracy involving many men of means." He paused.

I might as well put it out there.

"Your name was among the initial list." Damon stood and fetched the ledger, opening it to the relevant page. He handed it to Evercreech.

Several moments passed, and Evercreech's brows knotted as he read the entry. "Explain this," he ground out, obviously trying to keep his anger in check.

"From what the investigative agency deduced, you were brought to Chellenhome at the age of four when your mother died. Gerald Simpson took you in less than a year later."

"Yes," Evercreech nodded. "He was a retired policeman, and he and his wife were good to me. They saw that I received an education, a loving home, and a chance at a career. They are both gone now. They were in their early sixties when they took me in, never had children of their own."

"I am glad you had a good home and people that loved you. That is more than most of us ever have."

"Dora Mitchell. I never knew my mother. I have no memory of her," Evercreech said, his voice full of emotion. "I asked my father once why he never named me Simpson, and he replied that I should carry on the name I was born with. It turns out I wasn't born with this name at all." Evercreech looked up, a dour expression on his face. "And what in hell has any of this to do with you?"

"You *are* the detective. Haven't you made a connection? We are half-brothers, and our sire is the aforementioned unfeeling son of a bitch. See the initials EC? That stands for Edward Cranston."

Evercreech sat back, and his anger whooshed out of him in a rush. "My God," he croaked, clearly shocked.

Damon sat in his chair. "My God, indeed."

"Did you know this when I attended the duke's death?"

"I had just returned from Spain. My mother gave me a list of eight names. It was the children that she knew of. I could not mention it then, not under the circumstances. And at that time, I had no proof. Once I hired The Galway Investigative Agency, I found that ledger and more besides."

"More?"

Damon explained about Chellenhome and the fact that hundreds of children passed through there, some sired by the late duke, others by men of means who paid a fee to be rid of the children. He told him of the children currently residing at Chellenhome.

Evercreech's eyes widened. "I have no memory of being at this Chellenhome. The Simpsons paid for me?"

"Yes. A tidy sum. Perhaps the man's life savings. That was the scheme my father had set up. But I am told it is not illegal. More's the pity."

"Why tell me all this? What do you want from me, to be your brother?" Evercreech asked incredulously. "Jesus. You nobs are all alike, thinking you can use people. Buy and sell them and bend them to your will."

Well, this was going differently than Damon had hoped. But what did he expect? This result convinced him not to approach anyone else on his mother's list or any he may encounter in the ledgers. The past can stay in the past, and it was for the best for everyone.

"You have a point, for that is what my father and his morally bankrupt acquaintances did." Damon stood. "I need a drink. I have scotch. Can I pour you one?"

"I'm on the clock, but hell. Pour away. This information has me completely rattled. I cannot believe this, but there it is. Proof, as you said."

Damon poured the drinks, then handed a glass to Evercreech. "Proof, such as it is. As far as a brother, I leave that up to you. You see, I did *not* have a loving home and people that loved me. Am I looking for a family? Perhaps. Rather pathetic when I say it aloud."

Damon took his seat and sipped his scotch. "But I will settle for us getting to know one another. Perhaps we can become friends. I do not have enough of those, either."

Evercreech studied him closely as if trying to ascertain Damon's motives. "And what about those other names on the list you spoke of?"

"I have come to believe the past is best left in the past. I am sorry I told you since it upset you, and I don't want to put anyone else through that. You and Olivia are as far as I will go regarding the original list. Besides, I will concentrate on caring for the five children currently at the home that my father sired. They need my assistance, as do the other children, and I aim to give it."

"Olivia?"

"Our half-sister recently discovered. She was also on the initial list." Damon reached for the ledger, turned it to the appropriate page, and handed it back to Evercreech. "She married a friend of mine. The Duke of Watford."

"My God. A sister married to a duke and five more siblings besides. I cannot fathom it."

Damon didn't have the heart to tell him it could be dozens upon dozens. The man was shocked and upset as it was.

The detective threw back a swig of scotch, then clenched his teeth at the burn. "I always hated the name Evercreech."

"Be Mitchell Simpson going forward. The name honors your mother and the family that accepted you into their lives. There is nothing legal to do. Just change it."

"Perhaps I will. I apologize, Your Grace, for my show of temper earlier."

"Understandable," Damon murmured.

Evercreech stood. "I will be in touch. I need—"

"To think on it. Take all the time you require." Damon placed his drink on the table and stood as well. Then he held out his hand.

Evercreech took it, then quickly released it and headed for the door. Once it opened, Kingsley stepped inside.

"Kingsley, hail a hansom for the detective."

And with that, Evercreech was gone.

"Christ," Damon muttered, slamming the door shut.

He strode to the sideboard, topped off his scotch, then headed to his desk and plopped into the plush chair. He may very well never see that man again. Well, it was up to the detective if he wanted to become acquainted. Damon was not going to ruminate over it.

He shuffled through the correspondence, which reminded him. He hadn't written Olivia yet and would do so later tonight. Finally, he came across his mother's letter. Special delivery; no wonder it arrived here so swiftly. Taking his letter opener, he slid it under the wax seal and removed the stationary.

MY DEAR DAMON,

Your steward, Mr. Arrowsmith, brought me the news of your father's death. I cannot say I was surprised, considering his lifestyle, but I was surprised to hear it was because of his heart, for I was convinced he did not have one.

And that will be the last sliver of bitterness you will hear from me regarding your father. He is gone, and I plan to move on with my life, and I suggest you do the same.

I have spoken with Tony and Sebastián, and we have decided to divide our time between Spain and England. Tony has enough that we can live quite comfortably. We will reside in a villa on his parents' property and rent a modest town house in London. Mr. Arrowsmith has offered his services in finding us one.

It seems, my darling boy, you are about to have a ready-made family descend on you shortly. By the time you get this letter, Tony and I will be married. Sebastián has expressed an interest in attending university in England, which will work out all around.

I had to cajole Mr. Arrowsmith to tell me about the status of the villa. I had no idea your father sold it. I have already contacted the owner and told him we would vacate as soon as possible. The furniture will be sold, and we are packing as I write this.

Mr. Arrowsmith will return to London in a few days, and we will be close behind. I will send a cable when we are ready to depart.

I cannot wait to see you and for you to meet your brother. He is quite excited at the prospect. We have much time to make up for.

We are free, Damon. Free to live and love and banish the past.

Your loving mother

HIS MOTHER—COMING HERE. With her husband and son. Ready-made family, indeed. Damon smiled. Free to live and love and banish the past. No one had ever written such valid words to Damon. How strange to go from an unfeeling rogue to embracing a patchwork quilt of a family and to have an older half-sister and possibly an older half-brother. And those children at Chellenhome.

He would have more family than he knew what to do with.

But isn't that what he wanted when he started this venture? He had pondered over it enough, more often than he should have. Of course, he could use the pretext of seeing if the duke's illegitimate offspring needed assistance, but Damon could admit now that the actual reason is he wanted some semblance of a family. A connection. He said as much earlier to Althea. Yes, he had two or three close friends, but regardless of what some say, friends are not family. Not to Damon's way of thinking.

He was about to attend to the rest of the correspondence when Kingsley knocked and entered the room.

"Your Grace, there is an August Donaldson to see you. He claims to be a footman at Chellenham Park."

Well, the fates continued to churn up all around him. Why was the man here?

"Send him in."

Kingsley showed the young man into the study, and Damon remained seated. Donaldson looked to be in his late twenties, and he had dark blond hair and those piercing Cranston blue eyes and high cheekbones. How astounding that so many were tainted with those distinct characteristics.

"Mr. Donaldson, Your Grace," Kingsley stated.

"Thank you, Kingsley. You may leave us." Damon motioned to the chair in front of his desk. "Take a seat. What can I do for you?"

The man was guarded, his mouth pulled into a taut line. "I wish to leave for North America, and I want you to help me. Seeing we share the same father."

He remembered Christian saying people would be lining up with their hands out. It seems his friend was correct.

"How did you discover this?" Damon asked softly.

"The duke told me two years ago. He enjoyed revealing it. He knew my mother by name and said he got me the job at the estate. I confronted my mother; she did not deny it. I would have quit then and there, but I couldn't afford it. All I want is to put this behind me. I want a new beginning, far from here. When I heard of the duke's death, I quit my position and came here."

Damon noticed Donaldson was not using 'Your Grace' when addressing him. Typical of his father to tell the young man, the late duke no doubt received perverse pleasure out of Donaldson's vexatious response.

"And how much do you require to put the past behind you?"

Donaldson scowled. "I'm not here for blackmail. I want enough to travel to Liverpool, catch a steamer, and start fresh in either Canada or The United States of America. I don't care which."

"So, I will not be contacted by you in the future, looking for further funds?"

"No. I am cutting all ties."

"Even with your mother?" Damon asked, his voice quiet.

"Even her. We weren't all that close anyway. She lied to me my whole life. Besides, she married when I was six. My mother has a husband and other children to keep her company."

Damon could not fault the man. "Will one hundred pounds be sufficient? The dukedom is not all that wealthy, and funds are tight. It is all I can spare."

"Yes. It's more than enough."

"I do not have the money on me. Return tomorrow afternoon and ask for Kingsley. He will give you the funds." Damon stood and held out his hand. "I wish you luck on your journey. If I may offer one bit of advice, it is the guidance I will try and take as well. Put all bitterness aside, as it will eat away at you. Embrace your new life."

Donaldson looked at the extended hand. Then he took it and shook it. "Thank you, Your Grace."

The man turned and departed, closing the door behind him.

"Goodbye, August," Damon murmured.

Kingsley entered the room.

"Send Baldwin to me."

"At once, Your Grace. Will you be here for dinner?"

"Yes. Nothing too fancy, a light meal."

As his butler left, Damon rubbed his temple as his head ached like the devil. He pushed aside his drink. This would be his life going forward, one melodrama after another. Best to get used to it.

"You wished to see me, Your Grace?" his valet asked.

"I need you to head to the bank and withdraw one hundred pounds in notes. I surmise there is enough in the account?"

"There is, Your Grace. I received a dividend payment from your automobile venture, thirteen hundred pounds. As I said, this will keep the dukedom afloat; I am happy to relate. There is much to discuss. Are you available after dinner?"

And there will be no getting away from his duke duties either.

Damon willed away his headache, for he had no longer time or patience for such indulgences. August Donaldson was not the only one embarking on a new life.

"I am. I want to finalize the staffing as well. We will meet here in the study at seven sharp. Withdraw one hundred and seventy-five pounds, instead."

He could afford a little extra for Donaldson.

"Yes, Your Grace." Kingsley bowed and departed.

Damon raised his glass to no one in particular. "To a fresh start."

Chapter 21

FIVE DAYS HAD ELAPSED since Althea last saw or heard from Damon. Thankfully, she had plenty to keep her occupied, enough to distract her from missing him terribly. It also kept her from reflecting on her complicated health question. During this time, Althea also concluded that many others had had worse health news than she had and dealt with various maladies in everyday life. So, if Althea has to use a cane for whatever reason for however long it takes—so be it.

No more lamenting her fate.

Althea sat at the dining room table with the various ledgers in front of her. By cross-referencing the transactions, she formulated a pattern of the dealings and crafted a report of her findings. The scheme not only brought in vast amounts of money for the late duke but also showed numerous smaller payments made to numbered accounts.

She only left the house once, two days past, when Corbett showed up unannounced to say Doctor Stevenson had an opening, and if she came right away, he could do the biopsy. She had no time to contact anyone to accompany her. Perhaps it was for the best. Althea asked Corbett to keep it to himself for the time being, for there was no need to alarm anyone. The results would take a week or less.

She reached down and gently touched the plaster on her leg. Corbett told her there would be a general soreness and tenderness that would soon dissipate. Would Damon and her family be annoyed when they discovered she traveled to the appointment without letting them know? No doubt. But this was something she had to do for herself. To face her crisis head-on with her chin held high.

Mrs. Bartle entered the room. "A telegram for you."

Althea hadn't heard the bell; she had been so deep in thought. She took it from the housekeeper; the note was from Edwina Callen.

"Miss Callen has located Adina Desmond's mother and asks if she can bring her to London."

Over tea yesterday, Althea explained the case in general terms to Mrs. Bartle and updated the housekeeper on her ongoing health issues. Mrs. Bartle had been with her family for years, and Althea adored her.

"That is good news. Do you want the lady to stay here?" Mrs. Bartle asked.

"It depends on when they arrive. You had better prepare Eleanora's old room just in case. Miss Callen says she has enough money for two train tickets. I must send a response."

"As luck would have it, Archie is downstairs having a bite of lunch, and I'll be leaving once he's finished. There is a meat pie in the icebox for your supper."

Althea smiled at the housekeeper. "Thank you. And how often does Archie drop in to see you?"

"Bah, he likes my cooking, that is all. He's a good lad and growing like a weed. He'll be off to school soon, and I won't see him as much. If I can give him a little mothering now and then, all the better. For both of us." Mrs. Bartle dabbed at the corner of her eye with the hem of her apron. "Drat it. I never expected to get so attached to the boy."

"I am glad for you both. With all the lonely and orphaned children out there, we all should do what we can."

"It will never be enough, will it?" Mrs. Bartle sniffled.

"No," Althea replied sadly. "We can't save them all."

"That randy duke of yours has turned out to be a bit of a dark horse. Who knew he had a compassionate heart under that perfect exterior?" Mrs. Bartle said, her mood brightening. "I'll send Archie up as soon as he's finished eating."

Dark horse, indeed.

Archie arrived ten minutes later. "Miss Althea. Mrs. Bartle says you want a telegram sent?"

"Have a seat for a minute, Archie." The lad took the seat opposite. "Are you happy here, working for us?"

"Yes, miss. You've all been good to me. Allenby is working to secure any money from my father's will, and I'm off to school in September."

"Are you looking forward to that?"

Archie nodded. "I am, hard to believe. I want a good life."

"Have you thought about what you want to do when your schooling is complete? I ask because Miss Eleanora will not be able to continue to work on full caseloads, not with a husband and possibly children in her future. I also may have impediments on my full attention."

Archie gave her a crooked grin. "You mean Chellenham? He's an impediment, all right."

Althea chuckled, then sobered. "Yes, Chellenham may be part of it. But there is another issue. A possible one. Why do I mention it? I wish to know once you complete your studies if you would be interested in being the head investigator and eventual administrator of The Galway Agency. Only if you wish it. I don't wish to pressure you in any way."

Archie's light brown eyes widened. "You mean it? You would trust me to take over running this agency?"

"My sister and I will still be involved, as will my cousin, Sybil. But yes, you would be running the day-to-day business. I thought to locate a suitable place to open an office, but perhaps we will turn this house into the headquarters. It is the Galway family home, bought and paid for. A few female investigators can live in the rooms above, and I will insist that most employees be women. But first things first."

"Miss Althea. I want to work here and help you all run the business. I won't disappoint you, and I'll study hard. I can't thank you enough. You and your sister, Allenby, and Miss Sybil and Mrs. Bartle. You're like my family."

Archie's earnest speech genuinely touched Althea. "We think of you as the little brother we never had. You can call me Althea since we are family now." She passed him the folded note. "Here is the telegram. Miss Callen located the woman in question and will bring her here to reunite with her daughter. Will you look after the particulars and make arrangements with Mrs. Bartle?"

"Yes, Althea. I will."

Althea nodded. "Good lad. Come for dinner here tomorrow night, around six o'clock. With the family."

Archie stood, his eyes glittering with emotion. "I will." He departed.

Althea sat back in her chair and exhaled. Her heart ached at the prospect of possibly stepping back from running the agency, but she must plan for all conceivable scenarios. She would invite Damon and tell everyone that she had the biopsy.

The bell rang. Drat it; she was alone. Althea gingerly approached the front door to find a young messenger boy holding an envelope.

"No need to pay, miss. I'm to wait for a reply."

She took the envelope.

"Wait here." After closing the door, she leaned against it and opened the note.

My Thea,

If you are available, I would like to take you to dinner Friday night at the Savoy Hotel, in The Grill Room. It is not fancy dress, and most patrons are men, but I know you do not mind that. I chose it because it's quiet and private, and I want us to enjoy each other's company without speaking of the case. Send your answer along with the messenger, and if you agree, the carriage will be by to collect you Friday at seven.

Damon ♥

He had drawn a heart next to his name. Her own heart skipped a beat. When was the last time Althea had taken a meal at a restaurant with a man? Close to two years ago, with a solicitor. The evening had passed pleasantly enough, but there were no sparks, no pull, at least on her end. He had asked to see her again, but she demurred politely.

All sorts of eateries were cropping up, from pubs serving food to tea rooms, bistros, and formal dining. It was the latest craze in London, and it sounded like The Grill Room stood between a pub and formal dining, which suited Althea right down to the ground.

Pulling out a sheet of paper from the drawer, she then dipped her pen in the ink bottle and wrote,

Dear Damon,

I will join you for dinner Friday night. I look forward to it. Speaking of dinner, I am having a small, informal gathering tomorrow night. I would like for you to attend. Very much. It is a family dinner. Please arrive at about six. I assume you are coming if I do not hear from you.

Inviting Damon will show her family how important he has become in her life. And he had, beyond all sense. Why deny it or try to ignore it? She was falling in love with him.

Dipping the pen in ink, she signed the note.

Althea ♥

She opened the door and handed the note to the messenger. The boy touched his forelock and scampered off.

What to wear Friday night? She had a few gowns that were not quite formal but suitable evening wear for a social event. Althea smiled. She knew just the one.

It was copper and brown; the skirt was cream-colored with copper-shaded flowers with a dark brown velvet overlay. The copper puffed upper sleeves narrowed down to the elbow, where the rest of the sleeve was the same dark brown velvet as the overlay. The front of the gown resembled a laced-up bodice, with dark brown up to the high neck. She had a matching velvet hat to finish the look. It would be perfect for a night out with her duke.

Althea slowly made her way to her room. After laying the note flat, she carefully smoothed it. She removed a journal from the top drawer of her desk, then placed the letter inside it to join the other message he had sent her some weeks ago. Also pressed between the pages was a cornflower from the convent, the one Damon had given her.

Yes, it appears she was a romantic sentimentalist at heart. At least as far as her duke was concerned.

Gossip be hanged.

Althea would enjoy her dinners—especially the one alone with Damon.

Chapter 22

CLEVELAND STREET HAD been a hotbed of activity all day, with Mrs. Bartle in the kitchen preparing the meal to Eleanora showing up mid-afternoon to make the rolls and scones. With input from Mrs. Bartle, Althea planned the menu and decided on steamed clams as an appetizer. The main meal was herb-roasted chicken, mashed potatoes, corn, and wild mushrooms, served with Eleanora's American cloverleaf rolls. Then, assorted cheeses, biscuits, Eleanora's scones, and a raspberry-filled sponge cake.

Eleanora, Christian, Archie, Sybil, Corbett, Uncle Reece, and Aunt Wilhelmina will be in attendance. And, of course, Damon.

As Althea wished for a word, Uncle Reece and his wife arrived earlier. She had already asked Uncle Reece to come by a few days ago, where she brought him up to date on her health concern. Now, she wished to discuss another sensitive subject. Damon.

They were alone in the study, her uncle holding a tumbler of Jameson Irish whiskey. It was also her late father's favorite. Uncle Reece resembled her father, and it hurt to look at him at times. But in another way, the similarity brought comfort, as if her father were still here in the physical sense.

"You look well, Uncle. How goes the crime-fighting?" Althea teased. Uncle Reece was a detective inspector at J Division, Bethnal Green, in the East End.

"Same as it ever was, my dear. It fills my days, never a dull moment."

"And Aunt Mina fills your nights?" Althea smiled. Wilhelmina was a police officer's widow whom Reece had recently married.

Uncle Reece raised his glass. "That she does, bless her. And what do I hear about *your* nights?"

"The Duke of Chellenham," Althea replied with a wistful sigh.

"A duke. Just like your sister. You girls have aimed high and more power to you. Your father and I only wanted the best for you both, and in society's eyes, dukes are right up there."

Althea laughed, then sobered.

"Is it serious?" her uncle asked softly.

"Yes. We've all but said the words to each other. I have fallen in love. Oh, what an alarming prospect. My insides have been in knots for weeks. Perhaps even months, ever since we first met. He has a terrible reputation."

"Does he?" Uncle Reece murmured as he sipped his whiskey.

"Ellie informed you of everything. She told me that she asked you to investigate Damon," Althea exclaimed.

They were close to their uncle. He had lived with them for years, helping his older brother raise his two active daughters. Two gruff policemen bringing up little girls? In theory, it shouldn't have worked. But the brothers arranged their shifts, so one was always nearby when needed, and Mrs. Bartle kept up the housekeeping and meals end of the bargain.

"Don't be cross. Your sister was concerned. Eleanora wanted to know if I knew anything of him, criminally speaking."

Well, her sister is an investigator. And Althea wasn't angry. Not when Eleanora first informed her of the inquiry or now. "I am not cross, Uncle. Truly. And is there anything beyond the gossip?"

"Nothing. But as you know, the elites rarely find themselves entangled with the law. Regarding his reputation, it has been my experience that most titled young men go too far regarding vices. I sent my share on their way when I came across them staggering out of brothels or pubs. There was and is no point in arresting them for misdemeanors. I found out early in my career that all it causes is problems. For the coppers."

"Hardly seems fair," Althea replied cynically. "But it is the way of things. Why would I fall for a dissipated, bored aristocrat? I loathe everything he stands for, and I can't make it—make any sense."

"Love isn't supposed to make sense, Niece. You would not have given your affection to a complete reprobate. Come now. There must be *some* good in him."

"There is. It took some doing, but I dug deep enough to find it. Damon has been nothing but supportive and caring since my diagnosis."

Uncle Reece smiled. "Then, I like him already."

"He has uncovered horrible information about his late father, which is why he hired the agency." Althea gave her uncle a condensed version of the past several weeks and the discoveries made.

Her uncle placed his near-empty glass on the table. "I thought I had heard everything, but apparently not. And Chellenham is going to take in these discovered young half-siblings?"

Althea nodded. "I believe he is. Damon wanted a family, and he has certainly found it. From an older brother and sister to the young ones living at the home. Damon had a terrible childhood."

"Evercreech. I've never met him, but I heard of him. At Westminster, I believe. He has a good reputation, both as a detective and a man. And as far as childhoods, I am sorry to hear of Chellenham's. I often wonder if Hollis and I did you girls any favors keeping you with us. It was unconventional, to be sure."

"I wouldn't have wanted it any other way. Cleveland Street was a loving home when we were growing up, and no mistake. I was quite bereft the day you moved out," Althea smiled sadly.

"Hollis had passed, you and Ellie had your new investigative business, and it was time to get on with our lives. And you both have. God above, I miss my brother. But I have you girls as a reminder."

"And we have you, Uncle. As a reminder. And you also have moved on with your life."

Her uncle nodded. "Aye, and I'm happy. I want the same for you, Althea. My bright shining star."

Uncle Reece hadn't called her that for many years. Tears welled in her eyes. Her uncle stood and opened his arms, and Althea stepped into them. He held her tight and kissed the top of her head. Not difficult to do since her uncle was quite tall.

"Embrace all life has to offer. I know your analytical mind will eventually sort it all out. Take your time, don't rush anything. But if this complicated duke makes your heart beat faster, don't deny your feelings. Live and love, Althea."

She nodded.

Eleanora opened the door. "Sorry to interrupt, but everyone is here. The meal is ready."

Uncle Reece held out his arm toward Eleanora. "Ellie, come join the hug. Just like when you girls were small."

Eleanora smiled and came to them, and they all embraced. Laughing, they headed into the parlor. Althea led Uncle Reece directly to Damon. He looked splendid, as always. Tonight, Damon wore a black suit with a silver waistcoat.

"Uncle Reece, this is Damon Cranston, the Duke of Chellenham. Damon, my dear uncle, Reece Galway, Inspector at J Division, Bethnal Green."

Damon extended his hand. "A distinct honor, sir. Althea speaks highly of you."

Uncle Reece took his hand and shook it. "Does she, now? Well, Althea speaks highly of you, Your Grace."

Small talk commenced among the guests until Corbett raised his hand. "Could I have your attention for a moment before we enter the dining room? Sybil has honored me by agreeing to become my wife. We are engaged."

Excited chatter broke out as hugs and handshakes were shared by all.

"When is the wedding?" Eleanora asked.

"Not until next summer. We have to arrange a trip to Yorkshire to meet Sybil's parents first," Corbett replied. "And get their blessing."

"My aunt and uncle will love you, Corbett. As we do," Althea enthused.

"That will be one of many toasts we will make once seated," Christian said. "To your happiness."

Everyone headed to the dining room, and Althea took Damon's arm.

"My God, your uncle is tall," he whispered.

"Close to six and a half feet. My father was almost as tall as that. Look at Eleanora. Somehow, the tall height family trait just skimmed past me."

"You are fine as you are."

Once everyone was seated, Mrs. Bartle brought in the appetizers. As she served, the bell rang. "Who would come right at dinner time? I'll go." She placed the platter of clams on the table. "Serve yourselves until I return."

The housekeeper hurried off, and everyone passed around the pitchers of water, bottles of wine, and clams while the conversation remained lively.

Until everyone saw who had rung the bell. The discussion ceased rather abruptly.

Doctor Stevenson removed his hat. "I have disturbed a family dinner. My apologies. I stopped by your boarding house, Corbett, and the landlady said I could reach you here. I have news. Miss Althea, if we could speak privately?"

This is it. My future lay bare.

Althea stood. "You can speak freely. Everyone here knows about my condition, save Archie." She turned toward the lad. "They found a growth on my leg, which Doctor Simpson biopsied."

"Ah. The possible impediment," Archie murmured, a worried expression on his face.

"Very well, I will speak freely," the doctor said. "The tumor was benign."

Althea had to hold on to the table to keep from falling. Damon was at her side, slipping his arm around her waist, holding her upright. A whoosh of audible relief filled the room, and everyone exclaimed happily.

Doctor Stevenson held up his hand. When the excitement died down, he said, "It is good news, but I should remove the tumor in a timely manner. Miss Althea, you may have to use a cane for several months after the operation. And there is a slight chance you may have to use one for the rest of your life. But I doubt it will come to that. We will know more after. My guess is several months."

A knot of disappointment settled inside her, and Althea struggled not to show it outwardly. *Again, so many other people have had worse news than this.*

"My Thea. The news is good—more than good. There is no cancer," Damon urged.

He knew what she was thinking, and Damon was right. Relief washed over her, and she turned and threw her arms about Damon's neck, and he held her close.

"All is well, my Thea," he whispered.

"Doctor Stevenson, why not join us?" Christian asked. "I am sure there is enough food. Mrs. Bartle?"

The housekeeper dabbed the corner of her eye with the hem of her apron. "That there is. More than enough."

The doctor placed his hat on his head. "The invitation is tempting, and I thank you. But I have other appointments tonight. Enjoy your dinner. The diagnosis is to be celebrated. I will be in touch soon." Doctor Stevenson smiled warmly at Althea, then Mrs. Bartle escorted him to the front door.

"And celebrate it, we shall." Christian stood and raised his glass. "To Althea, the best possible news. And to Sybil and Corbett, all the happiness for your future." Everyone toasted.

"Now, Mrs. Bartle," Eleanora said, coming from behind the table as soon as the housekeeper reappeared. "You are to join us for this meal. Sybil and I will assist in the serving. As you can see, there is an empty chair next to Archie. It is for you. We planned it that way."

Mrs. Bartle looked puzzled. "Why?"

"Because you are part of the family, Susan," Uncle Reece stated. "And have been for years, in case you didn't know. The Galways are not the most outwardly demonstrative people, but we feel things deeply."

"Why, Reece. You're an old softie," Mrs. Bartle laughed merrily. Althea had never heard her uncle and Mrs. Bartle refer to themselves by their first names. They must do so when alone.

Eleanora and Sybil followed the housekeeper into the kitchen, and they served the rest of the food. Mrs. Bartle removed her apron and sat next to Archie. She gave the lad an affectionate smile and squeezed his hand. "Thank you for including me."

"How could we not?" Althea replied. "We are all family."

The meal was delicious, and everyone made short work of the food in between overlapping conversations and laughter. Afterward, Althea took Damon's arm and walked to the front door, then assisted him in slipping on his long coat.

"We are alone," he murmured. Damon pulled her into his arms and kissed her thoroughly. "Until Friday night. We have much to discuss." And with that, he opened the door and rushed to his waiting carriage.

"Embrace all life has to offer. I know your analytical mind will eventually sort it all out. Take your time, don't rush anything. But if this complicated duke makes your heart beat faster, don't deny your feelings. Live and love, Althea."

Her uncle was correct on all fronts. Althea needed to sort it all out. It was her way of dealing with things. But she would not take long, for it was time she tossed away any remaining doubts about Damon—and her feelings.

Live and love, indeed.

Chapter 23

AS THE CARRIAGE APPROACHED Cleveland Street, the horses' hooves clattered against the cobblestones. Damon felt surprisingly calm, and his deep-seated ego must have caused this burst of confidence.

This was a first. Damon had never eaten at the Savoy Hotel, let alone accompanied a woman to a meal. As he relayed to Althea, he usually ate alone at a pub or musical hall.

The carriage pulled up in front of Althea's house, and Damon waited until Dawson pulled down the metal steps. Damon exited the carriage and rang the bell; mere moments later, the door opened, and a vision of loveliness stood before him. The copper and brown gown suited Althea perfectly, showcasing her beautiful dark brown hair and eyes.

"You are stunning, my Thea." He took her arm and assisted her into the carriage. He then sat on the bench opposite.

"I hope I am not too overdressed for The Grill Room." She laid a medium-sized case at her feet.

"Not at all. You will turn every head there, I promise you. Be prepared for a plethora of meat dishes, as it caters mostly to men. There is no fuss or frills. And the bar is equipped with female bartenders."

"This sounds like a men's club. Do they bring slabs of meat to the middle of the restaurant and grill it on large braziers?" Althea teased.

"How humorous. Theatergoers, different classes of folk alike, and men of business frequent the place, so there is quite an eclectic mix. I thought you would thrive in such surroundings. Was I correct?"

Althea smiled. "Yes. Absolutely. I cannot abide formal dining, although I have only been to one, and I felt so out of place, regardless of who had accompanied me. Eleanora claims she will hold a formal dinner this Christmas, so I must brush up on the cutlery and goblet rules."

Damon cocked an eyebrow. "You were out with a man?"

"Yes," she laughed gently. "I am twenty-six. I haven't been wrapped in wool and stored away these past years. I have gone on social occasions with men."

That declaration sent every predatory and envious nerve ending in his body on high alert. It made no sense, except it was a typical response for men in general. Arrogant men like him. How Althea tolerated him, he could not say.

"You must tell me about those occasions, each and every one," Damon purred.

"Oh? And you will tell me about all your social occasions?" Althea laughed.

"This is it."

She ceased laughing. "I'm the first woman you are taking out to dine?"

"You are. Remember your report on me during Christian's case? I took in a musical and dined—alone. I do not attend balls, grand dinners, parties, except for those debauched country revels that led to even more depraved activities."

Althea looked astonished; then she shook her head. "I am curious why anyone would even attend such an event. You *are* speaking of orgies?"

Damon stared out the window at the passing scenery, observing that the sun was low in the sky. Dusk would soon be upon them. "I cannot explain why I acted in such a way—"

"Damon, look at me."

He turned slightly and met her frank gaze.

"I was asking the question in general, not requesting that you root around into your past. Perhaps someday, we will discuss your historical doings. But I see it pains you, and I do not want to cause you any pain. Are you still interested in such supplementary happenings?"

"No. Not at all," Damon replied honestly. "Historical doings and supplementary happenings, very amusing."

"Then let us leave your disreputable reputation in the ash heap of the past—where it belongs. I am only interested in the man who sits before me here, in the present. The man I have come to know better. The man I am falling in love with."

Damon could not be more shocked if she had pulled out her revolver and shot him between the eyes. He banged on the roof.

The small window slid open. "Yes, Your Grace?" Dawson asked.

"Pull over by the side of the street."

"Yes, Your Grace."

It took a few moments, but the carriage inevitably parked. Their gazes remained locked.

"You *are* falling in love with me? You're certain?" Damon asked, still incredulous. He knew she found him attractive, but this? His heart soared. "What happened to you needing time to think, jumbled feelings, and all that?"

"Well, it is all I have thought about these past several days. This health crisis brought much into focus—once the initial shock passed. I have no idea what the future will bring. Do any of us, really? I still have more to work through, but I will."

"Kiss me," he murmured.

Althea launched herself into his open arms. She rubbed her nose against his, and a rumble of laughter left his throat. Never had he felt such complete and utter joy. Then, Althea cupped his cheeks and leaned in, giving his lips a gentle brush, a feather-type kiss. It was enough to arouse him to the point of pain. Damon moaned and allowed Althea to set the pace. She hungrily nibbled on his lower lip, then dove in, tangling her tongue with his, all but devouring him.

"Oh, you taste so delicious," she whispered between kisses. "I will never get enough."

"I hope you never do," he replied.

"Oh, we mustn't muss ourselves," Althea said as she reluctantly moved off his lap.

"I am tempted to tell Dawson to take us home, hang dinner," he growled seductively.

Althea took her seat on the opposite bench. "It is tempting, but I want to have dinner with you. Eat red meat and drink bold red wine."

Damon banged on the roof, and the carriage lurched forward. "Dinner it is. And conversation. What *is* in that case, by the by?"

"It's for later. If you wish, I thought I would drop by your town house after dinner. I can only stay until midnight."

"Oh, I wish indeed. Stay as long as you like. The rest of our lives."

Althea gave him such a welcoming smile that his heart hitched again as it often did when she was near. He kept a book of memories in his mind for every dazzling smile she had ever given him. Basking in her generous warmth made him realize how barren his life had been. Devoid of love and acceptance. Damon never wanted to return to that tedious, cold existence ever again.

They arrived at the Savoy. The luxurious hotel, located on the north bank of the Thames, opened its doors in 1889. Its electric lighting cast a bright luminescence over the heart of London and the West End theater area.

Damon gave directions to Dawson to park around the corner where carriages generally congregated, then took Althea's hand and slipped it through his arm as they stepped into the front lobby. The brightness was almost overwhelming as electric bulbs shone from chandeliers, wall sconces, and desk lamps.

"Gideon tells me there are electric lifts brought from America, where they are called elevators," Damon whispered in her ear as they headed toward The Grill Room. "The formal French dining room is upstairs. Ah, here we are." Damon turned to the Maître d. "Reservation for Chellenham."

The uniformed man snapped to attention. "Welcome, Your Grace. Your table is here, as requested. Private and overlooking the Thames."

Damon assisted Althea in taking her seat, and after they ordered their drinks, the waiter brought the menus. They removed their gloves. "I hear the lobster salad is delicious," he said while scanning the menu. Asher Colborne had recommended it.

"Oh, let's have some. And I love this place with all the wood walls, moldings, and ornate paneled ceilings. Very cozy."

They ordered it along with prime beef with mushrooms in a red wine sauce and grilled asparagus and lyonnaise potatoes.

Left alone at last, Damon raised his glass. "To the future. We can have one, my Thea."

She gave him a quivering smile as she raised her glass. "I still have to work through that possibility as long as my health doesn't hamper such dreams. I hadn't planned on using a cane either for a few months—or the rest of my days. But I will adjust."

The fact that Althea did not immediately embrace the idea of a mutual future sparked a flicker of doubt within him. But he wouldn't let such toxic feelings overtake him. Not tonight.

"I refuse to allow such an outcome to damper my complete bliss. And neither should you. We can adjust to any scenario. I know you must work through things at your own particular pace." Damon paused, then smiled warmly. "Know that I will be at your side, always. If you want to lean on me for support for whatever reason, I welcome it gladly. No one has ever needed me before, and I quite like the sensation."

"Oh, Damon. I do need you, most desperately." Althea's eyes glistened with unshed tears.

They clinked glasses and sipped the wine, their gazes still locked.

"I know others that need you as well," Althea said softly. "Have you given any thought to your five half-siblings?"

"I have. I cannot abandon the children to fate. I assume Adina's mother is enroute?"

The waiter brought the lobster salad, then moved away to wait on other patrons.

Althea picked up her utensils and cut the leafy dish. "Archie is handling the details. So much for not speaking of the case."

Damon smiled. "Well, we are discussing family more than anything."

"And Archie is family, a younger brother I had always wished for. I am so glad he came into our lives."

"I am part of your inner circle, then?" Damon asked as he sipped his wine.

"Most assuredly. I invited you to our family dinner, after all. Now, what about your younger siblings?"

"I assume Adina will return to Cornwall with her mother. I will offer a yearly stipend and leave it up to the girl to stay in contact. As to the other four, I might as well rip the plaster off the wound, as it were, and bring them into my home. But not until the renovations are complete and I have had time to hire a governess, nurse, and possible tutor for the oldest boy, Hugh. In the meantime, I will visit Chellenhome often, get to know them, and see if they want to come live with me."

"In fact," he continued between bites. "I went to Chellenhome the day after your dinner. All went well, and I spoke with MacClery about renovations, and the children talked to me freely, without hesitation."

He glanced at Althea.

One of those unshed tears had trickled down her cheeks. "You *are* going to give them a home?" she asked tremulously.

"Yes, blast it. Adorable moppets galloping through the halls, creating a ruckus, and eating me out of house and home. How tedious."

Althea laughed as she brushed the tear away.

"I wish I could take all the children in. But I vow to ensure the others have good homes and the best possible future."

"I agree."

"And you will never guess who was waiting at Clarendon Place after I left you several days ago," Damon added.

Through the salad and partway into the beef course, Damon told Althea of Evercreech and Donaldson coming to see him. He held his hand aloft to show her the ring Mitchell Evercreech had brought.

"Perhaps they will stay in touch," Althea offered hopefully.

"Not Donaldson. Perhaps Evercreech. Time will tell. And I have other interesting news. As you know, extensive renovations are underway at the duke town house. You will never guess what the workers found when tearing down my father's bed chamber walls?"

"A secret room for deviant doings of the physical nature?" Althea replied sweetly.

"I do love your dark turn of mind. A good guess and not out of the realm of possibility. The workers found a strong box hidden in a cache. Thankfully, they are honest men and brought it straight to Kingsley. I thought I would have to contact your cracksman Cleves, but we managed to open it. There were over six hundred pounds in the box. My father's secret stash, which his solicitor knew nothing about."

"The late duke was devious to his core," Althea replied. "He had that money and ignored Mrs. Seddon's letters for financial help? Left them to stave? What an evil man."

"That he was. His hubris and egomaniac behavior fueled his devious doings. I suppose I came by it honestly."

"Perhaps a healthy ego, but not the rest. Not even close. There is decency in you. Your father had none at all. What will you do with the money?" Althea asked as she sipped her wine.

"First, I gave the workers a small token of gratitude. Next, I will pay my father's outstanding debts. The rest? Sink it into the renovations at the town house and Chellenhome. I will put it to good use."

"It was a lucky find. What if you hadn't been doing such renovations?"

Damon shrugged as he cut his asparagus. "Then I suppose some future owner of this property would have found it decades from now. Lucky find, indeed."

"I have something to tell you. I had the biopsy several days ago."

Damon stopped mid-bite. He swallowed hard. "I wondered how Doctor Stevenson had the results, but then, he mentioned a biopsy when giving his conclusion. Everyone was so happy and relieved there were no questions. Why didn't you send for me?" Yes, damn it, he was hurt.

"It came about so fast I had no time to tell anyone. Doctor Stevenson had a late cancellation. Don't be angry. I wanted it over with."

"I am not angry. A little annoyed, for I wanted to be there for you." There was no use brooding over it, as Doctor Simpson had already revealed the satisfactory results. Perhaps his former peevish self would sulk moodily. But not now. Not ever again.

Althea reached across the table and took his hand. "You were there with me, in my heart."

"How can you be falling for me? I cannot fathom it. You will be taking on a decidedly arrogant, not-all-that-wealthy duke with a brood of half-siblings and extended family. My new steward, Willis Arrowsmith, will find my mother, stepfather, and half-brother a place to live." He explained the details of his mother's letter.

Althea clasped her hands together. "Oh, what exciting news! When will they arrive?"

"Soon, I expect. I have invited my family to stay at Clarendon Place until they find a town house or large flat to suit them. So, it is good you are coming back with me tonight, for I do not know when we will have any privacy again."

Althea smiled. "Then we should forgo dessert and head to your place immediately."

Damon threw down his napkin and snapped his fingers to gain the waiter's attention. "I cannot agree more."

After paying the bill, they stepped outside.

"We will have to walk to the next street to the carriage. Are you able?" Damon asked worriedly.

Althea slipped her arm through his. "As long as I am with you."

Damon could not resist. With a quick move, he gently swung Althea around until he concealed them in the shadows at the head of an alley. He removed his hat and quickly captured her lips with his, kissing her deeply and meticulously.

With a gasping moan, Althea looped her arms around his neck and stood on the toes of her shoes to return the searing kiss, all but devouring him. Her passion sparked his to unknown levels, arousing him. She grabbed fistfuls of his hair as he pulled her close, right against that hard part of him. The part that ached to join with her.

"Bloody hell. You two are a pair. Never could keep your hands off the ladies or the lads. Eh, Brookton? Like your immoral father. Right, it's Chellenham now. I nearly forgot," a voice rumbled with mockery.

They broke apart and turned toward the voice.

It was Silas Browning, and he held a revolver on them.

Chapter 24

ALTHEA GASPED. DAMN it all, her revolver was in her case in the carriage, though she had a small knife in her garter. But that was no match for a gun.

And any sudden movement and this man could shoot one or both before she lifted her gown enough to access the weapon.

"Silas Browning. What do you want?" Damon asked, his voice steady.

Browning?

But, of course, he referred to Damon by name.

Damon stepped forward, but Althea touched his arm to halt him. Any perceived attack could cause Browning to fire the weapon.

"My bleedin' money. Where is it?" the man demanded.

"Yes. It *is* blood money," Damon spat. "Buying and selling children as if they are bales of cotton to barter at a market. You disgust me."

Browning growled. "Don't act high and mighty with me, you bleedin' hypocrite. You lot take advantage of those less fortunate as quickly as taking a breath. I worked hard for that money. I earned my coin, and I want it. Take me to it, or I will shoot you both in the alley. I got nothing to lose."

Before Damon could respond, a dark figure dropped down on Browning from above, knocking him off his feet. The revolver skittered across the cobblestones, and Althea reached to grab it. It was hard to see what was happening as most of the alley lay in shadow. Browning was getting to his feet when this strange person pummeled Browning with quicksilver punches and a roundhouse kick to the chin that sent Browning reeling across the ground.

The dark man stood over Browning and then kicked him in the face. The sickening crunch of bone followed by a high-pitched scream became silenced when the dark man grabbed a fistful of Browning's thinning hair and banged his head against the cobblestones, effectively silencing him.

The burst of violence was shocking to observe. Althea held the revolver close to her side in case this mysterious man decided to attack them.

The man turned and stepped out of the shadows. The nearby gas street lamp illumination cast him in an eerie glow. The tall man wore black leather from head to toe and was a remarkable sight from his wide-brimmed hat, face mask, long flowing coat, waistcoat, trousers, and boots. Tucked in his belt was a cudgel of some sort. He took off the hat and gave an exaggerated bow. A black scarf even covered his hair. He resembled a highwayman from another era.

"The Sentinel, at your service." The voice was deep but muffled, the words hard to make out. The man plopped his hat on his head and sprinted from the alley.

"What in the hell?" Damon muttered. He moved forward as if to give chase, but Althea held up her hand.

"Let him go. He assisted us, and that is all that matters."

Damon pointed toward the street. "Did you see his costume? The Sentinel?"

"Guardian, sentry, lookout. Watchman. He is a vigilante. The East End is notorious for them and has been for centuries. How many ghosts and shadows have existed in the past and present? More than we know. There is something familiar about him, and I will have to puzzle it through."

"You do that. Meanwhile, keep the gun on Browning, and I will fetch the carriage and bring it here. We will stuff the man in the conveyance and take him to Clarendon Place. We have questions." Damon crouched down and placed the tips of two fingers against Browning's neck. "Bloodied, but still alive."

Damon stood, looped his arm about her waist, and kissed her hard. "That was an exciting end to the evening."

Althea nuzzled his neck. "The night is not over yet."

"How true. Keep an eye on him." Damon kissed her forehead and rushed from the alley.

Althea kicked Browning with the toe of her shoe. Out cold, and no doubt would be for some time. Then Althea looked up. The building before her had a long staircase to the flat above. How long had this Sentinel been up there? Had he followed them to the restaurant, keeping watch? It was the only explanation that made sense. Unless he came upon them by chance. Althea would get to the bottom of it soon enough.

The carriage pulled up, and Dawson and Damon jumped down, and with Damon taking his feet and the driver taking Browning's shoulders, they carried him toward the carriage. Althea hurried as quickly as she could to assist in holding the door open, and the men effectively dumped him within. Then Damon aided her in and then followed. The door slammed, and they were off at a brisk pace.

A groan came from the crumbled figure on the floor, but he remained unconscious. Althea kept the revolver pointed at Browning.

"What are we going to do with him?" she whispered.

"I am not certain. Question the blackguard. I could call the police as he held a gun on us and threatened to kill us. I could say he tried to rob us and play up the incident. But that would be a blatant lie. Low, even for me. We will do as you suggested: hold his money in exchange for information. And a promise he leaves the city never to return."

Althea nodded. "I believe that is the best solution."

In no time at all, they arrived at Clarendon Place. Browning started to stir.

With Dawson's assistance, they dragged Browning upright into the town house, and a startled Kingsley held the door.

"Kingsley, bring gauze, plasters, and a bowl of hot water. Quickly, now," Damon demanded as they headed to the study.

"At once, Your Grace." The butler hurried off, and the men dragged Browning to a chair and sat him on it. His head lolled, and Damon grabbed a fistful of Browning's hair and slapped him hard.

"Wake up, you cretin," Damon hissed.

Well. Althea stood closer, still holding the revolver on Browning. Althea was rather impressed by Damon's command. This was a surprising side of him and not unwelcome.

"What in the bloody hell," the man rumbled as he struggled to focus. He shook his head as if to clear the cobwebs.

"We have questions. Answer them to our satisfaction, and you will get your money," Althea stated firmly. "Then you will leave London, never to return. Or we will have The Sentinel hunt you down. The man who beat you into submission? He works for me."

Damon turned and gave her an approving nod, then swung his gaze back toward Browning. "And Miss Galway will use the pistol on you, make no mistake. She has shot miserable men like you before. And she never misses."

Browning gave Althea an assessing gaze, then touched the back of his head and came away with blood on his fingers. "I'm bleedin'."

"We will attend to that. Questions first. Do you agree to the terms?" Damon asked, his tone deadly serious.

"I just want my money."

"You could have approached us without threats," Althea admonished as she took the seat opposite, still keeping a firm grip on the firearm.

Browning grunted. "Right. Sure. Ask your questions."

"How was it done? Explain the process of Chellenhome," Althea demanded.

"The duke gave me names, gents, and aristos with by-blows they wanted gone. I was to collect a fee, then bring the bastards to Chellenhome. Then, we sold them to businesses, factories, or people who wanted a child for whatever reason."

"We figured that part out," Damon snapped. "I want to know why an earl or viscount or whoever would pay to have their progeny taken away when all they had to do was ignore the child, as many have done in the past. There had to be something in it for them."

Browning squirmed in his seat. "I'm feelin' sick. I need attendin' to," he complained.

"Once you answer me," Damon replied, his tone thunderous.

"There was a small fee paid back to the gents. A finder's fee. Some greedier ones started snatching orphans off the street for ready cash. When the inventory was low, the duke bought street waifs and sold them for thrice the price or more. Those names were not written in the ledgers. I got a cut for every sale, but the duke made the most of anyone. For a while there, he was in high clover."

"A top-down scam, in other words. My late father told me of these. The scam relies on recruiting new members, bringing in more money, and the late duke sitting on the top took the most profit. But then it all started to unravel, correct?" Althea interjected.

Browning grunted his affirmation.

Kingsley entered with a tray and placed it on the table near Browning. "I can take care of this man's wounds as you continue questioning him, Your Grace, Miss Galway."

"Thank you, Kingsley. Have at it. I believe the nose is broken. You may want to check that as well," Damon replied.

"Not the first time," Browning muttered. "And not the last; I'll be bound."

"No doubt," Althea replied. "So, it all started to unravel?"

"Aye. The older members started dying off or were too old to run the streets for whatever purpose. The duke did his bit to maintain the inventory, but he alone could not keep it a going concern. He tried to recruit newer blood, but it all fell apart. The newer gents were not as reckless as the old ones."

Browning's verbal cadence moved between his East End upbringing to his exaggerated gentleman's accent. Althea stared at him, assessing his character, such as it was. He had held a gun on them. Would he have used it? Desperation can cause a man to do all sorts. Yet, he was being cooperative. Perhaps even telling the truth. His words had a ring of veracity.

"The boys at Chellenhome, Byron Holloway and Jack Benton. Tell me what you know of them," Damon questioned.

Kingsley worked efficiently, wrapping gauze around the brute's head and laying plasters on his nose and forehead.

"They're his, the late duke's. They're brothers. Why do they have different last names; I don't know or care. Of all the women Himself had, this one he kept tucked away for a while. Got attached to her as much as he was capable. I only knew the woman as Christabel. She died when the oldest boy was four. Maybe the duke didn't care, for he hardly turned a hair at the news of her death. Told me to take the boys to the home but not to sell them until he said. He never said."

Damon and Althea exchanged looks. How strange that Edward Cranston kept the boys. But who knows why the old duke did or did not do anything? The more Althea learned of the man, the more of an enigma he became. A thoroughly despicable being, but a puzzle, nonetheless.

"The boys have no family to speak of?" Althea asked.

"None that the duke told me. I don't think he knew. Knowing him, I doubt he was concerned about it. I don't know where the woman is from or her people."

"And Hugh Crossingham?" Althea asked. This question would test whether Browning's story matched what Hugh had given them.

"The duke gave me the name of an orphanage and said the boy was there and to fetch him. As soon as I saw the lad, I knew it was his. When the boy's mother died, the local vicar whisked this Hugh away to an orphanage before we could get him. It took months to track him down, as the boy was transferred many times. But I found him and took him to the home."

Browning glowered. "Seddon got too attached to them all: delayed purchases and the like. I went to complain to the duke some weeks back, and he told me it was over and to forget about Chellenhome. Why would I? It was my livelihood, and I decided I would continue without him. Then the bastard up and dies."

"Are you the least aware of how reprehensible the scheme is, you included? Are you aware the children were hungry?" Damon asked incredulously.

The man shrugged. "I know what reprehensible means, and I wasn't breaking the law. And I was going to get them food. You got in there before me. Some of those snotty-nosed youngsters went on to a better life. Most of them, I'd wager. Seddon always insisted on havin' the final word about where they went. She made me inspect like, and I did. I'm not a complete monster. I just wanted to make money. A better life, like those kiddies."

"Are there any more after Chloe?" Althea asked. "Any children out there still living with their mothers? Children that the duke sired?"

"Nah. If there was, the old duke never told me." Browning tapped his temple. "The man kept a lot of that information up here.

Smart, he was. He told me it was his calling to make offspring wherever he could. Superior blood and all that rot. It sounds a bit barmy when I say it out loud. Anyway, all we dealt with in the past few years were street waifs. I snatched them up to sell. Better than living on the streets."

Damon stood, a disgusted look on his face. He departed and returned with the strong box, tossed it at Browning, and the man barely caught it.

"Here now, no need to be like that," Browning said as he opened the box and ran his fingertips along the bundles of notes.

"All five hundred plus pounds are there—your blood money. Collect your belongings at Queen Anne's Gate and be gone before the sun rises. Leave London. In fact, leave England. Or this Sentinel will hunt you down and beat you until you cease to breathe. Or I will do it. Now get out of my house," Damon hissed through clenched teeth.

Browning rose and started to lumber toward the door, then he halted. "We did some good. Kids starving on the streets got good homes or places to work."

Damon scoffed. "You keep telling yourself that if it salves whatever conscience you have. In truth, you facilitated a maniacal egotist's twisted view of human life and profited from it. You served him and obeyed his every warped request. And that makes you a sniveling weakling of epic proportions."

"Aye," Browning said softly. "I am that. A fancy way to call me a miserable bastard. I'll be gone within the hour."

Browning departed.

"Kingsley, see that Browning *is* gone within the hour."

"With pleasure, Your Grace."

"I am not to be disturbed the rest of the night unless this place is on fire."

Kingsley gave a slight bow and quit the room.

Althea threw herself into Damon's arms. "You handled that magnificently."

He held her close, nuzzling her neck. "And I like it when you embrace me like this. It seems I am indeed saddled with four half-siblings. Will that be an impediment to any possible future between us?"

Althea pulled back and gazed up at him. He looked a little worried. "No. Not an impediment at all. What would you have done if I said yes, it is?"

"Send them all off to school, anything to keep you. But it would not sit well with me. Not at all. I believe it would eventually drive a wedge between us. And that would break my heart."

Althea hugged him tight. "Never, ever, send them away. I will never ask it of you. Unless they want it. You said Hugh expressed an interest in further schooling, and the others will, too, at some point. But that is different. It appears your future may entail a ready-made family. Moreso, with your mother and her family arriving soon. It is what you wanted, Damon. A family. Someone to love. And love you in return. Isn't that what most of us want, after all?"

"I have dreamed of it for many months, being in a happy family—with you. From the moment I held you after you tripped that first time. It started then, and I tried to deny it. I became convinced I would never deserve you. That you could never love and trust me. Or respect me, for why would you? My entire adult life up until that moment had been a vast wasteland of dissipation."

He gently kissed her forehead. "But you sent me into a whirlwind, and I started to feel. But know this; I cannot bear it if anything were to happen to you—it would shatter me. If I were broken before, *this* would destroy me."

The anguish in his voice tore her heart asunder.

Althea cupped his cheeks, making him look at her. "We shouldn't speak of a future until my health situation concludes. My

THE NOT SO PERFECT DUKE

condition is not a conflict plot point in a fiction book. As I said, it is called life. It can be messy. Unpredictable events, as well as health crises, are all part of the bargain."

"In sickness and in health?"

"Yes, it is an aspect of those vows for a reason. If you genuinely love someone, you stand by them no matter what."

His beautiful eyes glittered with emotion. "Then I shall be at your side through it all. I love you, my Thea. As I never thought I would love anyone—ever. You. Are. Everything."

His emotional words arrowed straight to her heart. "Then take me to your bed and love me."

Damon lifted her into his arms and headed toward the stairs.

"Wait, my case," she cried. Damon set her down, grabbed her case, handed it to her, then swept her into his arms again.

Once inside his room, he lowered her and leaned in to kiss her.

Althea laid her hand against his chest. "Let me change into something I brought. Do you mind?" She sat the case on the chair, then unbuttoned his waistcoat. "You looked rather magnificent tonight. The gold waistcoat, the light fawn trousers." She loosened his cravat. "There. Now, sit on the chaise. Do not undress further. Not yet. I will return in a moment."

Althea snatched up her case and ducked into his bathing room, quickly changing into her silk turquoise blue gown. It had matching stockings and garters, which she had worn under her copper and brown-flowered dress. The night dress flowed magnificently, and Althea pulled the short sleeves off her shoulders as a finishing touch. She left the first few hooks in the back undone, for she could not reach them.

With a quick exhale of excitement, she opened the door and entered the room. Damon sat on the chaise longue; his legs spread, his erection more pronounced with the tight trousers. She was in his arms in an instant.

"God. You are beautiful," he murmured as he grasped the back of her gown. "I love this color on you. Perfection."

Althea laid her hand on his shoulder and gazed into his half-lidded eyes. "I want you, Damon. I love you. Nothing and no one else matters at this moment, only us."

"I couldn't agree more. I love you, as I thought I would never be capable of feeling. You haunt my soul."

Then, Damon took her to paradise.

Chapter 25

ALTHEA SAT UPRIGHT in bed. "Oliver Wollstonecraft!"

Damon opened one eye and glanced at the mantel clock. It was closing in on midnight. "I do not appreciate calling out another man's name while in my bed," he grumbled. "Especially since we've made love twice."

"It was three times. I especially loved being on top, like in the carriage."

"I stand corrected. And I like that position as well. So, indulge me. Why call out the name?" Damon yawned and sat upright. The sheet slipped down, barely covering his naked and aroused state. "So, Wollstonecraft?"

"I think he is The Sentinel."

Damon sputtered, then laughed. "Why would you think that?"

"This Sentinel followed us to the restaurant. I am certain of it. I do not believe he came upon us by chance. This vigilante was aware we might be in danger. And who knew of this outside of our immediate circle? Think back. Oliver Wollstonecraft was in the room when we discussed Browning and how he may break into one of our homes to look for a safe." Althea nodded, crossing her arms across her sheet-covered breasts. She looked entirely pleased with herself.

"A particularly adroit deduction. However, if you recall, we also spoke of Silas Browning attacking Mrs. Seddon and the fact that he was a danger in Doctor Buchanan's presence."

"Oh, well done," Althea enthused. "But Corbett acting as a vigilante? I cannot fathom it."

"On the other hand, why would an heir apparent to an earl swan about the slums rescuing random people? It makes no sense."

"Most vigilantes of the past patrolled an area that policemen would not dare to enter. St. Giles was demolished during a clearance in the '70s to make way for better roads and transportation, and the poor ventured further south into the Seven Dials. Also located in the West End is Notting Dale, another slum home to poisonous jobs such as pig farming and brick kilns. And Cut-throat Lane is there; the name says it all."

Althea exhaled and continued, "Then there is the East End and its many slums. Why did vigilantes patrol these areas—a sense of justice and fairness? My father said, in general, the coppers left the vigilantes alone as they served a purpose. For the most part. Perhaps Wollstonecraft wishes to carry on his family's good works in his particular way."

"My God, you are magnificent," Damon murmured, impressed. "You may have the right of it."

"We should do our part to protect Wollstonecraft—if he is The Sentinel—and keep his identification private."

"I agree." Damon grabbed the sheet and flung it from the bed, causing Althea to squeal playfully. "But I have something else in mind."

"It is near midnight. I must head home."

"One more time, my Thea. And it is one of *my* favorite positions."

Damon encircled her waist and brought her up on her knees. He knelt behind her.

"Oh. This is different. Like the animals?" Althea said, clearly curious.

"Exactly." Damon affixed another sheath, then caressed her feminine core until she was wet and ready for him. Then, grasping her hips, he slid in slowly as Althea moaned. Holding still, Damon once again savored the way she fit him perfectly. All those empty encounters, cheap debaucheries, none gave him the satisfaction of joining with Althea, not even close. He could stay like this for the rest of his life.

"Um, Damon?" Althea rolled her hips to gain his attention.

"Right." No leisurely strokes here. Damon pounded hard, giving in to his base instincts. Judging by the whimpers, then the demands that he go faster, Althea enjoyed this as much as he did. She met each thrust by taking him deeper, if possible.

It was wild, abandoned, and utterly soul-stirring. Althea reached her peak in no time at all since he was at such an angle to directly stimulate her swollen clit. Damon did not slow the pace.

"Again, my Thea." His demand came out as a raspy growl. A roil of colors swan in his vision as he was beyond all consciousness.

Moments later, Althea came again, and her passionate cries tore through him straight to his heart, swelling it beyond its size as if it were pounding against his ribcage.

My God, he loved her with every fiber of his being.

Then came his release. "Jesus!" He yelled as his climax slammed him hard. He nearly collapsed from the intensity, for he shook and shuddered for several moments. Then he flopped to the bed, pulling a breathless Althea into his arms.

"That position didn't aggravate your leg?" he gasped as if trying to gain control of his breathing. "Damn it all. I should have thought of that before selfishly taking my gratification."

"I am fine," she purred as her fingers trailed through his damp chest hair. "You must escort me home. But let us catch our breath first."

"As I said, this may be the last time we can be together like this. Until our wedding night."

Althea grew very still.

"We've mentioned a possible future more than once, although we haven't discussed it at any length," Damon continued. "I say we make our commitment permanent. I have said how much I love you; I have shown you just how much. That will never change, no matter what life throws our way."

Then he heard a sniffle. "This was not part of my plans, falling in love. And certainly not with you—a duke. But I have, and I cannot imagine you *not* being part of my life."

Silence.

Damon's insides began to twist with anxiety. Would she refuse him? She didn't precisely squeal with delight at his heartfelt declaration and hug the stuffing out of him. "But? Are you having doubts? Is it my past as a notorious rake that gives you pause? My so-called standing in society? Do you not trust me?"

Althea kissed his cheek. "I *do* trust you and love you with all my heart. The only doubts I have are my own. I have seen what Olivia and Eleanora are subjected to. How Christian and Gideon are all but given the cut by society for supposedly marrying beneath them. They all say they do not care, but it *will* matter. Especially when and if they have children. I have to consider that."

Damon did not give a fuck what anyone thought. He never had. But he was in a position not to care. Althea was not, and society would always be harsher toward her, and it was not just.

"My love, it will be a new century in two years. If this were eighty or more years ago, there might be some merit to what you say. Society ruled all at one time. Not anymore. They do not have that kind of power, which will only diminish as the years pass. Within our circle of friends, it will not matter at all. They are the only people I care about outside of my family. Hang everyone else. We will hold our heads high. And as far as children? If we have any, it will be on your terms. And we will raise them to respect others regardless of class. What other concerns do you have?"

Althea sighed. "My health. We still do not know the outcome regarding the operation."

"No. But whatever the result is, I will still love and want you." Damon laced his fingers through hers. "We can face anything as long as we are together."

"Can you give me a little more time? Not much, mind."

"You mentioned this earlier, and I will. I understand that you need to think this through logically. But I had to tell you how I feel and what I want for us."

She stroked his cheek affectionately. "You do know me. And I also appreciate that you are telling me how you feel. I want us to be able to speak of anything."

"As do I." Damon pulled her on top of him and kissed her hard. And that was not all that was growing hard.

Althea broke the kiss and laughed. "Oh, no. You are going to take me home."

"As you wish," he grumbled. Then he gave a brilliant smile. "You know, I really am happy. And it is all due to you, my Thea." Althea tossed him his trousers. After slipping them on, Damon halted in his dressing. "Do you remember what Sister Rose said to us? Love bears all things, believes all things, hopes all things, endures all things. How true. That applies to us. And remember, she said to be courageous as if she knew you would face a crisis. And you have, Althea. You are the most courageous woman I know."

Althea clasped him tight. It seemed she hugged the stuffing out of him after all.

Yes, everything would be absolutely fine as long as she was in his embrace. As long as they were together.

Damon had fallen madly in love—for the first and last time in his life.

DAMON ESCORTED ALTHEA home, only to return to find a strange carriage sitting in front of Clarendon Place. At half past one in the morning?

Kingsley greeted him at the door. "The Duchess of Chellenham, Your Grace. And her husband and son await you in the parlor. I brought tea and biscuits."

"Thank you." Damon hurried toward the parlor. He entered to find his mother seated, holding a cup of tea, and two men standing nearby. One was De León; the other must be Damon's brother. The lad was tall, perhaps close to six feet. Was he finished growing? It was hard to know. Dark hair like his mother and father, and of course, handsome.

Damon went to his mother, leaned in, and kissed her cheek.

"Forgive us. I insisted we come straight away after the ship landed in Liverpool, and we arrived later than I had planned," his mother smiled. "Mr. Arrowsmith traveled with us and says he will stop by tomorrow afternoon."

Damon held his hand to De León, and the man shook it heartily. "Good to see you, Damon."

"And you." Damon turned to the young man. "And this must be Sebastián." Damon held out his hand, but to his utter astonishment, Sebastián embraced him.

"I always wanted a brother," the young man whispered.

"As have I," Damon replied as he patted the young man on the back. They separated. "It is much too late to find a hotel. Stay here for as long as you like. I sent an invitation stating such, but I suppose you had already departed. Kingsley!"

The butler stepped into the room. "I have prepared two guest rooms, and the trunks are already in the rooms, Your Grace."

"Mr. Arrowsmith arrived before your letter, and we thank you for the invitation," his mother smiled.

"If you don't mind," De León said. "I want to head straight to bed as I am completely exhausted. Sebastián? Come, allow Damon to have a visit with your mother."

"Of course. Kingsley will escort you. We will speak more tomorrow. Good night."

Damon was alone with his mother. All at once, the years melted, and they forgave the past.

Damon sat on the settee. "Much has happened since I visited you in Spain."

"Yes, for us both," His mother replied, placing her teacup before them.

"The night the duke died. I had the strangest dream." Damon told his mother of the dream, wandering through Chellenham Park and finding his father in the same position he had been in at two in the morning.

His mother shook her head. "So that is how he was discovered. I am not surprised. Edward would have been mortified as he was such a stickler for outward appearances. To a point."

"Will he haunt me the rest of my days? Will he always hover nearby in my consciousness, his debauched legacy staining my life?"

His mother took his hand. "Only if you allow it. Edward Cranston isn't worth remembering. You are *not* your father's son. Do not ever doubt it. You are capable of love, fidelity, and honor. I can see it in your eyes. It is all within you."

Damon laid his hand on top of his mother's. "I believe it is." He told her of Althea and the young siblings he discovered at the foundling home.

"Then embrace it. You are taking in your half-siblings and giving them a home and a future. But more importantly, you are giving them a family. Love. Security. We can be a large, loving family, my darling boy. All you have to do is put aside your doubts and fears. You deserve to be loved. And happy. Make Althea part of your life, or you will regret it if you do not."

"I have asked her to marry me. Can you imagine? And the intelligent woman that she is, Althea is considering the prospect. Althea knows what I am and loves me regardless. I don't deserve her."

"What you *were*. You are no longer that man, not that you ever were deep down. You deserve everything. Love, most of all."

"I love *you*, Mother. Welcome home."

MORE THAN TWENTY-FOUR hours had passed since he had heard from Althea. When he received the note that Althea would drop by at ten the following day, Damon hardly slept a wink. Had she made up her mind that swiftly? He thought a few days more, at least. Should he be worried?

He paced in his study, awaiting her arrival. He told his family he had an appointment and would join them for breakfast later. One surprising development is that Anthony De León expressed an interest in buying Clarendon Place. It would be part of Sebastián's inheritance and give them a place to live while he attends university. When Damon offered to knock some off the asking price, his stepfather wouldn't have it. Why not keep the property within the family?

His thoughts were interrupted by Althea's prompt arrival. How beautiful she looked, wearing a burgundy wool skirt and matching jacket.

"Shall I bring tea, Your Grace?" Kingsley asked.

"No, thank you."

The butler departed and closed the door behind him. There was no use prolonging the agony. Best to express his feelings once again and make his case.

"So, you thought it over?"

"I have."

"Allow me to make one last appeal. I am, as society claims, a besotted rake so in love with you that he has renounced his former wicked ways to be devoted to you the rest of our days. And God, how I love you. I will agree to any terms you lay forth because I cannot be without you. My world will be hollow. But you fill it. *You* fill me."

Damon took a step closer. There was no stopping him now; the words tumbled out of him in an emotional rush. "You will be taking on quite a lot, children running underfoot, extended family everywhere we turn, but you must also have your own life. Continue with your investigative agency. You will anyway, as you hardly need my permission. What is the saying? 'Make me the happiest of men.' Say yes, my Thea. End my agony. Join your life with mine. I will never make demands on any aspect of your life. I give my solemn vow. There is no rush to have children, if you want them or if we are even able—"

Althea came to stand before him and laid a finger on his lips. "Yes, I will marry you. I accept and embrace your family with my whole heart. But more importantly, I embrace *you*. I love you, Damon. So very much. We will face everything life throws at us. We can have it all, my love."

He took her hand and kissed it. Damon's heart soared. "And I do hope this will not be a long engagement."

"I apologize for not saying yes right away. I needed to work the rest of this through. There was and is no doubt of my feelings. I admit I momentarily doubted if we could blend our lives, and I briefly doubted you would even be capable of it. I am sorry for that, too. I cannot explain why I needed to think this through. I've always puzzled out every major decision in my life."

"I understand, and I am not upset in the least."

"And *that* is also why I love you." Althea raised their joined hands and kissed them. "A small Christmas wedding is all I want, as Eleanora had with Uncle Reece walking me down the aisle."

"Then it shall be done." Damon kissed her passionately, then scooped her into his arms and hurried into the dining room. "Althea has agreed to marry me!" he announced to his family.

They surrounded them, offering congratulations. The scene was as comforting as a warm blanket.

Damon would never be lonely again. With Althea, he had the love he so richly deserved—at last.

He would spend a lifetime proving to Althea how honored he was to have it.

****Farther ahead is a sneak peek of Book 6 in The Rakes of St. Regent's Park series, *The Viscount of Shadows*! It is Oliver Wollstonecraft (grandson of Aidan, from book 3, *Love with a Notorious Rake* in the Men of Wollstonecraft Hall Series), and Claudia Ellingford, who first appeared in the Rakes series in book 4, *The Duke of Pain*, as Mary O'Toole. Check it out! And after the epilogue, check out the 2^(nd) author's note relating to historical facts! ****

Epilogue

TEN YEARS LATER
Chellenham Park, Essex

What a whirlwind decade since Damon and Althea had agreed to marry. His mother, her husband, and Damon's half-brother lived in London while Sebastián attended university. Damon got to know his family, and life-long bonds formed. Sebastián was now one of the youngest judges at the police court at Guildhall in northern London and a full member of The Rakes of St. Regent's Park. His mother and stepfather spent summers and early autumns in London at Clarendon Place and wintered in Spain at their villa.

As for the rest of his found family, Adina Desmond reunited with her mother, and they returned to Cornwall. Damon paid a small yearly stipend as agreed upon with Adina's mother. He tried to offer more, but they gently refused, saying they only needed enough to live comfortably. They exchanged letters once or twice a year, but Adina preferred to remain apart from the rest. Damon respected that.

As for Althea's operation, the doctors successfully removed the benign growth, and she used the cane for nearly two years. They married at Christmas, at Queen Anne's Gate. It was a small affair with friends and family.

Now fully renovated and every trace of his loathsome father gone, they moved in with his younger half-siblings. A ready-made family, indeed.

Archie Fitzgerald eventually took over as manager of The Galway Agency, with the sisters keeping a hand in. Althea continued with her investigative agency, slowing down only long enough to give birth to their son and heir three years later.

Damon and Althea named their son Rory Galway Cranston, the Marquess of Brookton, after Althea's grandfather. Rory's birth held its share of drama. The delivery was difficult, and both mother and son were in peril for a time. Those agonizing days were the worst of Damon's life. They recovered when it was all said and done, although Althea had to have a life-saving operation, which meant no further children.

But as Damon told Althea, it didn't matter as long as she regained her health. And Queen Anne's Gate was filled with children regardless—and happiness, as Damon never imagined he would ever experience.

As for his older half-siblings, though Mitchell Evercreech was initially reluctant, they became friends and brothers. His half-brother even took Damon's advice and changed his name to Mitchell Simpson to honor the older couple that had raised him. Mitch also joined the Rakes of St. Regent's Park after some convincing.

And Olivia? They had grown closer still, and their families were inseparable. As were all The Rakes and their families.

Mrs. Seddon married MacClery, and they took over the daily home and nearby farm management. With Clarendon Place sold to Anthony De León and the Daimler shares reaping ever-growing profits, Damon more than kept the dukedom afloat. Because of it, Chellenhome became a legitimate orphanage and expanded in size and scope.

As for the children residing at the home when Damon had first discovered it? The Rakes of St. Regent's Park took them under their wing. The group sponsored the children for further education and training, took some on as wards, or informally adopted in Gideon and Olivia's case. The oldest girl, Helena, trained to be a nurse, and Hugh Crossingham decided to pursue medicine. The Rakes started a university fund for the children; some became barristers, doctors, or teachers. The fund still benefited any children passing through Chellenhome's doors.

Chloe ran into Damon's study, waving a letter in her hand. "Papa! The summer party invitation to Aunt Eleanora and Uncle Christian's has arrived!"

When Damon had taken in his half-sister, the child insisted on calling him Papa from the beginning and shortly thereafter referred to Althea as Mama. They tried to explain that Chloe was his half-sister, but the little poppet wouldn't have it, even to this day.

"Can we take the Tourer, please?" Chloe cried, practically bouncing on the tips of her toes.

The 30/40 HP Tourer was a Daimler automobile and one of the most popular ones of the past year and made at the recently opened car factory in Coventry. To say The Rakes had somewhat benefited financially by investing in Daimler was an understatement. The future looked bright in all ways, but financially as well.

"Yes, we will take the auto, along with the carriage. Go and pack and round up your brothers and sisters."

Chloe squealed joyfully and ran from the room, almost knocking Althea off her feet.

"Slow down, Chloe!" Althea called after her. Turning to Damon, she smiled. "Already a handful; imagine when she discovers boys if she hasn't already."

Damon slipped his arms about Althea's waist. "Good God, what a prospect."

"Gideon and Olivia and family are coming for dinner tomorrow night."

Damon nuzzled her neck. "Hmm."

"And I invited Mitch and his family as well."

Damon trailed kisses along her jawline, stopping long enough to nibble on her earlobe.

"Are you listening to me?" Althea chuckled.

"Always, my love. A big family dinner. That is a matter of course around here. I expect it."

As most do in married life, Althea and Damon had their ups and downs, but thankfully, the downs were rare.

The love and respect only grew through the years, and as of yet, the physical aspect had not diminished.

"I say we slip upstairs while everyone is running about and packing," Damon murmured.

"Why go upstairs?" Althea replied silkily. "Lock the door."

Yes, life was good, indeed.

Author's Note #2

In the late Victorian age, women couldn't join the Metropolitan Police in London except as a matron. The first female police constable with the full power of arrest was Edith Smith. The Met Police hired her in 1915. Like Althea Galway in my story, many women joined or created private investigative agencies. Lady detectives were also popular in fiction books during the Victorian era, starting in the 1860s.

The London City Police was officially formed in 1832 and became The City of London Police with the passing of the City of London Police Act of 1839. It made the force independent and separate from The Metropolitan Police. They preside over 1.1 square miles in the heart of the city to this day.

The study of classifying blood types did begin in the late Victorian age, but it wasn't until 1901 that Karl Landsteiner placed them under four types. Scientists did not use blood types to establish paternal links until the 1930s.

In 1889, Johann Friedrich Mieschers discovered nucleic acid. Its full name is deoxyribonucleic acid, or as we refer to it today, DNA. Its use for paternity tests didn't occur until 1988.

In the Victorian era, being a surgeon differed from being a surgeon today. Surgeons were doctors who performed tasks such as pulling teeth and treating wounds and skin diseases. These doctors had no medical degrees but learned their trades through apprenticeships with established doctors. Doctor Corbett Buchanan is a trained physician but often labors as a surgeon.

Unwanted children had been abandoned for centuries. In Britain, it wasn't until the Adoption of Children Act of 1926 that adoption had legal status. Before then, it was informal, if it happened at all. Most found jobs in factories or apprenticeships; others wound up on the streets. An unmarried woman could not name a man as the father of her child on the birth certificate unless she gained an affiliation order against him, so most children had no idea who their fathers were.

Top-down schemes are what we call pyramid schemes. This scam has been around for ages, but one of the most famous occurred following World War I by Charles Ponzi. (Thus, the term, Ponzi Scheme) Scams of this sort were described in two of Charles Dickens's books, *Martin Chuzzlewit* (1844) and *Little Dorrit* (1857)

Adamantinoma makes up less than 1% of all bone cancers and appears more in males than females. Why give it to my heroine? Because life can be messy, as Althea stated in the story! That type of tumor gained recognition in 1827 but not classified. Scientists named it Adamantinoma in 1885, and it wasn't until 1930 that it was given the name Ameloblastoma that we use now.

Early X-rays, or Röntgen rays (discovered in 1895), were very dangerous, and they often caused burns and hair loss and led to various cancers. Thomas Edison did develop the first commercially available fluoroscope in the late 1890s, and that fundamental design is still part of present-day X-ray machines.

The Grill Room at the Savoy Hotel is still open to this day. The inside of the restaurant has some of the Victorian-era architectural designs intact. Although, after a renovation in 2010, it has more of an Art Deco look. The chef Gordon Ramsay has run The Grill Room since 2003.

I love researching Victorian-era meals and food preferences, so forgive me if I go into too much detail at mealtimes!

CHARACTERS OF MINE mentioned or appearing in this story:

TREMAIN HORNSBY. CHECK out his story in *The Vicar's Frozen Heart* (The Hornsby Brothers #2)

Harrison Hornsby. Check out his story in *The Marquess of Secrets* (The Hornsby Brothers #3)

Aidan Wollstonecraft. Check out his story in *Love with a Notorious Rake* (The Men of Wollstonecraft Hall #3)

Simon Wolstenholme, Baron Stonecliff. Check out his story in *The Governess and the Beast* (Blind Cupid #2)

THE CRIMINAL OR VILLAINOUS-leaning men on the late duke's list for Chellenhome:

DUKE OF WHINSTONE. *The Duke of Pain* (The Rakes of St. Regent's Park #4)

Earl of Southen. *The Copper and the Madam* (Blind Cupid #3)

Sir Anthony Crossley, baronet, and the Earl of Oakby. *Knight of Christmas* (The Rakes of St. Regent's Park #3)

Jonathan Wolstenholme, Baron Stonecliff. (Whose son, Simon, now the baron, was an original member of The Rakes and the main character in *The Governess and the Beast* (Blind Cupid #2)) Jonathan is mentioned several times in TGATB.

Author Biography

A multi-published author from the East Coast of Canada, Karyn Gerrard loves to write sensual historical and contemporary romances. Tortured heroes are an absolute must.

Karyn's been happily married for a long time to her own hero. His encouragement and loving support keep her moving forward.

To learn more about Karyn and her books, visit www.karyngerrard.com[1]

Also, visit her on Facebook, Twitter, Pinterest, Instagram, and Bookbub.

"Looking for a swoon-worthy read? You can't go wrong with the lovely and emotional romances from Karyn Gerrard." ~**Vanessa Kelly, USA Today Bestselling author**

"Karyn Gerrard writes very enjoyable, richly textured historical romances." ~**Kate Pearce, New York Times and USA Today Bestselling author**

---

1. http://www.karyngerrard.com/

More Books by Karyn Gerrard

~H istorical~
    The Spinster and Mr. Glover (Book #1 Blind Cupid Series)

The Governess and the Beast (Book #2 Blind Cupid Series)

The Copper and the Madam (Book #3 Blind Cupid Series)

Protecting the Duke (The Rakes of St. Regent's Park #1)

The Baron and the Mistress (The Rakes of St. Regent's Park #2)

Knight of Christmas (The Rakes of St. Regent's Park #3)

Duke of Pain (The Rakes of St. Regent's Park #4)

Bold Seduction (of Professor Hornsby) (Book #1 Hornsby Brothers Series)

The Vicar's Frozen Heart (Book #2 Hornsby Brothers Series)

Marquess of Secrets (Book #3 Hornsby Brothers Series)

Beloved Monster (Book #1 The Ravenswood Chronicles)

Beloved Beast (Book #2 The Ravenswood Chronicles)

Marriage with a Proper Stranger (Book #1 Men of Wollstonecraft Hall Series)

Scandal with a Sinful Scot (Book #2 Men of Wollstonecraft Hall Series)

Love with a Notorious Rake (Book #3 Men of Wollstonecraft Hall Series)

The Not So Perfect Duke (The Rakes of St. Regent's Park #5)

COMING SOON! The Viscount of Shadows (The Rakes of St. Regent's Park #6)

~**Contemporary**~

My Highlander Cover Model (Heroes of Time Travel Anthology Series #1)

Timeless Heart (Heroes of Time Travel Anthology Series #2)

My Wicked Soul (It's Never Too Late for Love Anthology Series #1)

That Christmas Feeling (It's Never Too Late for Love Anthology Series #2)

Wild Pitch

He's the Wicked Bad (Wicked Men of Rockland City #1)

His Wicked Celtic Kiss (Wicked Men of Rockland City #2)

His Wicked Cold Heart (Wicked Men of Rockland City #3) is coming soon!

Sneak Peek of The Viscount of Shadows (The Rakes of St.
Regent's Park #6)

Prologue

A*ugust 1898*
 London, England

MARY O'TOOLE BECAME a prostitute after finding herself alone and on the streets at age sixteen. At least, that is how society saw her, judgmental as they were. And no doubt what the two women sitting across from her in the Ten Bells pub in the East End of London assumed. Mary couldn't make out their expressions, for they kept them maddingly neutral.

One was quite tall, the other about average stature for a woman. Mary guessed her height was somewhere in between the two. Both ladies stared at her with clear-eyed astuteness.

"I am Althea Galway," the shorter one declared. She reached into her case and placed a card on the table. With the tip of one finger, she slid it across to Mary.

Mary picked it up. "The Galway Investigative Agency. Looking for a lost soul? There are plenty around here, love," she said sarcastically.

"Actually, we were searching for *you.* Olivia Durham suggested we seek you out at the Ten Bells, where you take lunch. You came to her rescue this past spring. Do you recall the incident?" the tall one asked.

Mary remembered everything. Olivia Durham had been cornered in a dark alley by two repulsive men who had abducted her from a duke's town house. Mary had been with her prostitute compatriots. Pulling a knife from her garter, Mary stood them down, threatening to cut them from their throat to bollocks. Perhaps she hadn't quite verbalized that aloud, but she had thought it. And she was tempted to do it if they hadn't fled like the cowards they were and no doubt still is.

Mary placed the card on the table. "I remember Olivia. Pan tells me she married her duke. The best to her and all. She doesn't owe me anything. I sought out the job at The Velvet Vine as she suggested. Thank her for me, yeah?"

Miss Althea Galway inclined her head to the tall woman next to her. "My older sister, Eleanora Galway-Bamford, and co-owner of our agency."

Mary nodded in acknowledgment. You did not hear about two sisters running an investigative agency every day. Good for them.

"Olivia, now the Duchess of Watford, has recommended you for our agency. We wish to hire you," Eleanora Galway stated.

What?

"You cannot be serious," Mary balked.

"We most certainly are," Althea Galway replied firmly. "You know the streets, are obviously smart, can handle yourself with a knife. You would be perfect for undercover work and other assignments. We cannot pay the wages you may be accustomed to at your present labor, but we offer steady employment and adventure."

Adventure? Mary had quite enough of that in her life. As far as money was concerned?

"I am not making as much as you think," Mary said, her mouth quirking into a half-smile. "And I am not ashamed of how I made money to survive these past years."

Mary had taken the position at The Velvet Vine and Tackle brothel to see that her friends had a comfortable place to stay. It had taken a good deal of negotiating with Pan, the owner, to take them all on, with Mary agreeing to assist him in running the club while smoothing the rough edges off her friends. As part of the deal, Mary refused to service any customers. To her utter astonishment, Pan had agreed.

"We offer room and board, all meals included. You would have your own room," Eleanora Galway interjected. "And as to your current work? It is not a factor to us."

Well, that was good to know about her current living. As far as a room, she had her own now. In fact, it was Olivia Durham's old one. "I don't know nothing of being an investigator."

But the notion had taken root. Mary was tired of street life, not knowing where the next crust of bread was coming from or if she would have a roof over her head for more than one night—these past months had been a blessed reprieve from survival on the streets. And to use her survival skills in a compelling career or to begin a new chapter, a diverse journey? It was enticing.

"We will train you. You read; do you write as well?" Eleanora Galway asked.

"Aye."

"The majority of our clients are women seeking a divorce, but we have had a few important cases beyond that," Althea Galway stated. "You would be living at our place on Cleveland Street. Our cousin, Sybil Norton, lives there with another investigator, Edwina Callen. The rate of pay would be two pounds a week. To start."

Yes, it was less than she was making now, but not by much. It was an excellent wage, more than a clerk at a bank would make. It would be hard to leave her comrades after all they had been through. Mary would have to confer with them. But she knew they would encourage her to pursue a new life. Maybe even an exciting one.

Wait. Galway-Bamford?

Mary hardly read the papers, for who had time? But her sharp recall flipped through her well-ordered memory to an article of a lady investigator marrying a duke. She swung her gaze toward Eleanora.

"Are you the Duchess of Allenby?"

"I am. And my sister is about to marry the Duke of Chellenham. But we are still running our agency." The duchess pointed to the cane leaning against the table. "At the moment, Althea does not get around as well as she used to, and we have more clients than we can possibly take on. It is why we approached you. We need the assistance."

Well, you could knock Mary over with a feather. Dukes? How fascinating. "Don't you want to know anything more of my past?"

Althea shrugged. "Not particularly. That is your business. If you take this job, you leave the life behind. Except where it may be useful for any investigations, such as gathering facts. Your street smarts will be invaluable."

The wheels in Mary's mind were turning. She tapped her fingers against the table. "You do not know me. Yet you both are willing to take me on. Why?"

"Because Olivia recommended you, and I trust my friend implicitly. And sitting here conversing, I can see you are frank, confident, intelligent, and perfect for our needs. If you prefer a trial period to see if you would like the work, we can arrange that," Althea replied.

Mary took a sip from her pint mug of bitter. "Can I get back to you? I need to think this through. I want to speak to the owner and my compatriots before deciding."

"That is satisfactory," Eleanora responded.

"Let me tell you a little about myself, for it is best you know this now. My name is not Mary O'Toole. I am twenty-six, the illegitimate daughter of a duke. I have been alone and on the streets since age sixteen. And though you may hear a slight Irish accent, I am not from Ireland."

Mary dropped the accent and spoke in perfect upper-crust English. "Although the first years of my life were spent living on Eaton Place not far from Belgrave Square, as soon as my so-called duke father tired of his mistress—my mother—we were turned out. The subsequent addresses made their eventual slide into abject poverty."

"Do not tell me your father was the Duke of Chellenham, my fiancé's late father. He was a disreputable rake of dubious morals," Althea whispered. "He left children in all corners of London and beyond."

"No, the name on my birth certificate states Claudia Ellingford. My mother put my father's last name on the certificate because she thought it sounded posh, even though my father is not legally named on the official documentation."

"Whinstone," Althea Galway whispered. "My God."

"The very one. I see the duke's reputation precedes him."

"Olivia's case," Eleanora Galway interjected, "Whinstone was the villain, her husband's loathsome stepfather. He was the one behind Olivia's abduction. What are the odds?"

"It is a small world, after all. In the scheme of things. And I am not surprised he was the villain." Hell's bells, her so-called father was worse than she had initially supposed.

"Whinstone is in prison, and plans are in motion in the House of Lords to have his dukedom stripped from him," Althea Galway added.

"A good place for him. May he rot." Mary frowned, thinking back, going to her father on bended knee, begging for a couple of pounds so she could find clean lodgings to care for her sick mother. The cruel man had her turned away without even granting her an audience. Good riddance.

Mary stood and held out her hand to the women. They each shook it. "I will send word to the address on this card when I decide. Give me at least ten days to mull this over."

"Very well. And if you agree, we will have a more comprehensive interview and tell you about the agency and the cases you may be involved in," Althea Galway replied.

Mary pulled her shawl across her shoulders and strode from the pub with her head held high. The ladies could pay for her lunch.

It may be time to become Claudia Ellingford again.

Chapter 1

L *ate September 1898*
London, England

MARY O'TOOLE TOOK THOSE ten days to consider the offer. With the encouragement of her friends, she began her new life using her real name Claudia Ellingford.

Tonight, she lurked in a dark alley, following a baronet, Sir Tristan Nottingham, as her first assignment with The Galway Investigative Agency. Her partner for the night, Edwina Callen, awaited her in a hansom cab on the next street.

Claudia had a few weeks of training, but nothing like the practical application to truly learn investigative skills. They were handling a divorce case, as Sir Tristan's lady wife suspected him of stepping out, and the lady in question had had enough of the man's infidelities and wanted solid proof to present in court.

Sir Tristan was unquestionably seeking out the lower forms of vice in the East End if he was heading where Claudia imagined. Not that there were many dilapidated buildings left in this section of Bethnal Green, as a clearance was taking place by the London County Council. But the poor and criminals would find another place to take root. Evictions have occurred for centuries to make way for the railways above and below ground—and supposed urban enhancement.

But the East End was not alone in these types of slums, as there were pockets throughout the city. Claudia came to find out that fact when she and her mother moved to the West End Avernus—as it had been referred to recently in the papers—around Notting Dale, or hell on earth as the locals called it. The newspapers also referred to it as The Potteries and Piggeries—where fifteen people shared a toilet and forty out of a hundred children did not live to see their second birthday.

Claudia shook away the horrid memories and concentrated on the task at hand.

Sir Tristan moved with swift and decided purpose, his long cloak snapping in the wind. Deeper, Sir Tristan traveled into the rookery through twisting, dank alleys and courtyards. Sounds of off-key piano music filled her hearing. Then she was correct. The man was heading toward Kelly's Paradise, which was anything but. But the back-alley venue offered an abundance of cheap gin, gambling, bawdy shows, and of course—sex.

Claudia was not wearing her newly purchased wool skirt and jacket, but to blend in with the locals, she wore a tattered dress with a patched shawl wrapped around her head and shoulders and fingerless lace gloves. And she had two knives on her, one in the holder attached to her garter and a smaller one in her boot.

The doors were open since it was a warm night. It allowed some semblance of fresh air to circulate. Not that the air was fresh, far from it. Claudia stood in the doorway and peeked in. A tobacco smoke haze hovered over the large crowd. On stage, four scantily-dressed women were doing a lewd dance eliciting hoots and applause from the general male audience. In one darkened corner, a man had a woman against the wall, rutting her, with a small group of men watching as if it were part of the show.

She scanned the crowd and found Nottingham. By all accounts, he was good-looking if your preference ran toward smug, middle-aged elites. Already he had a pint of bitter in one hand and a plump woman in the other. He buried his face in the woman's generous bosom, his mouth latching on to the barely-revealed nipple peeking out of her low-cut blouse. The woman laughed naughtily, whispering in his ear.

Someone grabbed Claudia's shoulder and spun her about, pulling the shawl from around her head. The garment fluttered to the ground. Three men stood before her; their gazes were lascivious and threatening. She had expected this. A woman alone was not safe anywhere in this area.

"Here, sod off and all!" she yelled, using her Irish accent. "I belong to Grindhouse Pete, eh? So, you'd best shove off and leave me be, you bleedin' muckshites!" Claudia had no idea if Grindhouse Pete was still in control of this part of the rookery, but the men's hesitation meant the name still carried some weight.

"Pete won't mind if we have a taste," one man rumbled. "I've never had me a redhead afore. Wonder if she's red—down there?" The other men chuckled salaciously.

"A taste?" she slowly raised the hem of her frayed dress, giving the men a flash of leg. Claudia stealthily reached for her knife. "A taste of what, ducks?"

With the men now distracted, she grabbed the knife from her rawhide holder and swung around in an arc, making contact.

One of the men screamed, his hand to his cheek. Blood oozed between his fingers. "The bitch cut me!"

Before Claudia could react or reply, someone dropped down from above. In a flash of dark leather, the tall man—she assumed it was a man considering the width of the shoulders and the muscular build—battered one of her attackers with what appeared to be a truncheon.

He then turned to the other men, pulling a large dagger from his coat. "This is my territory," the muffled voice hissed as he held the blade to one of the men's throats. "Leave now if you want to live."

The men needed no further inducement. They grabbed the beaten man, brought him to his feet, and hurried out of the alley. The tall man turned to face her as he tucked the knife away.

His territory?

Claudia will not wait for this leather-clad rookery boss to lay his hands on her. Claudia lifted her leg and kicked him right in the bollocks. Or at least she hoped so, as ascertaining the target in the dark was challenging. She must have made at least partial contact as the man descended on one knee, his breath expelling in wheezing gasps.

"I was trying to help you," he bit out.

"I do not need any assistance," she replied, speaking in her own voice. "I had the matter under control. Who *are* you?"

The man grunted as he stood. "The Sentinel, at your service."

www.ingramcontent.com/pod-product-compliance
Lightning Source LLC
Chambersburg PA
CBHW070101030726
47506CB00002B/547